IN THE SLEEP OF DEATH

A NOVEL

KIMBERLY
VAN GINKEL

Supervising Editors: Caitlin Chrismon, Emily Oliver
Associate Editors: Erika Skorstad, Shannon Marks
Internal Formatting: Shannon Marks
Cover Designer: L. Austen Johnson

ISBN: 978-1-952919-17-6

GenZPublishing.org
Aberdeen, NJ

To my parents, Jack and Patricia Brown.
You are with me every day.

CONTENTS

PART XII
IN THE SLEEP OF DEATH

PART XIII
FLIGHT

PART XIV
INTERLUDE

I
MEIN TREUER

1

MONDAY, JUNE 14, 1886

SHE WATCHED the men of the posse milling about in the darkness, like phantoms along the outskirts of the campfire. They had been ordered to spread out with their bedrolls in case she tried to run. They needn't have bothered; fatigue had already dug its claws into her.

Stay awake, Lorena, begged that familiar voice in the depths of her mind.

Raising her chin ever higher, she sat stiff-backed and proud, legs crossed demurely at the ankles, as though serving tea in her mother's parlor rather than perched on an overturned crate somewhere on the barren plains. Prisoner or not, Lorena Adalwolf was a wellborn lady and intended to be treated as such. The haughtiness that came second nature to her now also appeared to be a good tactical choice. Most of these local rubes knew just enough about polite society to realize they were not equipped to function in it. A few well-chosen words left them fumble-footed and backing away like disobedient servants.

She sensed their fear as well. The newspapers branded her "The Hellfire Witch of St. Louis," which set every home in the state abuzz with differing versions of her exploits. The one thing everyone agreed upon is that if you were fool enough to look straight at her, she'd curse you with the *Evil Eye*. Little wonder, then, that the men scampered off as soon as they erected her tent, leaving her with only her two traveling companions and George for company.

From the way the others deferred to him, she pegged George as the leader. Unfortunately for her, he seemed unfazed by her reputation. Clearly a different breed, this one didn't falter when he spoke to her but held her gaze steadily. Indeed, his eyes rarely left her.

It wouldn't do to encourage his attentions by staring back, so Lorena scrutinized him over the rim of her goblet as she pretended to sip her wine. Though the men guzzled applejack, she'd been presented with the prime pickings of their larder—a burgundy so dark it tasted of vinegar and reeked like a bloodletting. Her stomach twisted at the scent. In her moment of distraction, George caught her eyes lingering on him and returned a bold wink.

Clad in a homespun shirt and blue striped slacks with a short-barrel Peacemaker thrust through his belt, he eyed her with a possessive smirk that would have scandalized her Eastern society friends. But the palpable lust was not for her body. She could practically see the silver dollars tallying in his mind. Within a day's ride they would reach the St. Louis Sheriff's Office, and George's gang would collect the bounty before she took her first proud step onto the gallows.

At the moment, she had more pressing concerns. Better to face an enemy outright than one masquerading as an ally.

Across the fire from her, Giles Colquoit, her late husband's apprentice, twisted his lanky body to sit cross-legged like a soggy pretzel as he sucked at his long nine cigar. When he grinned, he reminded her of a ferret. Perhaps it was the brown snaggletooth tucked over his lower lip or the way he raked his thinning hair over his dirt-smeared forehead.

Lorena sighed, thinking what a shame that she had fallen dependent on this intractable bastard.

Her young servant, Bo, appeared with a long stick with which to stoke the fire. He worked in silence, so close to the flames that his dark skin glowed orange. Without turning his head, he swept the goblet from her hand and poured the wretched wine over the outermost embers to keep George from noticing that Lorena was wasting her portion of the provisions.

Dear, sweet Bo! When he finished, squatting on his haunches by her side, Lorena discretely patted his shoulder. Her fingers lingered on the frayed collar of what in better days had been Bo's Sunday suit. The only remaining link to her home, he shone as a beacon of faith and loyalty in this fetid landscape of scalawags and sinners.

Her husband's words, "*Mein Treuer*," echoed in her ear as clearly as if he was standing beside her now. That was his pet name for her, a phrase that translated to "my faithful one." It occurred to her now that her devotion to her beloved Diedrick mirrored Bo's constancy to her. A flash of insight showed her how she could fulfill her husband's final request.

The promise of serenity bowed before her even as she shivered under the horrifying image of what she must do.

"If you're cold, ma'am," George drawled, "I could call for more wood for the fire."

"Spare me your concern, sir. I am quite well."

Bo sprang to his feet. "I'll fetch more anyhow, Miss Lorena."

She turned to watch him scamper off, amused that whereas Colquoit's inane grin never flickered, Bo had so nimbly caught the social nuances. Under her tutelage, Bo had become well educated in mannerly chit-chat, the art of hiding ugly meaning beneath polite words.

When George expressed concern for her comfort, he was letting her know how closely he was watching her, that even her slight shiver was cataloged in his mind. Her direct rebuff of any act of kindness from her captor was bold enough that even Bo caught the lady's disdain and stepped in before the man could take offense.

And when Bo returned, laden with scrub brush, and resumed his vigil at her side, she murmured, "Thank you, Bo. You'll never know how grateful I am." Her benign words became Bo's eulogy, for she had just resolved to murder him before sunrise.

2

FRIDAY, APRIL 16, 1886

UNTIL THE PRECISE instant the German schismed her world into conflicting forces of passion and manic compulsion, young Lorena Whittaker was the model of a spirited post-war debutante.

"Girls! Is that you on the veranda?"

That five-second warning transformed two girls of leisure into their mother's concept of modest ladies. Lorena's kid boots, which had been curled beneath her on the serpentine-back sofa, met the floor with a thump. Her younger sister, Viola, discreetly spat the mint leaf she'd been chewing into the shrubbery lining the porch. A borrowed copy of *Doctor Faustus* made its way from Lorena's hands to the bottom of a pile of throw pillows. By the time Mrs. Whittaker burst through the French doors, both girls were sitting upright and proper, their hands occupied with ongoing embroidery projects. Their mother despised idle hands, even while they were enjoying the first spring day warm enough to rest on the porch without a shawl.

Built atop a hill that overlooked all of downtown Allegheny, Pennsylvania, the Whittaker home, with its ornate Indian-red gimcrackery and lavender cupolas, captured the eye of every passerby. Snuggled in amongst the opulence, the fashionable Whittaker girls loved relaxing outside to avail themselves of impromptu visits from any friend or gossip-stoker on her way home along Ridge Avenue.

Their mother approved of the socializing—provided her poised and polished ladies proved to the world that they were not work-shy. By her standards, that meant an almost constant burden of sewing, knitting, tatting, and other ladylike frippery.

Lorena had barely poked her needle through a random spot in the fabric when Mrs. Whittaker spotted them.

"There you are! I've been calling all through the house for you. Upstairs now, and dress for dinner. Your father just sent word that he's bringing a businessman home tonight."

Once a carefree Southern belle, Mrs. Whittaker now sported a perpetual frown and worry lines, though no greys were yet visible in the tightly drawn bun at the nape of her neck. Lorena watched her mother's nervous hands clinking the chain of her crucifix back and forth over the strands of beads around her ruffled neckline.

"Someone we know?" Viola asked.

Her mother avoided her eyes. "No, a new acquaintance. One he hopes to impress."

Color rose in Viola's cheeks as she ventured, "I'll change into my brown muslin."

"You will wear your new lavender dinner gown," Mrs. Whittaker snapped. "Your father wishes us to dress to the nines—especially you."

"Oh!" With an inarticulate howl, Viola stomped into the house and slammed the door.

Mrs. Whittaker glanced quickly at the neighboring porches to see whether anyone important had witnessed the tantrum.

As Lorena swept past her mother in the entryway, she muttered, "You might at least allow her to retire early with a headache."

"Your father knows what's best for all of us."

Lorena paused with her hand on the banister of their grand staircase before replying thoughtfully, "You say that so frequently, Mother. I wonder whether you would repeat it so emphatically if you truly believed it."

Mr. Whittaker, renowned for being a shrewd financier, often reminded Lorena that she enjoyed a life of affluence solely because he'd been astute enough to sell his Carolina plantation and reinvest his profits in the expanding steel industry in the North. Privately, however, she found him a bit too cold and calculating, particularly in the way he carefully allocated his daughters.

Her oldest sister, Grace, headlined the social pages for months when she wed a genuine U.S. Congressman. The next girl, Mabel, became daughter-in-law to the second largest banking institution in Philadelphia. Anna, the fourth girl, united his family with the coal mine that supplied Mr. Whittaker's steel mills. And although Viola, the baby child, mooned over a boy whose financial prospects were unmentionable, it did nothing to daunt his nuptial scheming.

Lorena took her time dressing for dinner, her primary concern being to stay out of the way of the spectacle attending to Viola. Two Polish serving girls worked to braid fresh flowers into Viola's hair while her mother looked on from the bench in the center of the dressing room. All the while, Viola scowled at her pretty reflection in the mirror.

"That's it. You've hit upon it," teased Lorena. "If you can manage to keep that expression plastered on throughout dinner, this Romeo might forget about your inheritance."

"Just you wait!" Viola hissed, her eyes blazing with tears. "After I'm married off, he'll turn on you next!"

Lorena wisely kept her tongue in check, despite the parade of witty rejoinders that came to mind. She'd eavesdropped on her parents enough to know they'd given her up as an old maid by her twenty-sixth birthday.

Miss Lorena was generally said to be just as attractive as the other girls—if a bit darker of features and less in need of the prominent bustle that padded the rumps of modern women. Her milk-and-honey complexion offset her dark chestnut eyes. Every bristle of her coarse black hair settled into place like an oil painting. A calmer demeanor could rarely be found. On the surface, she'd have made an ideal bride.

Her defect lay in her love of learning. After finishing school, she'd insisted on hiring local professors as her private tutors—only literature and arts at first, then more of the masculine tracks as, year upon year, she craved a fresh challenge. It had seemed to Mr. Whittaker like a harmless diversion to keep her occupied and single until he'd readied a match. But the sweet, young thing began speaking her mind in mixed company, contradicting any man she disagreed with and even unrepentantly boasting that she was better educated than any young man in the county. One embarrassed suitor after the next either balked or was given the boot until even Mr. Whittaker was forced to concede that perhaps not every woman was suited for marriage.

Her sisters confided in her that they wished they'd have caught onto this trick. Being raised as pampered China dolls had not prepared them to take a Lord and Master. Anna, in particular, had it so tough that when the labor bill passed that gave her husband a half-holiday each Saturday, she stopped speaking to her congressman brother-in-law.

Lorena remained quite content to languish in spinsterhood until the arrival of the enigmatic German.

The fuss over Viola continued until the ladies heard carriage bells clang in the drive below.

"Stop!" Viola screeched. She grabbed both serving girls by the wrist, pulling them to the window so she could peek through the curtains. Lorena took advantage of the vacancy at the mirror to adjust her own hairpins.

After a moment, one of the girls giggled, though the other emitted a series of choked snorts, trying not to laugh aloud. Viola turned back to the room with a radiant smile. "He's old! Mamma, you must have misunderstood. Pappa brought a little old man home for dinner."

Mrs. Whittaker abandoned propriety to run to the window herself.

"Land sakes!"

After she'd gotten a good eyeful, she turned to her youngest daughter with a broad, relaxed grin and cupped a gloved hand around Viola's soft cheek. Viola glowed at the sign—however muted and restrained—that her mother might not be quite ready to have her married off.

"That's quite enough adornment for her hair," Mrs. Whittaker told the working girls, who still had their hands full of braids as they followed Viola back to her bench. "Tie it off quickly. We must meet our guest."

Lorena linked arms with her sister for the long walk through the upper hall. They dutifully pinched their cheeks for color and donned their best artificial smiles.

Mr. Whittaker stood in the foyer, appraising his ladies as they descended the staircase. His left hand fumbled with his pocket watch, struggling to reinsert it in the vest pocket that rode taut over his well-fed belly. Greeting his wife with a kiss on the hand, her father exuded his sunniest manners, but Lorena sensed he was a mite embarrassed by the shrunken creature trailing in his wake.

Something just shy of Methuselah, the newcomer shuffled in wearing an expensive, stiffly starched suit to the odd effect that it was the *old man* who looked as though he'd shrunken in the wash and needed a good ironing. He supported his weight against a gold-tipped walking stick clutched in his right hand. Dusky grey hair hung over his ears as though he hadn't met a pair of shears in months, though his moustache and beard were manicured to a stiff point. Through a pince-nez perched askew on his crooked nose, his blue-grey eyes scanned the room, lingering on nothing until the Whittaker women gathered before him. His hands trembled noticeably as he removed his top hat.

"Mr. Diedrick Adalwolf," his host began, "allow me to present my wife, Mrs. Rose Bradwell Whittaker—of the Savannah Bradwells."

Before Mrs. Whittaker could speak, the man corrected, "*Master* Adalwolf."

Lorena saw her mother's lips purse at this exalted form of address and knew they'd all share a hearty laugh over it at the breakfast table the next morning. Too well-bred to contradict her guest, Mrs. Whittaker handled the situation neatly by lapsing into her sweetest Southern Belle accent.

"*Mah*ster Adalwolf, we are del*ah*ted you could join us this evening."

"It gives me great pleasure, Frau Whittaker."

Adalwolf spoke with such a thickly layered Germanic accent that Mrs. Whittaker paused, her lips moving slightly as she mentally translated his speech, before she smiled again. "Yes. Of course. And these beauties are my daughters, Viola and Lorena."

Lorena dropped a curtsy a beat behind her sister.

The butler stepped forth to take the gentlemen's hats as well as Adalwolf's voluminous traveling cloak.

Right on cue, the cook rescued them from aimless chit-chat by announcing dinner.

"Miss Lorena Whittaker, may I escort you inside?" Adalwolf asked.

Lorena thought she might fall through the floor. Unable to speak and mindful of everyone's eyes upon her, she gingerly took his proffered arm, and together they sauntered unsteadily over the threshold.

3

1885 - 1886

THOUGH SHE WOULD NEVER BE able to explain it, even to herself, Lorena knew him—knew him intimately—long before they met.

This man, this shriveled little creature, was somehow already her secret lover. She'd been dreaming of him for—what? months? years?—so long she could have filled several private journals with florid descriptions.

At first, the nondescript figure passed as no more than a recurrent sensation in otherwise mundane dreams, perhaps just there long enough to hold a door for her, help her into a carriage, or retrieve a fallen book at the library. When she revisited these locales in her waking life, she often felt a déjà vu about the stranger that left her increasingly unsettled.

Then one morning, she woke with a clear vision of Diedrick: handsome, blond, and tall. He seemed only slightly older than her, though his mode of dress was something you might see in an old portrait. She even caught the lingering scent of his cologne and kept her eyes shut tight until she identified its traces of sandalwood, nutmeg, and orange peel.

Ambrosia.

The night before this, she'd attended a soiree thrown by one of her father's associates. Lorena had danced the night through, splitting her time equally among all the single men of families her father wished to impress, until she could hardly keep her eyes open on the ride home. But in her dream that night, it transpired differently; this one dashing, young gent filled her entire dance card and held her close waltz after waltz.

Thereafter, his arrivals marked an abrupt transition in her dreams; no matter how the dream began, each storyline was abandoned the moment he took her arm. Musty Pennsylvania buildings dissolved to a lush landscape featuring a grand, colonial mansion like the one she'd known as a child. He took obvious pleasure in showing her every room of his estate, every rare statuette or scrollwork bookshelf. Sometimes Lorena would be left to explore by herself, always looking around corners for him as she strolled the rich labyrinth of his home. He would appear almost out of thin air, coming up behind her to hook an arm around her waist and nuzzle her neck.

And then one night, the nocturnal visits took a twist that left Lorena unspeakably thankful she'd never shared her dreams with anyone.

She found herself waiting for him on a moonlit hillside wearing nothing but a thigh-length chemise. When he appeared, he froze in shock, then bounded toward her with a roguish grin. She blushed crimson as he circled her, appraising her form, but she answered his smile with her own and did not resist when he swept her into his arms. Though her lingering maiden's virtues initially forced her to squirm away from his probing hands, her ultimate submission was passionate and absolute.

Every night after that, he returned to ravish her. Sensations a lady could never admit to knowing burned inside of her, leaving her restless and distracted through the bulk of her waking hours and almost wanton in her efforts to retire earlier each evening.

Potential suitors ambled through her life, but Lorena invested no emotion in them, smiling in secret pleasure at her "imaginary" lover instead.

On the night Mr. Whittaker brought the elderly Master Adalwolf to dinner, she felt exposed to the world, while at the same time in possession of a beautiful, fragile secret.

She recognized her lover as soon as he spoke her name. For a moment, she wobbled under the bewildering notion; it was as though a child's painting had been scribbled over a work of art. Wrinkles and liver spots masqueraded the once-attractive man. But she discerned the untroubled brow and smooth cleft chin underneath and, hint by hint, retraced the roguish features of the young man she'd loved. If she imagined he still had the long, wavy blond head of hair, Lorena could almost see both men—past and present—standing before her.

All this passed in the skip of a heartbeat.

She knew without doubt that the man of her dreams had come to call.

☙ 4 ❧
FRIDAY, APRIL 16, 1886

THAT EVENING, Mrs. Rose Whittaker presided over precisely the type of meal she loathed: one fraught with boring conversation. Despite her attempts at engaging them with a discussion of the arts, the men persisted in talking business.

"Do you mean to say that you survey the routes yourself?" asked Mr. Whittaker.

"Survey? For calculating and telling how to build? *Pffft.*" Adalwolf fanned the air with his hand as though slapping a repugnant horsefly. "I ride trains as a passenger, *ja*? To see where are needed more connections."

While Rose sat wishing they could send the man away until he hired an interpreter, her husband persisted, "So you want to build more stationhouses?"

"No, no, no. Connections. Tracks. So many are there long tracks from Atlantic to Pacific. Is good for freight, but is needed more short tracks for people crissing-crossing."

Mr. Whittaker's smile broadened. "Your interest is in splinter lines between cities! Fascinating!"

Rose failed to see anything fascinating in the least, particularly when her top-dollar meal had gone largely unnoticed. As soon as she received her husband's note that afternoon, she'd sent a runner into town for fresh oysters and descended upon the kitchen staff to realign the evening's menu. They'd laid out the best china on an imported rose-accented tablecloth and prepared a fare of roast beef, filet of flounder, and deviled oysters. A tureen of pepper-pot soup sat flanked by bowls of glazed sweet potatoes, creamed chestnuts, stewed turnips, and aspic jelly. To round out the meal, both apple dumplings and a decorated plum pudding were cooling on the sideboard. A snifter of brandy waited in the south parlor, where the men would retire to conclude their business.

Unfortunately, Mr. Whittaker remained too keen on delving into Adalwolf's affairs to observe the niceties of the formal dinner. "Which railway do you invest with? Union Pacific, or one of the New England lines?"

"Any of them. I say where lines are needed, they are happy to do with my monies."

"You own shares of connecting lines between various major railroads? Astounding."

The rising steel magnate salivated so much at his guest's speech that Rose itched to dab his mouth with her own napkin.

"Are you involved in any of the production decisions?" Mr. Whittaker faked nonchalance. "Perhaps the teams hired or... the steel suppliers?"

Adalwolf crammed his mouth full, forcing them into tense silence until he could respond. The victim of her own seating plan, Rose watched her guest masticate his meat. Naturally, she'd taken the foot of the table, her husband at the head, with the German tucked in between her and Lorena for appropriate boy-girl-boy-girl arrangement. Her subtler notion was placing Viola both across from the guest and in the most flattering light, yet another detail unnoticed by either man.

After an eternity, Adalwolf answered. "Of course. Is my monies, is my stipulations. They must use my approved business associates."

Throwing subtlety to the trade winds, Mr. Whittaker suddenly announced, "Our Viola is old enough for marriage!"

Rose glared at him while the poor girl choked on a sweet gherkin. Fortunately, the bachelor feigned a deaf ear.

Turning instead to Lorena, he said, "Your father tells me you have a fine education. What languages do you speak?"

Lorena startled, spilling her glass of cordial, but responded, "I am fluent in French, sir. And, of course, I can read and write Latin. I'm afraid my German is only cursory. I am in need of a proper tutor."

For the duration of the meal, Rose noticed with raised eyebrows the attentions he paid to her elder daughter and the ever-present blush Lorena wore as they engaged in conversation.

The instant their desserts were finished, the men strolled to the parlor to savor their pipes while the ladies cloistered themselves in the conservatory. Mrs. Whittaker barely waited for the hired girls to quit the room before venting her spleen with, "Land sakes! Inviting that wolf to dine with sheep! And, Lorena, whatever possessed you to go on so about yourself? It's unseemly. And worse, you'll put a notion into your father's head that—"

Mr. Whittaker rattled the pocket doors as he raced into the room. "He has requested a private audience."

Rose sprang to her feet before either girl could react. "No! Oh, Albert, please say you're only teasing. You wouldn't allow our child to marry a..." She dropped her voice, realizing the door to the south parlor also stood open. "He's older than *you*, for pity's sake. And who knows what family he has to speak of?"

Viola began to whimper. "Papa, I can't. I just *can't*."

"Hush, child. He wants Lorena."

All eyes turned to their middle child. She rose to her feet in one graceful motion, as if pulled by strings, then tossed aside her embroidery piece and dashed down the hall before anyone took a notion to stop her.

Rose turned to her husband, agog. There was no question of the outcome; Lorena refused every man. But why had she seemed so eager for what must become such an odious conversation? Did the girl take perverse thrill in collecting unwanted proposals?

Mr. Whittaker apparently entertained similar thoughts. "She had better demur gracefully and leave the door open for Viola. If she runs *this* one out of the house, I'll horsewhip her. See if I don't!"

"Albert! Please! You would never—"

He turned on her with such a severe temper that Rose dropped her gaze to the floor, afraid to utter another sound. Her husband normally did not incline toward violence, but with so much money at stake, his eyes were beginning to bulge.

She watched his feet pace the tiny room until Lorena returned.

The tête-à-tête lasted a scant ten minutes. Lorena reeled into the conservatory, clutching at furniture for balance, until she collapsed onto a couch.

"Not even a quarter hour," Mr. Whittaker scolded, then remembered the open corridor and dropped his voice. "You might at least have heard him out. It insults a man's pride to be turned down so fast!"

"She looks about to faint." Rose bent over her daughter, feeling her cheeks and forehead. "Poor girl."

"Poor?" raged Mr. Whittaker. "Rich and coddled is more like it. If you had an ounce of practicality about you, Lorena, you might have seen this for the blessing that it is. Why, by the looks of him, you'd be a widow in no time and wealthier than you can imagine! Willful, stupid child!"

"You're wrong, Father," Lorena said in a distant voice. "Wrong in every syllable. I have not refused him. I am his."

THE HIGHLY IMPROBABLE LOVERS SHOCKED THE household with both their unswerving resolve and their rush to the altar. Master Adalwolf insisted the wedding take place within a fortnight so that he could continue his scheduled travels.

Six topsy-turvy days later, Lorena's family assembled at the train station to watch the newlyweds depart. Adalwolf had rented a private train car, as befitted a man of his station, and Mr. Whittaker was bursting with happiness.

Mrs. Whittaker sported a wistful expression throughout the day and waved goodbye from the platform with the unshakable feeling that she would never see this child again.

EVENTUALLY, THE FAMILY STOPPED INSPECTING THE daily post with any hopes of hearing from Lorena. Mr. Whittaker was forced at last to admit that the man's business ventures must have been a bust. And years later, when the nickel rags brought sensationalized accounts of the Hellfire Witch of St. Louis, no one ever thought to connect them with Miss Lorena.

5
TUESDAY, JUNE 15, 1886

FIGHTING the anguish that threatened to shred her psyche, Lorena crept from her carriage and moved like the mist across the dew-laden prairie. In nearby farms, cocks poised to call the dawn. Her window for action blinked open.

She'd been permitted to sleep inside the two-seater coach for, despite the vulgar names the posse had taken to calling her, a married woman could not be expected to nest with drunken scoundrels. Fortunately, they hadn't ransacked it well enough to find the weapon stored inside her husband's valise.

After the initial ambush, the men were quick to steer clear of Miss Lorena. Only George stayed within spitting distance of her once they'd set up camp. At the moment, he lay propped against the front wheel of the carriage, snoring off a bellyful of apple brandy.

Lorena glided through the campsite, the trail of her dress kicking up dust as she squinted to locate Bo in the semi-darkness. At last, she found him curled up on his side in the dirt. Dropping to her knees, she gingerly shook his shoulder.

"I'm movin'," he muttered, knocking her hand aside with his forearm. Bo's walnut eyes fluttered open, and immediately, the boy grew alert and concerned. He dropped to a whisper. "What is it, Miss Lorena?"

Lorena caressed his brow with her fingertips and explained why he must die.

"God in Heaven, Miss Lorena! I cain't do that. It's Old Scratch talkin' through you, don' you see?"

"I'll make it swift," she continued soothingly. "Just relax."

"You acting crazy as a loon!" Sweat beaded on his forehead. He grabbed her left wrist none too gently, pushing it away. "It's that foreign man. He done put the voodoo on you. Ain't no how you could truly..."

Over Bo's desperate arguments, Lorena heard again the echo of her Master's voice—Mein Treuer—and music from another time soared in her ears. "Mephistos Hollenrufe," the first waltz they danced together on the night she fell in love.

Dee-dah-daah, BUM-de-BUM dah-aah...

6

EXCERPT FROM DIEDRICK ADALWOLF'S JOURNAL:

Everywhere I go in this country brings me closer to my goals. I have found my anchor and bound her to me. I go now to meet with a scholar of natives who published this translation:

"Cherokee Courting Song"

Across the meadow
Where the maiden is gathering berries,
The bee circles a flower.

Down the hill
The spider spins his web
In silence. Ha! He waits.

A maiden's heart
Flits and swoops like the bee
Carelessly changing directions.

Like the spider
You must ensnare her.
Spin a web around her soul.

Let her cling
Only to you, like the
Morning dew upon the flower.

Bind her heart
To yours
So it never roams free.

II
LADY LUCK

❧ 7 ❧
FRIDAY, MAY 7, 1886

"She's all horns and rattles, that one," groused the landlady as she hefted an armful of fresh linens and ascended the stairwell. "I've a mind to double the rent if they stay past Sunday."

"Think they'd pay it?" her daughter mused. "She dresses like they've got the money of Midas. Try it, Ma. I think I could even put up with her sour lemon face for two dollars a day."

They rounded the corner and nearly collided with Lorena as she stepped out of her room. Though her cheeks were flushed with embarrassment, she froze both women with a glare of royal disdain akin to the one Mrs. Whittaker reserved for naughty servants.

Looking thunderously abashed, the daughter hid her face behind the stack of blankets she toted while her mother tried to recover by saying brightly, "Back from your walk so soon, Mrs. Adalwolf?"

"Indeed... I shall take my tea in my room today."

"Very good. And will your husband be home for dinner?"

"How should I know?" Lorena whirled back into her room and slammed the door. Everything they said about her terrible manners was true, but it was better than letting them see the tears brimming along her lashes.

In the bosom of Allegheny, PA, she'd never known loneliness. Nor the depression of homesickness. Nor the panicked frustration of watching her life spiral down the wrong path.

Her marriage had been a mistake.

The young Diedrick of her dreams seemed so unlike this man she'd taken as the center of her universe. Master Adalwolf - as he insisted on being called - cared nothing for dancing, socializing, or sightseeing, let alone courting his new wife. Each time she recalled the affections of her dream lover, this cold counterpart seemed more distant. Sometimes when he joined her at breakfast, she would give a start upon catching in the corner of her eye a wrinkled, stooping old man. But when she turned her full attention to him and concentrated, she saw reminders of her young Diedrick again.

Adalwolf never discussed his income or his railroad investments in her presence; his studies consumed his waking hours. While she thirsted for his attention, he delved into one book after another, and it was quite impossible to dislodge his interest. Looking for new ways to draw him into conversation about his life's work, Lorena snooped through his appointment book and found it filled with a gamut of theologians, from Indian guides to German rabbis to Egyptian scholars.

At least he was a religious man, she comforted herself. Though if he wished to live as a monk, she wondered what part she was meant to play in his life.

She thought she might have been able to make the best of her fate—as her sister Mabel did with her own loveless marriage—by focusing on her home, community, and eventually a family. Then came the second blow: Lorena could never be the lady of the house in the wonderful, southern mansion she'd devoted so many nights to exploring. It apparently didn't exist. Adalwolf's permanent lodgings were in a modest home in downtown St. Louis, but his affairs kept them traveling the country, a week here, a few days there.

So, they began their life together rooming in a series of boarding houses until each one felt more like a paisley-wallpapered prison. Her days dragged on until she couldn't bear the sight of a novel, let alone needlework. She tried at first to spark conversations with the families they stayed with, but either the daughters were ill-bred and slow-witted or they were much too occupied to spend their days entertaining an increasingly churlish tenant.

Most days, like this one, she found herself trapped in her room with nothing to do but lie fully clothed in bed, wallowing in self-pity.

She'd lost Diedrick.

Sure, she was married to the man who *used* to be Diedrick. But they were so disparate.

When she first met Adalwolf, she'd been overjoyed at finding her lover. Learning that he was real—attainable, even—made her heart thump until she thought she might burst. No matter that decades had weathered him down, she saw the opportunity to exchange her precious stolen moments for an entire lifetime together, a vow she made wholeheartedly.

And perhaps foolishly.

Her husband appeared indifferent to her now, scarcely noticing when she entered a room, rarely attending to conversation. Her nights passed dreamlessly. She hadn't glimpsed young Diedrick—not even a fragment of a dream—since the night of her engagement. Had she somehow broken the link by allowing the elder Adalwolf into her life?

Was her lover gone forever?

The older landladies she stayed with were generally compassionate toward her, assuming her ill moods were the result of a young woman forced into relations with a gruff old man.

Actually, quite the reverse was true.

Lorena had leapt into matrimony flush with sexual awakening, then found herself bound to a man with no apparent interest in physical contact. On the eve of her wedding, Mother Rose bestowed the appalling advice to "close your eyes and suffer through it, remembering always that only dutiful wives get to have babies."

As she could hardly inform her mother that she'd jettisoned her virginity a dozen dreams ago, Lorena solemnly nodded while forming her own plan. She would not look upon him as an old man. If she concentrated, she was able to find the handsome man caged inside the wilting shell. When his tremulous hands reached for her, she would not shy away.

The night of their wedding, she held her breath as he moved over her. But after a long wait, he looked down at his groin, said, "*Verdammt,*" and rolled away.

Although it should have been a relief that he was apparently incapable, it left her fitful, tossing and turning through the long nights.

The rest of their honeymoon week, he did not join her in the bedroom at all. Thereafter, when he escorted her to whatever quarters he'd secured for the night, she fell asleep alone while he sat at a desk scribbling notes in his journal or poring over the leather-bound tome he kept always at hand.

By the end of their second week of marriage, she'd become spiritually defeated. Her love was dead, her life was over, and she no longer cared about pleasing anyone. She lay in bed, listening to the *skritch-skritch* of Adalwolf's pen as he took notes of his days' discoveries, and suddenly, she hated him for interrupting her enjoyable life for this nonsense.

Sitting bolt upright, she tore off her unappreciated silk nightgown and flung it to the floor. Just to annoy him, she flounced across the room, shivering and goosepimply, and draped his favorite black opera cape around her shoulders.

Adalwolf laid his quill down as she returned to bed and curled up on her side, facing the wall. Neither spoke, but she felt his eyes on her and listened to his uneven breathing. At last, he doused his candle.

That night, her enjoyable dreams resumed.

8
THURSDAY, MAY 13, 1886

As the Pennsylvania Railroad eased alongside the Ohio River, children pressed their noses to the glass of the dining car. The adults accompanying them craned their necks to catch the first glimpse of the approaching city.

Lorena watched her fellow travelers rather than glancing out at the scenery. Unique in her complete indifference to their destination, she dropped her napkin over the half-eaten plate of shoofly pie and signaled for the waiter to take it away. On her sixth afternoon train ride in the span of twenty days, she couldn't muster the optimism to greet another strange town that could never be home.

Although the menu on this line proved far better than the standard way-station fare, the primary reason Lorena left Adalwolf alone in their Pullman was to find interesting conversation among equals. But, though it was common for travelers to meet and share tables, the invisible barrier of class distinction kept the scattered groups of diners from approaching the well-dressed lady in the corner. She had to content herself with eavesdropping on the cheerful chatter of vacationers.

"Come sit down, Hattie," one matron called to a clump of girls playing Cat's Cradle. "Finish your turtle soup before we get to the station."

Hattie turned out to be the one in the peach-and-grey pinafore. She untwined her fingers from the string and clip-clopped up the aisle in shiny, new dress shoes. Just before she reached her seat, her left heel caught a worn patch of flooring and shot out from under her. She pitched into the back of a bench and came up with a bloodied nose.

The other children found this the most fascinating event yet, particularly when her mother began to henpeck her for being clumsy.

Lorena watched all of this with a wave of déjà vu and scrambled in her handbag for the dime-store booklet she'd purchased that morning outside the Vincennes station. Innocently titled *Woman's Intuition*, it promised to acquaint a woman with her hidden psychic abilities. Of course, it was a silly notion—she would never mention it to Adalwolf, and in her college days, she'd have been the first to scoff at such nonsense—but Lorena held a growing suspicion that, if such phenomena did exist, she had a more pronounced flair for it than the common female.

Her dreams couldn't be described as prophetic, exactly. If anything, she was seeing Adalwolf in his past, not the future. Then again, how had she come to dream of him before they'd even met? And was she only imagining the way that her dreams had brought them together? She'd never broached the subject with Adalwolf—how could she? —but even though she remained a virgin, her nightlong passions seemed to bring a wholeness to their marriage. He was more attentive now, as though he sensed it, too.

She laughed to herself, thinking that at least their way she would never have to endure "new-bride sickness" and watch her belly bloat.

Lorena flipped through the "amazing true stories" collected in her book—the woman who refused to open her mail because of her premonition that her son had been killed in combat; a mother whose arm developed a stabbing pain while across town her daughter had broken her wrist; a schoolmarm whose dream of a fire at school enabled her to have a bucket ready when she accidentally kicked a chair into the wood-burning stove —to find the mind-training exercises "designed to develop a woman's birthright."

The first challenge, entitled "Greeting Fate," instructed her to close her eyes, clear her mind of daily issues, draw five deep breaths, and allow her mind to sketch a rough portrait of the next man to cross her path.

Feeling rather silly and hoping no one would take notice of her, Lorena dropped the book to her lap, lowered the brim of her lace-trimmed bonnet, and gently closed her eyes. Clearing her mind was the tricky bit. She kept wondering whether it was truly clear when all she was thinking of was whether it was clear enough. Then she worried over how much longer she was expected to stay at it to call it truly clear. When the noise in the car escalated again, tempting her to peek out, she decided she'd better get on with the next bit.

She thought of a man immediately but realized that it was just the waiter, and he probably didn't count. Again, she tried, but no one came to mind, just the black inside of her eyelids. Growing irritated with herself, she mustered a vision of a white suit and tails she'd admired on a man back in Pennsylvania. It was easy to add to that a modern moustache and hairdo, but the face wouldn't come. She covered her face with her gloves to keep from accidentally looking around. For some reason, the only image that came naturally was that of a circling coyote.

Finally giving up, she lowered her hands and blinked in the brightness of the afternoon.

"What'cha doin'?"

Colquoit appeared beside her table, tipping his hat only enough to leave muddy fingerprints along the felt.

Lorena gave a start of unpleasant surprise that sent her book tumbling from her lap. Colquoit bent down to retrieve it and squinted at the cover.

"Doin' some reading? Learn ya how to be a good little missus after all?"

"Don't pretend you can read," she snapped, pulling the book from his hand.

He leaned closer to her, still sporting a smile as oily as his thinning brown hair, but his eyes hardened enough to let her know she had injured his puffed-up pride.

"Awright, Miss Independent, you been gallivanting

with the manner-born long enough. I mean to fetch you back to our car before we hit town. The master don't like to wait around."

Lorena shrank away from his hot, tobacco-charged breath, but she kept her voice level as her mother had taught her she must always do with her inferiors. "You forget yourself, Mr. Colquoit. I do not answer to *you*. You may tell my husband that I will join him at the station house."

They held one another's stare long enough for her confidence to waver. Lorena's eyes flitted to the bowie knife fastened to his belt. With a low, rolling chuckle, Colquoit fingered the edge of the blade, and she reprimanded herself for bringing it to his attention. Then he stood tall above her, doffed his hat once more, and strolled along the dining car, never looking back.

She sat rigid, watching him go, and only when she grew reasonably sure he wasn't coming back did she realize that her clenched fists were driving her fingernails into her palms.

Soon afterward, the long, arrogant whistle of the train signaled its approach to the Cincinnati station and set the car's remaining passengers into flutters of excitement. Lorena repacked her bag and made sure she was the first lady helped onto the platform once they had stopped.

Fifteen minutes later, she regretted her hasty words. If she had returned to Adalwolf's side, she'd have had an ample entourage to escort her to the nearest waiting buggy-for-hire while they unloaded her luggage. Instead, she stood, resolutely holding her ground against the surge of the animated crowd in the bustling station-house while she scanned the foreign faces for a hint of familiarity.

At last, Bo appeared alongside the tracks, hauling two trunks and a carpet bag. Lorena waved her handkerchief to catch his eye and saw the young man's grin split to match her own.

☙ 9 ❧

TUESDAY, JUNE 15, 1886

DURING HIS SHORT stint with the Pinkerton's National Detective Agency, George Tremont saw more than his fill of men shot, hanged, or bludgeoned to death. But nothing ever gave him the willies like the sight on the Missouri plains that morning.

The tandem camps sprang to life with a bellow that ratcheted toward a scream before being abruptly silenced. By the time the rest of his gang sprinted downhill, George was bent over, gasping for air. He retreated behind the line of horses and tried not to retch.

Bad enough the boy's neck was slashed—like enough he was dead the moment the screaming stopped—but why'd she have to split him from neck to navel?

George would never have believed a lady could be so soulless. His suspicions would have fixed on the creepy, sallow-skinned Colquoit, but the evidence was everywhere he looked. Blood and worse stained her hands, dress, and a path of tall grass from the body to where she perched stiff-backed on the step of the carriage, her eyes as vacant as a blind man on laudanum.

"What the blazes is goin' on here?" yelled the first man to reach him.

"She's a witch," George said between haggard gasps. "You were right."

The men gathered in a loose huddle, some pacing the perimeter, to rejoin the argument that had festered all night.

"I say we get clear of these freaks and forget the damned reward," said one of the paunchier cowboys, whose name George had forgotten.

"That ain't no way to end it," countered Jeb, a fellow ex-Pinkerton. "Can't leave them runnin' free to hurt innocent people."

A short guy beneath a felt-brimmed Kossuth hat fumbled with the holsters of his six-shooters. "I'll shoot 'em. Right here and now, I will."

"It didn't say 'Dead or Alive' on the poster. Just 'Alive' and just the woman," Jeb said, staring him down.

"Hang the money! I don't feel right about this."

Finally, the oldest man of the posse, a former lieutenant colonel from days when such promotions came two for a penny, said to George, "Still your call, Tremont. Was your cousin what she killed. How d'you want to avenge him?"

His face still pale with nausea, George braced himself with an arm on his friend's shoulder. "I told you once. I'm bringin' her back to St. Louis for trial. Even if I have to go it alone."

10

FRIDAY, MAY 14, 1886

ON THEIR SECOND night in Cincinnati, Lorena overheard Adalwolf interrogating Colquoit on the back porch of their boarding house. She suspected that the reprobate had added gambling to his innumerable sins because her husband cross-examined every answer he gave: which saloons he'd stopped in, who he'd drank with, and how much money he'd put on the table at each. When their talk concluded, Adalwolf joined Lorena in their quarters, seeming more agitated than normal as he waited for her to prepare herself for bed.

That night, she had a dream so vivid she was forced to ask Adalwolf whether it had been real...

Adalwolf startled her by bursting into their room and grabbing her by the wrists to pull her out of bed. He bade her get dressed immediately, no small task in the dark. She broke a fingernail securing her corset while he stood behind her stroking his grey beard and muttering in German.

As soon as she'd donned her hat, he hustled her outside. Hand in hand, they scurried along the block to Race Street. The strip overflowed with nightlife, including one scarlet-curtained bawdy house that Lorena spotted just in time to raise a kerchief over her eyes as they passed.

Every time she cast a glance behind them, more vagrants had migrated onto their trail. She held tightly to Adalwolf's wrinkled fingers, nearly in hysterics for fear they were about to be mugged.

"We should not be here at this hour," she whispered. "We're too well-dressed in their eyes."

As usual, Master Adalwolf's mind was too preoccupied to answer. They continued strolling the avenue until he bent to read a wooden plaque hung at a tilt on the side of a building: Cin-City Saloon. Est. 1869.

With a sardonic grin, Adalwolf opened the door for her. Holding her head so high that the black ostrich plume on her hat brushed the door frame, Lorena stepped trepidatiously into the world her sister's temperance league called "the demon drink."

Rolls of smoke enveloped them, leaving her light-headed for a moment. The floor was filthier than the streets outside. Boisterous voices paused a moment to inspect these new dandies, then recommenced with greater gusto.

Seeing that all the tables were occupied, Adalwolf led her toward the mahogany bar along the left wall, but she was too dumbstruck to take a seat; dominating the wall behind the barkeep hung an enormous lithograph of a nude woman smiling coyly over her shoulder as she covered her delicates with a thin feather boa. Lorena was certain the floor would open up and swallow them all.

"What'll it be," the bartender asked, tacking on a respectful, "sir?"

"Whiskey," Adalwolf said, and Lorena goggled at his nonchalance.

"Buttermilk chaser?"

Adalwolf fluttered his fingers to indicate an "as you will" acceptance and finally succeeded in getting his wife to demurely belly-up to the bar.

"And for the missus? We do a mean Strawberry-Do here."

Lorena's eyes flared. What would Mrs. Whittaker think to see her daughter here? Drinking in one's own home might be perfectly acceptable, but to be taken for the type of base working woman who would imbibe in public after the social hour!

"No, thank you," she replied stonily.

The barkeep rolled his eyes as he delivered Adalwolf's short glass and tumbler. "Perhaps some Wife Pacifiers?"

"A fine idea," agreed Adalwolf.

The man whistled at a sleepy-looking boy in the corner, who returned a moment later with a chipped tea plate full of bonbons. Lorena selected one and grew begrudgingly glad of the distraction while her husband turned in his seat to scope out the other customers.

Eventually, the whooping and hollering around one table grew too loud to ignore. Though unfamiliar with the rules of poker, Lorena had attended enough penny-euchre parties to immediately spot the man on the winning streak.

Slump-faced and walrus-whiskered, the man withstood several playful punches to his back and shoulders from his cheering supporters as he crooked his arms to rake in a pile of bills. Two of the other five players rose, sheepfaced, and gathered their paltry remaining coins before quitting the table.

"Drossie's buying a round for the house," the barman told Adalwolf. "You gonna want another?"

Adalwolf kicked back his whiskey and held the shot glass out for a refill. This second shot he carried, sipping the buttermilk in his other hand, toward the poker table.

"May I sit to play?"

Until that moment, Lorena had misguidedly believed that she knew her husband well. He rarely spoke in public because his accent posed a social hindrance; he had no need for pastimes because his private studies engrossed him; and common vices were foreign because he was such a refined gentleman. Seeing how easily he rubbed elbows with the wharf workers, gandy dancers, and other ruffians called all this into question.

The winning man looked up with a welcoming smile, but to his left, a thirty-something, tan-faced guy with biceps too thick for his calico roundabout jacket kicked the empty chair away from Adalwolf.

"Find some other place to squat. I don't know you from Adam."

Adalwolf responded genially, "Many apologies. I should have first introduced myself. I am Diedrick Adalwolf. I have of very recent moved into the German Quarter."

The mustachioed man lit up like a firecracker. "I knew you were from the Black Forest as soon as I heard your voice. Güten Täg! *I am Johannes Van Dross."*

The countrymen shook hands, and Adalwolf drew up the discarded chair.

"It's your funeral, Drossie," said the big man, gathering his own stack of cash. "I ain't staying to watch."

The final member of the original quintet said nothing, only continued patiently shuffling until Adalwolf anted his first dollar.

The door swung open again with two more motley locals smelling strongly of the Ohio River. When they took seats on either side of Lorena, she abandoned her bonbons. The minute she approached her husband's game, every man stiffened.

"Watch 'er! Watch 'er!" cried one of the crowd.

"Stand behind me, Mein Treuer," said Adalwolf. "They fear you will spy on their cards."

Lorena gasped at the fresh insult of being called a cheater. Tightening her shawl, she flounced to an open spot behind Adalwolf and vowed not to look at the men or their cards until this evening was through.

Adalwolf dropped most of his cards, and for a second, she thought he had changed his mind about playing, but the dealer quickly provided four more.

Van Dross stacked ten silver dollars and advanced them to the center of the table. Adalwolf procured a ten-dollar bank note from his breast pocket and set it alongside.

"I'm out," said the dealer.

Beginning to twitch, Van Dross carefully counted out twenty dollars. Holding his breath, he scrutinized Adalwolf's expression, then shoved it to the center.

Adalwolf did not hesitate before extracting a fifty-dollar gold piece of his own to lay on top of the pile.

Someone whistled. Several men bent over the table to get a first-hand look at such an unheard-of denomination.

Van Dross looked again at his cards, then Adalwolf. His cards. Adalwolf. He ran a hand across his damp brow and wavered over his remaining cash.

"Let us make this simple, ja?" Adalwolf said quietly. "How much money do you have to wager?"

Van Dross paled. The crowd around the table grew. The same men he'd won his stack of money from now hovered aggressively over him.

As Van Dross fidgeted, Lorena wondered what was going through his mind. A wise man would not discuss cash in front of these ruffians. On the other hand, he had provided the primary entertainment for much of the night, and the one thing she knew about seedy blackguards like these was that they possessed a keen eye for tracking money. They'd know if he lied.

"Roundabouts a hundred dollars," he finally said.

In one fluid movement, Adalwolf pulled out his billfold and emptied it onto the table, fanning the bank notes for all to see. In even the farthest corners of the room, conversation screeched to a dead stop.

Van Dross's eyes bulged. Muttering a prayer sotto voce*, he shoved his full stack of winnings across the table.*

His friends shouted curses that made Lorena squirm. But it was too late for their Drossie to course-correct. Squeezing his eyes shut, he flipped over his cards. Three queens. Two fours.

"Oh, my," Adalwolf murmured. His shaking hands revealed his own hand. Two pair. Aces over eights.

A war whoop carried through the crowd. Workmen linked arms and danced jigs.

Ever the gentleman, Adalwolf shook his adversary's hand before rising to depart. "Well played, Herr Van Dross."

Lorena felt like someone had pulled her corset three inches tighter. A hundred dollars lost! She watched Van Dross shoveling the bills into his pockets and fainted dead away.

❧ 11 ❧

SATURDAY, MAY 15, 1886

"IT WAS SO VIVID," she stressed to Adalwolf the next morning at the breakfast table. "I could even smell the liniment on the barman's arms when he poured your drinks! And the opium in the back room. And I could swear my gloves still smell of chocolate. See?"

He declined to sniff her fingers. "How must I convince you? I did not gamble away our finances."

"Of course not." She sipped her coffee and tried to content herself with this answer, but a minute later added, "I wonder if there is such a place as Sin City Saloon."

"No. This town is more civilized than you allow." He delicately sliced his salted pork before musing, "Your mind is overtired from travel. I have heard the local playhouse is highly received. You shall attend tonight with Colquoit."

"Oh!" Her enthusiasm peaked and valleyed over the course of his last sentence. She loved the theatre, but stepping out with the gauche apprentice would be a study in incremental miseries—particularly when people mistook him for her husband.

"I would much rather go with you," she said delicately.

He treated her to one of his rare smiles. "Colquoit is very rough, ja? I need your help to culture him. You will do this, Mein Treuer?"

"Of course." She beamed, always eager for the chance to be of use to him.

They lapsed into silence as the landlord's eldest daughter arrived to deliver fresh helpings of doughnuts, porridge, and potato fixins. Adalwolf preferred to rise early and be at his leisure before the rest of the house had convened for breakfast. The downshoot to this was that they often ate their fill before the entire meal was laid out.

Unbeknownst to Adalwolf, Lorena habitually tucked extra food into folded napkins and snuck it back to their empty sleeping quarters until she had a chance to pass it along to Bo. No matter how much she insisted, finagled, or tried to bribe their hosts, no boarding house would lodge a colored man. She couldn't claim to be surprised by this, but it did gall her that they turned sweet Bo away while admitting Colquoit, with his manifest poor breeding, repugnant hygiene, and habit of pocketing the silverware.

Adalwolf generally sent Bo to the nearest flophouse with a five-cent piece for his nightly rent, but apparently, he forgot that those venues did not serve meals. Bo so rarely complained that he might have dwindled into a skeleton if Lorena hadn't seen one of the flophouses for herself—a ramshackle single-room building crammed with cots for vagrants and reprobates. Her first instinct was to send him back home, where at least he'd have a guaranteed roof over his head and square meals in his belly, but after he'd said it "weren't nothing a body can't get used to," she'd changed her mind. He wanted so desperately to see the world. If there was any way to set Bo on a path to a better life than he'd have had in Allegheny, she promised herself she would do it.

"Would it be acceptable," Lorena ventured, "for Bo to attend the play as well?"

Adalwolf engrossed himself in the morning newspaper and did not answer. She held her silence this time, terribly afraid she'd offended him.

But that afternoon, an envelope arrived for Mrs. Adalwolf containing two front row tickets to "The Black Crook" ...and one balcony admittance for Bo.

12
SATURDAY, MAY 15, 1886

JOHANNES VAN DROSS was enjoying the best night of his life. Even when his cards were terrible, his opponents' were worse. A round of applause went up when he forced the Moretti brothers to call it a night. He bought another round for the house to celebrate.

An aged man in a German-style traveling cloak approached, stroking his pointed beard thoughtfully. "Pardon me to intrude," he began in an accent so thick Van Dross did not immediately register it as English. "I am Diedrick Schmidt, newly come to Ohio. You have an opening for cards, ja?"

"You ain't welcome, old man," Druffles said as he kicked the chair out of Schmidt's reach.

But Van Dross overruled him, introducing himself and inviting the stranger to sit. An inkling of a memory tickled his forebrain. Something in this man's face, his gestures—Van Dross felt he knew him somehow. Perhaps they'd met once in the Old Country?

"Suit yourself," said Druffles, standing to leave. "It ain't my funeral."

Van Dross was on the verge of politely inquiring about Schmidt's background when Whitey started dealing a new hand. Holding his cards to his chest, Van Dross took only a quick peek and saw nothing worth bidding on. They all called, and Van Dross threw back three cards. Whitey dealt his replacements: two more ladies, creating a healthy three-of-a-kind. Schmidt had dropped four, so unless his ace had found two friends, Drossie was sitting pretty. As usual, Whitey made a face at his own draw and blew any chance of a bluff.

Van Dross confidently counted out ten dollars in coins and stacked them in the center of the table.

The newcomer, Schmidt, shocked the house by withdrawing his wallet, fanning out a fistful of money, and placing it in the center.

"One hundred dollars," he said.

Van Dross scrambled to match the wager, pulling hoarded money from every pocket. He suddenly knew how this would end; he'd had a premonition the night before, detailed down to the very cards in both hands.

"Drossie, you ignorant lunkhead!" This was the politest charge thrown at him from the frothing crowd.

Drossie'd frequented this saloon nearly every night for three years. In that span, he'd surely lost more money than he'd won in a lump sum tonight, so nobody harbored ill feelings over it. Besides, they'd liquor him up tomorrow and recirculate most of his winnings.

But to see their own hard-earned money offered so

casually to this foreign dandy? Even the barkeep looked ready to launch a brawl.

"Easy, men," Drossie pleaded. With a flourish, he slapped down his queens.

"Oh, my," said Schmidt.

Drossie pumped a fist in the air as the stranger displayed his cards: two aces, two eights.

And... a third ace? It couldn't be!

Johannes Van Dross felt the whole world spin backward. He leaned forward and puked his dinner all over his shoes. When he looked up again, the stranger—and his money—were gone.

Inside the saloon, all hell broke loose.

III
BO

13

TUESDAY, JUNE 15, 1886

LORENA HAD no idea how long she'd been warming herself beside the campfire before she realized it had burned out. Odd. She was sure she remembered flames dancing before her.

More horseflies converged on her lap. She couldn't find the strength to shoo them away. Somewhere behind her, Bo's remains were sprawled over his bedroll. She'd have to write his family. But how could she ever explain?

Mounting heartache overtook the sense of relief and stirrings of pride she'd felt last night when she'd finally discovered a way to help her husband. A candle inside of her had been snuffed. The passionate sense of purpose washed into untempered despair.

Colquoit ambled up to her again after a period of muttering over Bo's corpse. He hadn't spoken to her yet, but added to their usual hostilities she sensed a thick layer of jealousy. They'd warred and jockeyed for Master Adalwolf's attention since Lorena's wedding day. For the first time, she may have found the trump card.

"So..." Colquoit began. Hands in his trouser pockets, he kicked at the embers of the fire pit. "You figured the boy would be easier to kill than me?"

Lorena shook her head. The simplest truth was that she couldn't trust Colquoit—dead *or* alive—to do her or her husband's bidding. But she replied instead, "He told me you are too valuable to him to lose."

The unexpected compliment hitched Colquoit's jaw up a few degrees. Whistling through his teeth, he wandered off again.

Lorena held her composure by pressing her lips together and squeezing her eyes shut, but two fat tears escaped down her cheeks.

14

TUESDAY, JUNE 15, 1886

George didn't say a word when Lorena took upon herself the task of administering to the body; sure enough, nobody else was going to volunteer. He watched as she tenderly closed Bo's eyes and wrapped him in a heavy cotton blanket.

"This deep enough, you reckon?" Jeb called from where the men were digging the grave. They'd only plowed about three feet down, but George didn't blame them for being in a hurry to finish the job. He nodded his approval and went to fetch the body.

Wouldn't you know, she was crying again? Women's tears always plucked at George's heart.

He removed his hat and cleared his throat. "Um, ma'am?"

He studied her face, the twitching lower lip, the long eyelashes brimming with tears. For just a moment, she met his gaze and looked so lost, so inconsolable, that his instinct said to hold the woman tight to his chest and let her have a good cry.

Then she wiped her eyes, and he realized her gloves were still crusted from slashing the boy's innards.

Blast it! He had to stop letting her pull his strings. She had less a woman's heart in her breast than did a rattler.

"Move over, now. We got the grave ready."

"What? No! You can't!" She scrambled to her feet and seized George's arm. "Please! Stop them! Don't let them bury my Bo!"

George ripped his arm out of her icy clutches. "Touch me again and you'll regret it."

"The boy!" she cried, pointing unnecessarily toward Bo's body. "They can't bury him!"

"You want us to leave him out for the buzzards?"

"Oh!" When she squealed, her blood-soaked glove flew to her mouth. "You wretched beast! We'll take his body back to town for a decent burial."

The men around the hole heard her and mutinied.

"The hell we will!"

"I ain't riding with no slaughtered corpse. You never heard of juju?"

George grabbed her by the shoulders and led her backward. "Lady, you are going to sit down and shut up. We got work to do here."

"But he isn't going to—" She bit off her words, staring down into the hole. "We can't leave him here in the middle of nowhere. How will I ever tell his mama there isn't even a marker to his memory?"

George goggled at her, his entire forehead scrunched up in consternation. "You got no trouble killin' the feller in cold blood, but now you want to erect a monument to celebrate it?"

Lorena looked away, her nose high in the air. "Really! There's no call to be like that!"

In all his years, George had never heard of a murderer being so tender and emotional toward their victim while at the same time not displaying a shred of remorse.

"You expect us to tote his dead body 'cross Missoura on horseback? It ain't gonna happen. This field's as good as any other, and we'll fashion something for a marker. Then we're setting off again, and don't you try stalling."

This time, she seemed to accept the iron in his voice. Recomposing herself, Lorena said levelly, "I'll need to change my dress first, of course. I'll ask you to put the hood up on my landau so I may use it as dressing quarters. Do I have your word that none of your men will impeach my honor by wandering too close?"

George spat on the ground. "Woman, what you got left of your honor wouldn't feed a hind-tit calf!"

Lorena spun on her heel and crossed the grounds, sashaying in her genteel way as though she were off to an ice cream social. George watched her move, disgusted yet intrigued.

He needed answers.

With a few great strides, George overtook her and swung her around. "You know, I half believed you when you said you wasn't a murderer. But you *are* the Hellfire Witch. I know that now. How many men have you killed?"

"Don't you read the papers?" she said with the ghost of a laugh. "It's all there."

"Don't mind my curiosity," George's voice changed pitch, slow and dangerous as an impending tornado, "but it seems to me you soured on that boy awful quick. Thick as thieves, you two, and this morning you splatter his insides from here to Kingdom Come."

"Don't say that! It sounds so awful!"

"Don't it, now? You should've seen the full spectrum that I got fed. You dripping with blood, looking savage as a meat axe —"

"Stop it!" She buried her face in her hands, then covered her ears as the onslaught continued.

"Not only did you opt to kill him, but with at least a dozen rifles in the camp you haul off and go on a stabbing spree with that teeny dagger. Which gets me thinking you must've really taken to hating him to inflict that kind of—"

"I didn't hate him!" Tears gushed forth. She wrapped her arms around herself, somehow finding a chill amid the sweltering conditions. "He was my only hope. I loved him."

"Hush your mouth! I ain't going to believe that flimflam."

"Then you're a jaded fool. Of course I loved him! He was..." Abandoning all propriety, she admitted, "Little Bo was my cousin."

❧ 15 ❧

FRIDAY, MARCH 15, 1872

For Lorena, the truth unraveled just weeks before the family vacated her childhood home.

Mr. Whittaker had sold his entire plantation, lock, stock, and barrel, to some latter-day carpetbaggers so he could move closer to his fledgling steel factory in Pennsylvania. Though their new house in Allegheny was huge by local standards, he'd thrown most of their possessions into the sale. The girls were allowed to pack their clothing, jewelry, and assorted trifles, but nothing larger than a Jenny Lind trunk could hold. Many tears were shed over leaving behind their new Singer treadle sewing machine. Gone as well were the brass chandeliers, the lions paw dining set, and the beloved pinewood sleigh beds. He'd even sold their heirloom china and the frames to the family portraits.

The crushing blow for Lorena came when he traded off their entire library. Shelf after glorious shelf, empty!

So when she overheard her sister Mabel exclaim,

"Phew! Look at all these musty old books," she came running.

Three crates of their Grandmother Eleanor Whittaker's belongings had been pulled out of deep storage for one final sorting-through. In the East Parlor, Mabel busied herself sorting through dresses while Rose counted stacks of doilies to add to her own hope chest.

Lorena skidded through the door with one word on her lips. "Books?"

Rose pointed toward a discarded pile in the corner.

"What do you think of this?" Mabel asked, posing with a brown-and-blue printed, square-bosomed dress with leg-of-mutton sleeves.

Rose wrinkled her nose. "It's antediluvian! Why would you even consider being seen in such a thing?"

"I only meant to use the fabric..." Mabel began, but drifted off under her sister's withering frown.

Lorena's own excitement waned just as quickly as the first book she grabbed fell apart at the stitching. The next few failed to rally her spirits, as she held little interest in *The Science of Physiognomy* or *Experiments in Plant Hybridization*. Toward the bottom, she picked up a volume whose cover had been replaced with a hand-stitched sampler.

"Isn't this gaudy?" she said, tossing it to her sister.

Grace opened her knees to basket-catch it in her skirts. As it landed, it fell open to the center pages.

"Oh, my! Oh, oh, my!"

Soon, all three girls were gathered around to gawk and awe over the grotesque, French picture book. Every page held photos of naked men and women posing without shame.

Lorena stared so long she forgot to breathe.

"Why would anyone want a thing like that?" asked Mabel.

Grace answered in a faraway voice, "I suppose it's meant to teach women how to–"

"Not the book. *That*!" Mabel pointed to the man's groin. "Do all men have those?"

"Let us hope not!" Grace looked decidedly ashen. Lorena wondered whether she was thinking of her own impending nuptials to the senator.

With an unsteady hand, Grace turned the page. The next woman was lying down with the man on top of her. Grace fanned herself so heartily that Lorena considered running for a bottle of vapors.

"Will you have to do that when you get married, Grace?"

"Decidedly not! If I had to lie in that position, I would die of shame! Even with my garments on!"

"I wonder if they're hinged differently," Mabel mused.

"What?"

"Those French girls. Do you see how widely they swing their legs open? I shouldn't think that's even possible for a civilized lady."

To demonstrate, Mabel hiked up her skirts and squatted bowlegged before them, turning her toes outward until she forfeited her balance. With a squeal, she fell backward over the trunk, hoop skirt and stockings flailing in the air.

Grace dropped the book in her haste to rescue her sister. Only Lorena noticed the folded slip of yellowed paper that fell from the back cover.

"Mabel, you ninny," Grace scolded, though there was laughter in her voice. "You must learn to comport yourself like a lady or Mother will never consent to your coming out."

"What's the point of coming out if I have to do it in Pennsylvania?" Mabel countered, suddenly sullen. "Do they even have cotillions?"

Lorena ignored her sisters' relapse into bemoaning the drudgery of the North. The paper she'd found turned out to be a letter to her Grandmother Eleanor from her Great-Aunt Malvinia. After the usual wishes for good health, it dove into a report of some grand dinner she'd hosted for the governor—who'd attended, what they wore, where they sat. She'd crossed the sheet to save paper, only to waste it with a thorough account of every dish she'd served and the various ways the governor had complimented each serving.

Lorena was about to discard it when the postscript caught her eye:

Regarding the matter we discussed on the carriage ride, my advice is that you not question the girl. Where is the good in it, El? Do you suppose yours to be the first Southern home to spontaneously produce light-skinned babies in the slave cabin? You will be a happier wife if you will put this out of your mind forever.

"Grace, whatever does this mean?"

She passed it to her eldest sister, who scanned it

quickly, then brought it close to her face for a more careful study. Grace's lips twisted into a deformed pucker.

"What can she mean by it?" Lorena asked again. "Who cares what color skin a slave has?"

"It means nothing," Grace hissed, "because it isn't true." She tore the letter into thirds, then wadded it into her fist. "Don't you ever speak a word of this, Lorena, or Mother Rose will have you horse-whipped until you can't sit down."

Suddenly, Grace jumped to her feet and tugged at the bell pull.

The moment the servant appeared, Grace ordered, "Dispose of this mess. All of it. Come, girls, let us abandon this pursuit. Nothing from that trunk interests me. Grandmother Eleanor was a tasteless, old fool. Nothing of hers is worth cutting down for rags, even. We shall find such better fashions in Allegheny."

Lorena had never heard Grace sound so much like Mother Rose. As her sisters linked arms and she swept from the room, Grace chatted gaily, not a care to be had. But Lorena noticed she clutched the shredded letter tightly until she was able to chuck it into a fireplace.

Lorena followed, docilely, and nearly succeeded in putting it all out of her mind. Over the years, however, minor details flitted into her consciousness, like the fact that her father and his butler were exactly the same height and build.

Sam Whittaker - who'd taken the family name hand-in-hand with his freedom papers - stood behind her father so often that it was easy to forget he was there. But when Lorena truly looked at the man who attended her father day and night, it all became evident. They stood in identical poses: slightly duck-footed, one shoulder higher than the other. Shave off her father's beard and they had the same tapered face and jutting chin.

Lorena wondered whether Mother Rose had ever allowed herself to realize that her butler was also her brother-in-law. Surely not. Sam was a great favorite of Mr. Whittaker's, but even he had enough remnants of Southern pride to disavow that unwanted offshoot of the family tree. And yet...

Despite his pecuniary insistence on transporting the bare minimum of their belongings to their new home, they were bringing Sam and his entire family with them. Doubtless, it would be cheaper to hire local servants. And in her father's desperation to not be viewed as yet another Johnnie-come-a-Yankee, wouldn't it blacken his name to be bringing slaves with him, even under their new title of domestic servants?

Suddenly the fissure in Mr. Whittaker's otherwise smoothly polished career tactics made sense. And for the first time, she felt fiercely proud of her father.

All this dawned on her gradually, in dribs and drabs, until, a Southern Belle no longer, she acknowledged the truth. Standing in her own backyard in Pennsylvania one evening, she watched Sam's youngest children—her cousins—playing "Boogeyman."

Little Bo ran past, barefoot in breeches and an old straw hat. His wide, toothy grin captured her heart. From that moment forward, Lorena swaddled Bo in sisterly affection... until the day she splattered his blood across the Missouri plains.

16
SATURDAY, APRIL 17, 1886

THE MORNING AFTER HER ENGAGEMENT, Lorena slipped out before breakfast to share her news with Bo and encourage him to come along.

Within the hour, he told his pa he'd "tooken a notion to see the world." Sam forwarded the idea to Mr. Whittaker, who said offhandedly to Adalwolf, "Of course you'll take little Bo as a personal servant."

Lorena clapped her hands in delight. "Thank you, Father! What a wonderful present."

Mr. Whittaker beamed at her but kept an eye pasted on Mr. Adalwolf, waiting for his decision. Any answer—acceptance, denial, even a postponement—would have been taken as law by everyone involved. But Adalwolf turned in his chair to muse over an oil painting, acknowledging no one until they were called to dinner.

Lorena found it awkward to advance the subject again, so Bo was left in limbo. But when, on their wedding day, Bo arrived at the train station toting a rucksack of clothes, Adalwolf paid his fare without a word.

After that, they entered into a fragile accord of silence. Adalwolf spared neither word nor glance toward the boy, directing all messages through Colquoit. On the other hand, he provided for his charge financially at every stop as they crisscrossed the Midwest. Unsure whether Adalwolf's withdrawal stemmed from simple bigotry or jealousy of her affections, Lorena took care not to mention Bo when her husband was present.

And Bo never, ever confided to Lorena his growing distrust of the man in charge of their lives.

17

EXCERPT FROM DIEDRICK ADALWOLF'S JOURNAL:

LAST NIGHT I was weak and slept too soundly. I dreamt I was a small boy and heard again the song my nurse sang to me. Is my fevered mind trying to lead me to an answer?

Hush, naughty child
You will wake the house
Your father will be cross

You must learn
Not to fear the dark
In spite of what is there

Hush, naughty child
It shatters me
To see your punishments

Sleep through the night
And if we wake
I'll hold you tight tomorrow.

18
ELSEWHEN

As terrifying as his last moments of life were, what happened to Bo afterward petrified the marrow of his soul. He was sucked down. Down through the darkness, weighted by an anchor driven through his chest.

Not down! Oh, Lord, no!

And by some act of divine grace, he stopped, inert, prone on the unyielding ground beneath tortured skies. Not back, no. Not returned. But not *that place*, either.

Nothing moved. Not here, not in the distance. Nothing rustled in the wind. Even the sun changed its mind about rising, abandoning the plains to murky twilight. An ocean of untrampled grass surrounded him like the grave.

Bo didn't budge either, at first. Even breathing was no longer a useful habit. He supposed he was meant to wait patiently for the eternal peace he'd been promised.

After a while, it was hard not to fidget.

He kept picturing his last glimpse of the living world. Even with his eyes squeezed shut, he could still see those dark chestnut eyes staring down at him, haunted by her own private demon.

Miss Lorena, how could you? Sobs broke from his throat as he pictured that poor, sweet woman, all twisted up inside of herself. She'd done wrong, knew it was wrong, cried her heart out as she stabbed him, and even as Bo was fighting her off, he'd tried to save her.

It was him, girl. That damned old man. I should have got you away from him. Got us safe...

Bo reached up to wipe his eyes in grief and nearly gouged himself with the silver dagger clutched in his fist. He stared at it, amazed it had come through with him. Miss Lorena's final gift.

Resting place forgotten, Bo sat up, turning the knife in his hands, wondering.

She'd said so much crazy stuff at the end, wild ideas and foreign words, all a mishmash of instructions she'd meant for him to memorize. And somehow, she knew he'd land here, in this *other* place that no one had ever warned him about.

She'd killed him for her husband's sake—that wretched, twisted old fiend who'd never deserved her love, whose soul wasn't worth a plugged nickel. Bo had hoped he was dead, was glad he was dead.

"And the *devil take him*!" he roared, throwing his head back like a lion.

On his feet now, Bo stuffed the dagger through the belt of his trousers and took stock of his surroundings. A narrow path of reddish-brown dirt sprawled onward over loping hills toward infinity.

"If there's something I'm s'posed to do," he said

aloud, because hearing his own voice made the solitude less imposing, "best be gettin' on with it."

He threw back his shoulders, head high and proud like his daddy'd taught him, and took the road at a leisurely clip. A song rose within him, a spiritual from his childhood church, and it comforted him to replicate the deep baritone and rough drawl of the former plantation hands.

I KNOW DE OTHER WORLD AIN'T LIKE DIS
Fire in de East and fire in de West
I know de other world ain't like dis
Let God's children have some rest

I KNOW DE OTHER WORLD AIN'T LIKE DIS
Swing low, sweet chariot into de East
I know de other world ain't like dis
Let God's children have some peace.

IV
DREAM CATCHER

19

SUNDAY, MAY 16, 1886

Growing up, Lorena thought religion to be much like her father's carriage: wide, powerful, always there when she needed it, and a good excuse to dress up on a Sunday. She'd learned her catechisms and attended a séance here and there for amusement but left the deep deliberations to others. Like Mother Rose, she felt the point of being a loyal parishioner was to keep a pastor on retainer should circumstances arise.

So, she found herself completely at sea when she wed Adalwolf. Devoted to his theological research, he pored over his notes every waking hour. In the rare times that he set his studies aside, he always seemed distracted, as though he was still pondering the last thing he'd read.

Lorena spent most of her time with him reminding herself not to talk.

On the train to Peoria, they rode in terse silence, Adalwolf reading while Lorena fumbled with a bit of embroidery beneath swaying gas lights. On the bench across from them sat Colquoit and Bo; Adalwolf had abruptly taken a notion to leave Cincinnati and they'd arrived at the station too late to book separate passage for their servants. This gauche infraction of protocol left them all unsettled. All but Colquoit, chewing his tobacco and grinning like the devil.

She glanced up from her handwork and caught Colquoit in the act of wiping his nose on his sleeve. Momentarily abashed, he dropped his arm and tried to snuffle the phlegm back up. After a few moments of successively more distasteful noises, Adalwolf slammed his book closed.

"How am I to concentrate?"

Colquoit murmured something that had the tone of an apology, if not the words. It amused Lorena that her husband was the only man in the world Colquoit ever seemed keen on impressing.

"You are familiar with this next town?" Adalwolf asked him.

"Yes, sir. Been through Peoria a coupla times."

"Have you acquaintances to call on?"

"No. Nobody in Illinois."

Adalwolf pursed his lips. "You are familiar with the taverns, perhaps?"

"Uh ... well, yeah, but there are a darned lot of 'em."

Master Adalwolf said nothing, merely looking displeased.

"But you don't understand," Colquoit persisted. "They call it the Whiskey Capital of the World, for God's sake. You cain't swing a cat without hitting a distillery, bar, or whorehouse!"

Lorena gasped. Although she had actually grown used to his coarse phrasing, she felt it was unladylike not to take offense.

Adalwolf grunted and took up his book again. "That will do. Go to another car."

Colquoit fidgeted, not sure whether to try to stand in the cramped compartment. "Uh… Master Adalwolf, the train's booked up, remember? There ain't no other seats."

"Then ride in the baggage car," Adalwolf said, unruffled. As Colquoit indignantly stomped into the corridor, he added, "Take that one with you."

They all understood him to mean Bo. The young boy nodded a farewell to Lorena and took to his heels.

Lorena's mood improved immediately. They had hours left to ride, and she was almost never awarded time alone with her husband during daylight. She turned to look at him, but from this angle, all she could see was a hollow-cheeked old man.

Gathering her skirts, she slid across to Bo's empty seat. From across the aisle, his wrinkles seemed less deeply etched, and her imagination, coupled with his enchanting blue eyes, made him younger, virile once again.

"My dear," she said, "I worry that you will ruin your eyes trying to read in this poor light."

Adalwolf glanced up sharply, as though he'd forgotten she was still there. He closed his book but replied, "My eyes will last as long as this senescent body does."

Lorena tried again, "I would happily read it aloud to you."

"You read *Deutsche*?"

"Oh, I'm sorry. I didn't realize it would all be in German." She stole a long glance at the book that was a more constant presence in her life than her own conscience. Its wrinkled leather cover warped under the burden of inches of dog-eared pages, many of which were falling loose from the binding. It had no title, nothing on the cover or spine to give her a clue why he found it so eternally intriguing. "You brought it with you from your homeland, then?"

"Yes. These are my grandfather's studies. And my own appended to his."

Lorena perked up. Adalwolf had never mentioned his family to her before. She scooted closer to him.

"What field did he study?"

"*Höhere*—" he stopped, correcting himself. "In English you say Higher Criticism. Theism. He studied scriptures of all lands." Adalwolf's words came slowly as he carefully translated his thoughts. "He believed in historical analyses of the holy works."

He turned to the window, profiled against the storm lighting up the plains.

"My grandfather was Jürgen Adalwolf. You will not have heard of him, but he was long ago famous in Württemberg. He taught at the University of Tubingen, and his published papers, as they say, turned Europe on its ear."

Lorena smiled indulgently. "And you took up his work after he passed? What area do you study?"

Master Adalwolf returned his full attention to his wife, wandering his eyes over her features before responding. "That is not what he taught to me. That came before ... Grandfather was at the peak of his fame in the early forties, while I was just an arrogant rogue, interested in nothing beyond riding, games, and young women. He taught me nothing then. This was before the famine. The..." He tapped his tongue against his lips, searching for the words. "The potato blight. You have heard of the 'Hungry Forties?'"

She nodded.

"Terrible times, you see? There was simply," he raised his empty hands, "no food, ja? Such suffering. Not just the peasants. It began with the paupers, but by '45, even the aristocrats cinched their waistcoats to hide the shame of hunger. No food to be had for any price. So you see, my grandfather had power. Money. Fame. Knowledge. Yet he could do nothing but watch death gallop circles around his family."

"You lost someone—some people close to you?"

"Ja. My father and mother died. Then followed my brothers. Grandfather summoned me, and then we lived alone together."

The tremble in his voice hinted that his concise facts were steeped in loneliness. But it was an old wound, long since scabbed over.

"So your grandfather took you as his pupil?"

He uttered the slightest laugh at that, just enough to split the corners of his mouth. "No! Grandfather shared with no one. His remaining years he spent alone in his study. He traveled to the university only when he needed materials for his research. He spoke only to order food and necessities. Many days would pass that I did not catch even a glimpse of the man."

"If his faith was shaken, you should have consulted a pastor to intervene."

"That would have done nothing. My grandfather was not interested in faith. Truth was what he sought. In every book of truth ever written. My grandfather strove to learn about death. What happens afterward? What choices must a man make to determine his path? That is when he compiled this book."

Adalwolf stroked the manuscript on his lap like a favored pet. He sported a peaceful smile and Lorena felt intensely close to him.

"Grandfather died soon after. He left to me his money, his land, his mansion, but not his studies. This he hoarded, even in death. I discovered he had arranged to be entombed with this book. My servants would not disturb it, so I was forced to dig into his crypt myself." Stretching both arms toward her, he revealed thick, twisting scars inside both wrists, snaking up his arms. "So intent was I, I barely noticed how I cut myself again and again scrabbling on the stone."

"You robbed his grave?" Lorena couldn't stop staring at the book, imagining it in the corpse's embrace. "Why did you want it so desperately?"

"I grew very sick. Deadly sick. The crops grew again, and the world rejoiced that the Great Hunger was no more. I was young and rich and strong and happy and free. Then came my sickness. I grew weak.

Fevered. For two weeks, I slept, and the doctors feared I would never wake again."

"How did they save you?"

"Bah! They did nothing. I saved myself. I defeat death in sleep!"

He smiled once more, and this time, she saw nothing pleasant in it, only the skeletal sneer of thin lips drawn too tight.

"But when I wake, I do not remember how. I lose the understanding. So I seize my grandfather's knowledge, and I add to it my own. All my life, I study. And always I think of what is *not* written, what is lost. So now I am here."

Lorena shuffled in her seat, feeling their conversation had skipped a rail. "I don't understand. You mean in America? What do you seek here?"

"The savages."

"The...?" His answer knocked her so off-kilter that she was lost for words. "The *Indians*?"

"Ja, their theories of dreaming are most unique."

Lorena readjusted her shawl and fussed with the folds of her dress, a mannerism aped from Mother Rose when she was rankled. She had heard stories of Indians and their religious ceremonies and was quite certain she did not wish to hear any more.

"I have come to realize," her husband continued, "that the ancient truths may not be solely the property of our European continent. Ach! The years I will have wasted studying the classics if that is true. But no more wasting time. I came here to discover for myself the truth. I will soon be master of all."

Again, he stopped short. In the awkward pause that followed, he tickled the spine of his book with a yellowed fingernail as though the tome could be coaxed into revealing more information. Lorena watched with a strange jealousy.

"My dear, tell me what I may do to help you with your studies. I've always had a quick ear for languages. I would happily learn German if it—"

"No!" His sharp syllable silenced her, but after she bowed her head in submission, the words that followed were not unkind. "You have your own part to play. You are Mein Treuer. Sleep now."

Lorena knew better than to protest that she was not sleepy. She pressed against the compartment wall in a pose that supported her neck without compromising her dignity and concentrated on the rocking of the train.

20

SUNDAY, MAY 16, 1886

Like the pull of a magnet, slumber drew Lorena directly to her favorite spot in all the worlds: the master suite of her lover's mansion. Was it wrong to think of him as her husband when she was visiting him decades before they met? She was uncertain how God's laws on matrimony worked in such a case. She still did not understand how she was here at all, for that matter. But as to the time period, she now had a clue.

The aged Rococo furniture had puzzled her before. The veneer wardrobes with their lovely ivory floral designs were stunning, but the entire set had gone out of style long before Diedrick was born. She ought to have guessed that this was a bachelor's household. Apparently, he'd inherited it, in turn, from a man long widowed. They would have cared only that the thick walnut legs of the sofas were sturdy and unscuffed, not that the upholstery was faded and dull. She did not want to find fault with her new sometimes-home, but her eye immediately sought the few newer accessories, like the handcrafted clock on the mantle with its cunningly carved little cuckoo that peeped out on the hour.

Her heels tapped the parquet flooring as she crossed to the bedroom. Today, every window opened to a beautiful summer's day, allowing the light breeze to circulate the scent of fresh-cut flowers lining the dressing tables. His servants remained, then, even though she never encountered them, and he employed enough to tend to the trivial accents. Good.

This place, this time, must be in the 1840s, after he moved to his grandfather's estate. Likely the old man had already died and made Diedrick its master. But her sweet, carefree lover surely hadn't yet taken up his life's obsession with theological studies. She'd never seen him reading, had never even tripped over an open tome. Yet, if the servants again tended flower gardens and clipped the lawns, the Hungry Forties must be drawing to a close.

That left only one question: had Diedrick yet fallen to his month-long illness? He seemed too robust for a man who'd lain in a coma for weeks, but that could be deceiving. She needed to examine his wrists. If he had those horrible scars, the illness had already passed; if not...

She smiled when she found him, snoring in his favorite divan, muddy boots propped up on an ottoman, his riding crop still dangling from his hand. How he loved his morning rides!

Kneeling at his side, Lorena gingerly pushed up the sleeve of his blue frock coat and scrutinized the skin above his riding glove. No scar. Her heart leapt, and though she knew she was being insensible and that her dear husband was the same man at any age, in sickness and health, still she thrilled to the fact that this Diedrick, her one true love, was unsullied. Sickness had not claimed him yet, nor this twisted, myopic thirst for knowledge and power. This man was pure, with no secret agenda, and the love to which she so desperately clung must also be true.

It had to be.

Nothing made sense to her about these dream journeys. Rationally, she could not exist here, and yet everything—from the frayed seam near a missing button on his breeches to the stiffness of his linen cravat—felt as real to her as her own skin.

But if she was in his past, living with him as man and wife, why did his older self not seem to remember her? As cross as Adalwolf became when she mentioned her dreams, she dared not press him. Perhaps it was better if he had forgotten, if everything that happened here was known only to the young lovers.

No! *Pressing her lips to his gloved fingers, Lorena prayed that he would never forget her. Whatever ability allowed her to touch him in dreams, she must not lose it.*

Tears filling her eyes, she stretched up to kiss his cheek. Please, let this be real. It will break my heart if this isn't real.

Diedrick stirred, tilting his head to meet her with his mouth. She felt his body stiffen as he pulled her closer. His boots thumped to the floor, and he scooped her up by her padded rump and deposited her lengthwise onto the divan.

"Mein Liebling," *he whispered, grinning as he moved over her. The hands that worked the buttons of her bodice were smooth, manicured, and full of purpose.*

EXHAUSTED AND SWEATY FROM CONJUGAL BLISS, LORENA lounged in their feather bed. But it seemed silly to try to fall

asleep within a dream, so when the aftershocks of euphoria subsided, she opened her eyes again.

Diedrick was gone, but in the corner of the room lurked the elder version of Adalwolf. Stooped and grey-haired, with unheeded spittle in the corner of his mouth, he approached. The spark of love was never visible in this one's eyes, but the keen interest in Lorena never abated. She tugged at the comforter to cover her naked body. Illogical though it might have been, her lover was not *this old man. She'd never seen him like this in her dream home before, and it simply felt* wrong*.*

Adalwolf shuffled nearer and snatched the covers out of her grip. "Enough. Get dressed, insatiable woman. We have much work before us."

21
MONDAY, MAY 17, 1886

"LISTEN TO THIS ONE. You'll enjoy it," Lorena said.

Bo obligingly drew nearer to her on the grass-covered path so she wouldn't have to lift her voice. They had fled the boarding house for her daily constitutional as soon as the sky had cleared. Her newfound status as a married woman would have allowed her to roam the towns unescorted, but she preferred to keep Bo by her side—partly for company and partly to keep him out of Adalwolf's path.

Today, she carried an edition of *Lyrical Ballads* liberated from the landlord's study from which she read:

SHE DWELT AMONG THE UNTRODDEN WAYS
Beside the springs of Dove

AT HER SIDE, BO CHIMED IN:

. . .

A maid whom there were none to praise
And very few to love.

Lorena looked up, wide-eyed. Bo stood too far away to have been reading over her shoulder. "How on earth did you know that?"

He shrugged, scratching his belly through his woolen shirt. "Remembered it, I guess."

"But you couldn't have!"

"Really?" A grin broke across his face. Crossing his arms over his chest, he planted his feet and recited:

She lived unknown, and few could know
When Lucy ceased to be
But she is in her grave, and, O!
The diff'rence to me!

She gasped and ran her finger down the page to verify the poem. He'd gotten it word for word.

"But that can't be!" Snapping the book closed, she held the cover up before him. "This is William Wordsworth. I've never read it before. So, do you see, there is *no way* I could have taught it to you."

"Miss Lorena... it was you as taught me how to read. Did you 'spect I'd never pick up a book less'n you made me?"

Lorena stood speechless for a long moment. Then, from deep within, a giggle bubbled forth, and she clapped her hands in delight. Taking Bo's arm like they were schoolchildren, she led him traipsing along the path, drinking in the sunlight.

"Sweet, little Bo! Imagine you holding such surprises. Memorizing poems just for the enjoyment of it? Sometimes you strike me as smart as a Philadelphia lawyer, you do! Tell me another."

"Oh, uh..." He floundered, slowing his pace while he wrinkled his nose in thought. Then his brown eyes flashed. "There's a few by that Blake fellow that I always liked."

Standing tall with his thumbs tucked under his suspenders, he lifted his eyes to Heaven and intoned, "*O Rose, you are sick—*"

"I say! Watch your distance, boy!"

A short, stocky man barreled up the walkway toward them, one beefy hand holding his squat, round hat in place. He eyed Bo like he'd encountered a rabid dog that needed to be put down.

"Is he bothering you, ma'am?"

Lorena realized she'd let her hand rest on Bo's arm. She immediately separated from him, fluttering her fingers to fan her cheeks.

"Oh, no, no, not at all. He's my—my servant. My husband's servant," she amended, thinking this lie sounded more seemly.

It did appear to placate the stranger. Still puffing from the exertion of his run, he said, "Ah, well you cain't always tell nowadays. Why'n'cha run on back ta your chores, boy."

Bo stayed silent, his eyes darting from the man to

Lorena. Her heart racing, she sidled further away. Had she been too friendly with Bo? Would it have appeared to this man that they were enjoying each other's company too well, out here on the winding paths? How could she have been so careless?

Peoria might be as laid-back of a town as she'd ever seen, but even in Allegheny she had gotten Bo into trouble once by forgetting to treat him as a servant. Her father had intervened then to save Bo's hide. This time was up to her.

"His chore today," she said firmly, "is escorting me on my walk. I'm new to this town and don't wish to wind up lost."

"Ah, I thought you must've drifted in from somewheres. There's few enough comely young ladies in this end of town that I cain't name." He tipped his hat. "Welcome ta Peoria, Mrs. ..."

"Adalwolf. And you would be...?"

"Hubert Colby. I'm pastor of the Methodist church just up yonder." He pointed to a steeple just visible beyond the treetops. "And what church will you be attending?"

"Not likely any," she admitted, then flushed scarlet at his reaction. "It's not that I wouldn't wish to. It's just that we tend to travel every Sunday. For my husband's work, you see. We're only in town for the week."

Mr. Colby looked as pained as if he were vigorously jabbing himself with a needle. "I'm terribly sorry ta hear that. What line of work is he in?"

"Railroads. He invests in expansion lines."

"Well, I cain't look unfavorably on that. The railroad's the best thing to come through this town since—well since the whiskey barons, truth be told, but you won't be wanting to hear 'bout that." A sportive smirk played across his jowls before the pity returned. "But I am aggrieved that you should be forced ta travel on the Lord's day. How long has it been since you attended a proper service?"

"I remember well. It was the week before my wedding day."

Mr. Colby clucked his tongue in a wet *tsk-tsk*. "Mrs. Adalwolf, whilst you are staying in my city, would you allow me ta minister ta you personally?"

Lorena hesitated, wondering whether she ought to defer to her husband on this matter. Always intending herself for spinsterhood, she'd never asked her mother how to comport herself when encountered by a bachelor with a religious agenda. Then again, he *was* a Methodist and a clergyman...

"I think that would be acceptable," she decided.

Mr. Colby offered his arm and together they took another turn around the open lawn, talking animatedly on all topics that sprang to mind.

Bo tailed them home, nodding reassuringly whenever Lorena peeked over her shoulder.

22

MONDAY, MAY 17, 1886

LORENA KNELT by her bedside that night while her husband hunched over his studies as always. Mr. Colby's rebukes about falling from grace had left her conscience-stricken. She silently recited prayers until Adalwolf growled, "Stop dawdling and turn out your light."

So far, he hadn't commented on her newfound friendship with the pastor, let alone her request to stay in Peoria through the next set of services. Knowing well how he disliked disruptions when he penned his notes, she slipped into bed quickly and soon fell asleep.

That night, her dream did not begin in the mansion or its moon-drenched hillside, awaiting her lover. Instead, she found herself on the steps of an old brick church just as Mr. Colby emerged in his finest Sunday attire. His face lit up on seeing Lorena, and he held out both arms to welcome her.

Such a pleasant smile, she thought.

Then, suddenly, she was ripped from her dream.

Adalwolf shook her awake, his sallow face inches from her own. "*Nein! Nein! Nein*!"

Lorena flailed in his arms until the old man grew too tired to continue. She tumbled onto the floor, clutching at her racing heart. Adalwolf wheezed and lurched toward his desk chair.

When at last he'd recomposed himself, he straightened his spectacles and said in a clipped voice, "You are mine! You will invite no other men into your dreams. You understand this?"

"Yes," she whispered.

"Good. Return to sleep, Mein Treuer."

Lorena crawled into bed, facing the wall opposite him, and burrowed as far as possible under the linens. While her master watched, she closed her eyes and forced herself to breathe deeply, rhythmically. Pretending to sleep was all she could manage while her mind cowered.

He knew her dreams.

23

EXCERPT FROM DIEDRICK ADALWOLF'S JOURNAL:

Indian Origin Tale
Translated by Dr. Gerhard Becker

Before life began,
The skies were empty and dark.

The Great Bear of the Sky
Blew a mighty breath
And created the Earth
And all that live upon it.

He made the Darkness and the Light.
He made the Land Beyond Living
That is hidden from all but
The Raven of Death.

And the Great Bear created
The Morning Star that brings us Love
And the Evening Star that brings us Evil.

Listen now and remember!

The child of those stars is the Wind
Which blows through us all
And changes us with Dreams.

Sometimes she is loving and brings visions.
Sometimes she is evil and tells us lies.

So powerful is this child
That the Great Bear of the Sky
Forbid the stars to reunite.

He created Mother Moon and Father Sun
To watch over them
And keep them forever apart.

I see it now! This is the song I have been
seeking!

Raven = Thanatos?
Wind, Dreams, Power.
Next I must learn about their Dream
Catchers.

❦ V ❦
INTERLUDE

24
SPRING, 1886

P.H. Daniels, publisher notorious of the *Daily Missouri Democrat*, the most widely circulated of St. Louis's broadsheets, scowled at the copy he'd been passed. While he wasn't opposed to stretching the truth where it profited him, running obvious tomfoolery like this wasn't going to sell papers. He spat chaw in the vicinity of a spittoon, not caring that the wad clung instead to the corner of his desk blotter.

"Smithy!" he bawled. "What the Sam Hill are you giving me now?"

The stick-figured man in overlarge spectacles visibly started and swiveled his head toward the door as though belatedly mapping an escape route. P.H. rose and began rolling up his shirtsleeves, always ready to school a reporter the hard way if necessary. Smithy approached but kept a blockade of furniture between them.

"An Indian attack! I ask you!"

"Yes, sir. Nearabouts Terra Haute. About an hour west of the station."

"You an imbecile, boy? They ain't had Indian troubles in Illinois in over half a century."

"Yes, sir. But that's the story I got, sir. All three men swore to it." Smithy nervously readjusted his spectacles. Fingers black from typewriter ribbon left smears along the frame.

"What men?"

"Passengers from the train. Local folk. They'd been to Chicago on business and came straight to this office soon as they got back. I talked to them all morning while you was..."

Everyone on staff knew P.H. had been down with one honey of a hangover, but no one with a shred of sense would call him on it.

"You was indisposed," Smithy finished. "They seemed credible."

"Credible? And just how does a band of braves manage to stop a locomotive?"

"Well, uh... that hit into some confusion." By shuffling his feet, Smithy inched further away from his boss's clenched fists. "It all started with some rifle shots and someone jumped aboard and pulled the break line. Uh, this was the Pennsylvania Line you see, and most of the action happened around the bank car. I, uh... well, I think maybe it was local outlaws dressed up as redskins so's they wouldn't be recognized."

P.H. flopped back into his chair and tossed the article to the floor. Renegade Indians he could sell—maybe—but a bunch of white boys disguised as another race? His already dyspeptic stomach tightened.

"You didn't even read it," Smithy whined as he bent

to retrieve his submission. "You didn't even get to the weird foreigner."

P.H. grunted, his abusive way of inviting the young man to continue.

"Well, when it was all over and the bandits had got away, there was three men from the train lying dead on the ground, and one of them was the conductor! So while all the train crew are trying to decide should they send for help or try to push on, up comes this old German doctor and says he wants to inspect the bodies, right?"

P.H. raised his eyebrows, intrigued in spite of himself. The public loved a good necrophiliac story.

"So he gets out and circles around the bodies," Smithy continued, warming to the attention, "and then goes back to his car—rented out a whole, entire train car just for his personal use, mind you—and they wait and wait for him to come back out, but he never does."

"So?" P.H. barked.

"So 'bout half an hour later, the conductor they'd thought was dead stands up and says, 'We're a mite behind schedule, fellas,' and hops into the engine to take them home. Nice and jolly as you please. Whistling 'John Brown's Body.' And the whole time he don't realize he's sporting an arrow clean through the back of his head."

P.H. nearly swallowed his tobacco.

"Run it."

VI
OUTSIDE OF DESTINY

25
THURSDAY, MAY 20, 1886

ADALWOLF TAPPED his cane to the roof of their hired cab. The driver pulled up on the reins so sharply that Lorena's head banged against the frame of the brougham double-seater. Adalwolf, stooping forward in his usual crouch, was spared from injury.

"I will send the car back for you at this corner. One hour, ja?"

"Yes, that will be fine," she answered, clutching the handbag that held her spending money.

The driver hopped down to open the door and hand Lorena out. Just as she extended her arm, Adalwolf hissed, "Wait!" and she retracted it.

The cabbie looked puzzled for only a moment, until his attention was diverted downward. A petite Yorkshire Terrier appeared to come out of nowhere to attack the inch of exposed ankle below his corduroy trousers. The man yelped more in astonishment than pain and fell backward onto the grass trying to kick the dog off.

Lorena eased herself down onto the street corner

and walked away without a second glance. These moments of déjà vu did not even give her pause anymore. She knew from the previous night's dream that the man would end up with a bandaged calf, and the Yorkie would be returned to a distraught socialite two doors down.

Joliet's Eastern Avenue, known as Silk Stocking Row, presented a series of imposing mansions, three-and-four-story mammoths as ostentatious as their owners. One pink and powder-blue Queen Anne house reminded her of her parents' home, right down to the parapet at the crown. Lorena's heart rate sped as she traversed the blocks, her pace closer to that of the delivery boys scurrying between servants' entrances than the proper stroll of a young lady out to "get some air."

A rare freedom allowed her to walk alone through this new town. Adalwolf's old legs insisted on being driven everywhere, and he hated the idea of the upper-crust shopping in person. But he intended to send her and Colquoit to the Opera House the following night, so she'd requested alterations to one of her evening dresses. At least his vices didn't include being tight with money.

She'd wrangled an unsupervised hour. A stop at the dressmakers wouldn't take that long—she'd sent ahead the dress with a note containing instructions and measurements and would arrange for a fitting later—but Adalwolf did not know that.

She turned onto a merchant avenue and almost immediately came to the millinery. The perfect hat perched on a post in the front window—the one she'd come for. A squat straw design with a fan trim of rust velvet swooping along the brim. And she already knew it looked gorgeous on her.

Lorena gave a little sigh. It was a darling hat, but she'd love it more if it had come as a surprise.

All of her dreams—even afternoon catnaps—involved exploring new towns, meeting strangers, and chatting them up. It left her exhausted. And all of them had started coming true.

She knew before she entered the shop that she would be greeted by this rather dour shopkeeper wrapped in a tight-fitting draped polonaise and ruffled underskirt that might have been seemly and flattering on a woman half her age. And she was equally sure that, several blocks away, Adalwolf was being greeted at the local gentleman's club by a ruddy man dripping moustache wax who would be as impressed by Adalwolf's wealth as he was dismayed at his ethnicity. They would enjoy drinks and cold cuts before the early rush of members assembled, at which time Adalwolf would be kindly yet firmly turned away.

Lorena had foreknowledge of all of this. But what bothered her more was that Adalwolf did too. He'd prelived these events as truly as she had. As with the incident with the Yorkie and their driver, he wasn't even pretending ignorance of her dreams now.

Listlessly waiting on an over-padded Chesterfield, Lorena endured a parade of laces and ribbons in subtly different hues. They settled on a basic style, working backward to match the hat, and the matron enthusiastically pitched the latest local style of stiff beaded lace extending from the wrists, pointing toward the ring finger. Lorena remembered wearing this completed dress, and it itched something terrible. Of course, she couldn't tell the woman *that*, so she kept her tone chill and untenable.

"Plain cuffs, if you please. No, I do not wish to see any more styles. Keep it simple and elegant and bring it around to my address tomorrow at noon." She paused in the act of handing the seamstress her temporary calling card. Was she throwing away a chance to be out of the house alone? "That is to say... have it prepared by tomorrow afternoon, and I shall return for a final fitting."

The woman bobbed her head and twittered promises until Lorena marched outside and down the street. She was moving too fast again, but not enough to outrun her own tumultuous thoughts. She'd altered the dress design. She could change events. Even with pre-knowledge, she could still affect the outcomes. It gave her a glimmer of hope that she still had some control over herself, her life.

The *Woman's Intuition* booklet was still riding the Northern line, intentionally abandoned beneath her seat when she had perceived that all this, whatever it was, was not her doing. Adalwolf's pull mystified her, but beyond a doubt, his will over-powered hers. When she was allowed to lead her dreams, they stayed within the confines of the Southern mansion, she and her adoring young husband savoring one another's company; when Adalwolf took control, they were always running to noisy, smoky halls to rub elbows with the wrong element.

She felt like she was fighting a losing war every time she touched a pillow.

At the end of the block, she turned another corner. The homes here dropped drastically in size, the lots narrower. No carriages were on display, and no sunken windows affected the privacy of the very people preening to be noticed. This neighborhood marked the average homes of the less well-to-do. People here struggled against creditors but kept their heads held high, nonetheless, secure in the status that closely observed manners would keep for them.

Lorena had to stop to check the house numbers. She'd changed her pre-ordained path, and for once, she found herself traveling a road she'd never seen before in dreams or in life. Such a beautiful, freeing feeling!

The house she sought was typical, respectable, and nondescript. The only window not hidden behind a cherry tree displayed a discreet, hand-lettered sign that matched the advert in the Joliet weekly news: "Languages taught. Tea served. Inquire within."

Lorena felt bold as brass as she knocked. She could do this without Adalwolf's knowledge, for he never explored the past; her dreams only caught snippets of the very near future.

The door seemed to open itself. Then a voice drifted up from waist height.

"Greetings, my lady. How may I help you?"

Lorena bit back a grin at the girl, aged seven or eight, with corkscrew curls and a delicate lisp, endeavoring to seem so formal. She curtseyed like a royal courtier, exposing dirt-smeared stockings and the telltale double hemstitching of a skirt that had been flipped inside out for longer wear. Her eyes traveled over the intricate floral embroidery along the lace of Lorena's traveling dress, and her mouth formed an O of dazzled excitement.

"I wish to speak with Mrs. Tittensor," Lorena intoned.

The girl wordlessly led her into a small parlor just off the main hall. Lorena settled herself onto one of the settees and the girl bowed her way gracefully out of the room. As soon as she'd rounded the corner, Lorena heard her heels clacking on the floorboards as she ran full tilt to the back of the house, yelling, "Ma! There's a *fancy* lady here for you!"

Mrs. Tittensor wasted no time hustling to the front of the house. She was still in the act of discarding her apron when she reached the doorway, though, like her offspring, she glided in with the style of a grand dame. She rushed forward to take Lorena's hand, completely unconscious of the smear of flour along her jaw.

The ladies exchanged names, and the young daughter was dispatched for tea and cake before they sat down to business.

Lorena extracted from her bag a clipping from the local advertising sheet. "Your notice says you teach languages here. I would like to begin German lessons. Although, with my travels, I wouldn't be able to take on a steady tutor. I had hoped you—"

"I am so sorry! I cannot teach you." By the anguished look on Mrs. Tittensor's face, it was clear she was devastated at having to turn away business. "I only teach English. We have so many foreigners here these days. When I say I teach languages, that's only so people don't think... I mean, I wouldn't want to be accused of consorting with... I teach fine girls, you see," she insisted, as though she'd been accused otherwise. "Young ladies, mostly, looking to get on as hired help, and—"

"I see." Lorena saw her grand plan failing and could not restrain a little sigh. "I am sorry to have taken your time."

"Wait, wait. Don't rush off!" Mrs. Tittensor waved her hands frantically. "I'm thinking maybe I could find you someone. Mrs. Schlosser, now. She's a German lady I help out. Does cleaning and bleaching but she won't embarrass you none. I taught all four of her daughters how to speak proper and they helped teach her English enough to get around. Now they're grown, she comes 'round each week and I give her lessons in exchange for her doing our linens."

She stopped short, shamed at having admitted she was too poor to pay for cleaning services. Lorena pretended not to have caught the admission.

"You think she could teach me German?"

"Well," Mrs. Tittensor hedged, "probably not outright, mind you. But if I was to translate between you... I'd be happy to set up a meeting."

"That sounds acceptable. Tomorrow at three?"

Her hostess seemed to be waffling. "I would be

happy to do you this service," she repeated, looking down at her hands.

Lorena understood. "And, of course, I will pay you double, since you will be doing two lessons at once for my benefit."

Mrs. Tittensor beamed. "Tomorrow at three!"

26

THURSDAY, MAY 20, 1886

Lorena traipsed up the avenue, quite pleased with her exploits. In her young marriage, this was the first time she had dared to directly disobey Adalwolf—and it felt *good.* Though she couldn't articulate to herself why, she was driven to learn German, to get her hands on his studies, to try to deshroud the significance of all these eerie phenomena she'd come to accept into her daily life.

Then again, maybe she just needed to prove to herself that her mind didn't belong to her husband, despite his nightly intrusions.

She hummed to herself until she spotted Adalwolf and their hired cab already waiting at the corner. Amazing how he could make her feel chastised without even being near enough for eye contact! Lorena quickened her pace only slightly, wanting above all to appear dignified in her approach.

The driver, leg bandaged from the Yorkie incident,

helped her into the cab and sprung into his seat, bounding them away from the curb almost before she had settled against the pine bench seat.

Adalwolf said nothing.

Offering her brightest smile, Lorena prompted, "Your afternoon was enjoyable, I trust?"

"It had merit," he admitted. When he turned to her, Adalwolf gave such a start that he dropped his cane. "What happened to your hat?"

She raised both hands to her head to check that her beaded toque remained secured to her bun. She had no mirror, but the feathers seemed intact. Then she realized what he was really asking.

In her dream, she'd been so smitten with the new straw bonnet in the store window that she insisted on wearing it home. This time, she hadn't even tried it on.

"It seems you and I retain control of our own destinies," she said.

Adalwolf's face contorted as he scrutinized her. He mouthed the words, "control of our own destinies," and a wondrous metamorphosis came over him. He actually laughed, throwing his head back for a rich "ho-ho" that was so like his younger self Lorena's heart leapt with affection.

She slipped her arm in his and settled into the ride. Soon she started humming again, the waltz she always thought of as their song.

Dee-dah-daah, BUM-de-BUM dah-aah...

Adalwolf, who habitually demanded silence as they

traveled, surprised her again by tapping time with the melody. Her eyes were drawn to the tome that served as tympani to his fingertips. How was she ever going to wrest the research notes from his possession, let alone translate them?

27
TUESDAY, JUNE 15, 1886

"YA DIDN'T WANNA bury him? Why the hell not?" Colquoit snickered.

Their caravan had finally started down the trail, with Lorena and Colqoit riding as comfortable prisoners in the landau carriage. George and his men flanked them on horseback. Lorena stared straight ahead at the dusty horizon as Colquoit continued to bait her.

"Think you was gonna send Bo back to your family plot? Thinkin' of shippin' him Western Union? They got rules against packages seepin' blood and guts from every seam." He snorted. "Shouldn't a hacked at him so bad if ya was wanting to keep hold of the body."

Lorena inhaled slowly, incrementally. She felt as though she would explode if she let her breath out.

"Didn't think ya had it in ya. I always told the master I thought you were sweet on that boy."

Her head whipped toward him in shock, but she managed to keep silent. He had to be bluffing. He'd never have dared to be so insolent to Master Adalwolf. She began smoothing her skirts—a nervous habit she had whenever she worked too hard to appear calm.

"He sure *loved* you. Do anything for his Miss Lorena. Ya talk him into slicin' hisself up so you wouldn't ruin your nails? ...Naw, I reckon ya wouldn't a got so much o' his blood on ya in that case. So how'd it play out? A little smoochie-smoochie before the choppy-choppy?"

The scream that broke out of her started so high-pitched that it even hurt her own ears. She flailed at him, her fists pummeling every spot that her slitted eyes could see.

Colquoit slammed her against the seat with the weight of his body. She clawed at his lewd smirk until he slapped her face so hard that she felt like her brain had come loose.

Everything spun for her after that, and they fell together to the cramped floor of the carriage before she realized that the horses, spooked by her screams, were blazing their own path over the unplotted terrain. Men nearby shouted directions as their driver fought to keep control. But Lorena knew only the pressure of Colqoit's body on hers, the revolting stink of a man who had sweated through the same clothes for three straight days. Then a shadow blotted the sun as one of George's men jumped onto the carriage.

Colqoit jerked back in pain. A minute later, someone threw him over the side, into the path of a dozen advancing hooves. Her rescuer spared only a glance at Lorena, then jumped over the seat to help the driver rein in the horses.

Lorena stayed where she'd fallen until the ride bumped to an end. Behind her, several men surrounded Colquoit where he'd rolled to a stop.

"Want us to tie him up?" they hollered.

George had run his horse parallel to the pair pulling her carriage, helping bring them under control. Too winded to answer, he held his hand high with a thumbs-up sign. He turned his horse around and trotted in their direction. As he passed Lorena, he delivered a wordless, withering rebuke.

Conscience-stricken at last, she dropped her gaze.

28

TUESDAY, JUNE 15, 1886

Lorena found herself snuggled under layers of eiderdown quilts on the roomy feather bed of the mansion's master bedroom. She yawned and stretched luxuriously, then felt afresh the disappointment that none of this was real. Familiar as she found each detail, from the blossoming apple trees outside her window to her ruffled satin bedclothes, her husband's beautiful plantation home could be reached only in her dreams.

She sat and turned up the flame in the oil lamp provided on her bedside table. Adalwolf's chair stood empty, and when she sniffed, she caught no trace of the sweetgrass he tamped his pipe tobacco with. Odd that he wasn't expecting her; she must be catnapping.

"My love!" she called. "Are you here?"

A slamming door provided the response. Old Adalwolf hobbled in to greet her. Each successive visit found her husband more haggard, his skin and hair whiter, his wrinkles more deeply carved.

Did the shadows behind the door hint at another figure? She dared not look too closely.

"The boy," he demanded, "did you kill him yourself?"

"Yes, my love. And I gave him your—"

She clasped one, then both hands over her mouth.

The same force that always tried to draw her husband's name from her lips—the one Adalwolf constantly reminded her not to concede to—was at work now, overriding her will, making her want *to divulge the story of Bo.*

"No! He'll find out! He'll hear! Wake me up! Wake me up!*"*

29

TUESDAY, JUNE 15, 1886

George led his horse carefully down another forsaken hillside. He'd decided to take the rear-most position, directly behind the carriage, where he could keep an eye on everybody without having to meet the lady's gaze. Or smell her companion.

His stomach growled. He'd been wondering whether someone would call a lunch break soon or push on toward a stagecoach stop where they could get a hot meal instead of the rations they'd been subsisting on. Then it occurred to him that they were awaiting such a decision from *him*. Since his last bout of bravado had led him to call the woman *his* prisoner, by extension, that made it *his* posse. His decisions.

He decided against trying for a public area.

Mrs. Adalwolf might not cause a stir in polite company; everyone in these parts had heard of the Hell-fire Witch, but they were unlikely to connect those stories to such a refined Eastern-educated woman. That hollowed-out wretch Colquoit, on the other hand, was just devious enough to cause a panic by announcing he was a wanted man.

Whether he actually *was* wanted by the state remained a matter of some confusion. The posse had left St. Louis with only one name: Lorena Adalwolf. When they arrested her, Colquoit—acting drunk as a skunk at the time—laughed and taunted them, claiming he was the real killer, despite what the witnesses claimed. He and the young boy came along so willingly that the posse agreed it would be justice well served if what he said turned out to be true. Later that night, Colquoit insisted that his confession was somehow a trick of Lorena's, a case of the witch putting words in his mouth. George kept him as a prisoner, anyway, thinking he'd never met a man he trusted less.

Even now that they'd tied his arms behind him, he still seemed to have the upper hand, reclining contentedly in the open landau while the men around him grimaced from saddle sores. And all the time eyeing them with that greasy, lurking manner that suggested he'd recently pissed in one of their canteens and was hoping for a fight to follow.

The only reason that George had refused to drive the carriage himself was that he didn't want to have his back to Colquoit. It had taken a good span of talking, though, to keep old Henry in the driver's seat. Every one of the men was busting a gut to keep three yards away from her—somehow, they'd had gotten the idea that was the proper distance for avoiding the "Evil Eye."

Her little screaming fit did him no help, either. If they'd thought she was a loon before, well...

He couldn't help wondering how much of that incident had been Colquoit's fault, though. None of the posse had been close enough to hear their conversation—Henry being a mite deaf—so opinions were mixed as to whether her hired man was defending himself or attacking her. As for George, he'd caught a glimpse of Colquoit's face as he straddled Lorena, and it was enough to make George want to bite the sites off a six-gun.

He tried to remind himself that it wasn't his place to safeguard a murderess's honor. But still...

Just then, Lorena let out a squeal to wake the dead, crying, "He'll hear! Wake me up! *Wake me up*!"

George's horse reared, knocking him into the dirt. Before he could recover, his favorite stallion kicked him in the leg.

30
ELSEWHEN

Isolated in the unbound darkness, Diedrick Adalwolf secured the clasp on his traveling cloak. Unmoored from his anchor, he and The Other One reversed positions once again: the captive and the hunter.

31

EXCERPT FROM ADALWOLF'S JOURNAL

The song of the Sweat Lodge
Translated by Dr. Gerhard Becker

Come! Gather to the circle.
We pass the pipe
And tell of great deeds.

It is not the moon
That fills us with bravery
While the coyote howls on the hill.

Though a man is strong,
When the arrow finds him,
Still he may fall.

It is not the night
That gives us power.
It is the circle.

Come! Gather now.
To sit as men
And pass the pipe.

Smoke from the Sacred Bundle
Fills our spirits.
Death will not find us here.

WHAT CAN THIS MEAN? I feel this is the essence of their discoveries. Is the translation correct? I must find someone who has seen this Sacred Bundle.

VII
MEN OF MEN

32

FRIDAY, MAY 21, 1886

Something jolted her awake, but Lorena couldn't find the strength to rise. The room was dark, the bed lumpy, and she too disoriented to go to the trouble of discerning whether this was a dream or reality.

"Wake! Wake up!" Adalwolf's words were barely above a rasp, but his bony hands pinched her hard on the back until she squirmed away from him.

With a yelp, she rolled over. "What is it?"

"You must sleep for me."

"I *was* sleeping!"

"*Nein*!" He shook her by the shoulder. "First fetch my pipe. Then sleep."

Trepidation smothered her as she rose to a sitting position. With shaking hands, she lit the gas lantern at their bedside table.

Adalwolf looked like the residue of death. Feverish, shaking, and sweaty, his sallow skin shone beneath the blankness of his eyes. When he wheezed through his slack mouth, it sounded like a lady's fan being dragged across a xylophone.

Lorena jumped from the bed like a shot, almost dropping the lantern on the quilt.

"Are you dying?"

"My pipe," he repeated.

"Are you sure? Are you able to sit up enough to—"

"Fetch it!"

She rummaged through his travel bag. Her fingers found the carved wooden box that held his pipe and a small bag of tobacco. As she opened it, the whiff of sweetgrass and sagebrush almost overwhelmed her, and she found a new hope. Colquoit always referred to this as "the master's medicine bag." Perhaps it would indeed help?

Adalwolf had propped himself up against the wall when she returned with his package. He tamped it himself but allowed her to hold the flame for him as he struggled to inhale properly. At last, tendrils of smoke rose between them, and he seemed to relax.

"Sleep," he said simply.

Lorena curled up at his feet and obeyed.

33

FRIDAY, MAY 21, 1886 / SUMMER, 1857

THEY RODE TOGETHER on a narrow train, Lorena and Adalwolf. It was his older self, but healthier than he had been minutes ago. Still stooped and breathing heavily, he no longer looked feverish.

"Is the medicine working, my dear?"

He shushed her and turned to look around. Lorena craned her neck as well.

On the bench opposite them sat a matron with a worried expression. Lorena eyed her dress, an old-fashioned cut of plain, brown fabric. The woman idly patted the head of a small child resting against her while she fixed her eyes on a sullen boy sitting in the corner.

The rest of the train car—every single bench behind them—teemed with children. All ages, toddler through school age, huddled together in the bouncing, winding car, and their screeches, laughter, cries, and chatter mounted to an unbearable din. Lorena, who was raised in the "children should be seen and not heard" school of manners, thought about getting to her feet to rebuke them. But they obviously were not descendants of well-bred society. Most of the boys were shirtless and barefoot with only poorly fitting pants tied off with rope belts. The girls fared slightly better with straight-cut, sleeveless dresses that hit the vicinity of their knees.

Most puzzling was how they all afforded train fare. Then it came to Lorena with a shock—she had heard of The Orphan Trains Movement, of course, but had never given them much thought.

These children, likely rounded up on the streets of New York by the Children's Aid Society, were being shipped westward, to towns struggling to populate themselves, where more helpful hands were always needed. The younger set would likely be adopted into various families, while the ones nearing adulthood held the promise of at least an indentured servitude with a roof overhead and warm meals in their bellies.

Lorena's family had donated to similar charities in the past, but humanitarianism wasn't likely to explain why Adalwolf had picked this destination for her dream. What in the world could interest him in these children?

A great whistle sounded, and soon, a uniformed conductor hurried into the car.

"Almost there, ma'am," he said, tipping his hat to the lady opposite Lorena. "Might want to prepare the kids for stopping."

The woman heaved a great sigh but smiled up as though she'd found rescue in an Arthurian knight.

"At last," she said. Turning in her seat, she called, "Children!"

But before they came to any semblance of order, the brakes were pulled, and the great mass of metal heaved to a halt. A few children tumbled into the aisle with a considerable amount of shrieking and flailing about.

"But where is the station?" the woman asked, peering alternately through both sets of windows.

"This ain't a regular stop," the conductor explained. "The townsfolk asked us to disembark at a common relay station, so's the families wouldn't all have to travel so far."

"Sensible," she said, then clapped her hands for attention. "Boys and girls! Single file lines! I want to see the girls on the left and the boys on the right. No, my *right. There is no need for pushing. Let everyone see what proper gentlemen and ladies you can be. Do be on your best behavior, children. Oh, please. You must know how important this is."*

She seemed on the verge of tears but squared her shoulders and busied herself arranging them, comforting them, and wiping faces with her handkerchief. When all were accounted for, she strode back to the front of the lines. "Ready, then? Bright, shining faces, all. No, no, Giles, you stand with me."

Lorena leapt to her feet as the procession passed into the waiting sunshine. Giles? As in Giles Colquoit? She peered past Adalwolf through the grubby window, as the matron led her charges into the crowd. That sullen boy following half a pace behind her, his wrist gripped in her unyielding hand... could that be Colquoit?

She leaned back, trapped in the stuffy car until the orphans finished filing out, and thought that at least the rancid smells in the place made sense. They must be invading Colquoit's mind tonight.

"What are we doing here?" she asked her husband, vying to keep her voice light, indifferent. "Ransacking his memories?"

It rarely pleased Adalwolf to answer her questions, but he gave a terse nod. "Ja. I will see for myself if he has lied to me."

Twenty minutes later, Lorena's heels had ground divots into the dry earth from standing so long beside her husband. Only a small percentage of the original crowd remained within shouting distance of the smoke-belching train. Across the Nebraska plains, newly created families forged their way home. Apprenticeships were initiated on the way to neighboring towns. Only two children remained unaccounted for, Colquoit and a very sickly baby, and they were the subject of impassioned discussion between the remaining adults.

"I won't tell a fib, Pastor," the matron was saying, "he's a shady one. Probably come to no good. But if anyone can take him to task... Well, maybe this is the Lord's way of giving him one last chance. If we'd left him in the city, he'd have been in prison before the train pulled out of the station."

Lorena watched the man of the cloth fidgeting, clearly trying to talk his way out of a commitment to either child. "I just don't know," he kept repeating. "We have so many at home already."

"But the baby," she said quickly. Her method was to switch between the two, to keep him guessing. She clearly didn't intend to leave either child without a home. "Surely you can take in the baby. She don't eat much, and likely she won't be long for this world anyhow."

She said it matter-of-factly, but all eyes went to the swaddled lump in the basket by her feet. The preacher squeezed his eyes shut, his lips pursed, and made a muffled noise.

"I'll take her," he announced softly. "But not the boy!" And with that, he seized the basket and scampered off.

Then they were alone, the matron, the sheriff, and the rail-

road men, impatient to get the train moving again on its last leg toward Lancaster. One man handed the lady up onto the waiting platform and she ascended with her head bowed, whispering, "What's to become of the boy?"

No one had a ready answer. In the distance, Colquoit trudged wide circles, sneaking up on insects to stomp them into the dirt. He'd spared no time on any adult today once the lady had relinquished his wrist. Unlike the other orphans, he'd given no hopeful glances to the prospective parents, no angelic smiles or toothy attention-grabbers. He seemed indifferent, resigned to a life of catch-as-catch-can, even hundreds of miles away from the alleyways he'd haunted through most of his pickpocket life.

"I'll watch 'im." The declaration came from the sheriff, and it was as devoid of sentiment as if he'd just offered them a share of the chaw he was languidly packing into his bottom lip. The lady gasped and moved to shake his hand, to thank him. He waved her off. "He'll wind up in my jail anyway. Might's well keep 'im where I can see 'im."

Without another look at the departing trainsfolk, he walked past the boy. Not breaking his stride, he grabbed Colquoit by the scruff of the neck and led him along. "You. You're comin' with me."

34

FRIDAY, MAY 21, 1886 / FALL, 1857

LORENA FLUTTERED AWAKE, cramped from her fetal position beside Adalwolf. His skin was glossy once more, and the room had become so filled with smoke that she felt light-headed each time she inhaled.

"More," he croaked. "Sleep still."

She stretched flat on the bed and lay her head back down.

ONCE AGAIN, THEY FOUND THEMSELVES IN AN OLD prairie town. Several men rested outside a general store, their boots up on crates, just another afternoon shooting the breeze while it was too hot to work. Lorena recognized one as the sheriff who had taken custody of Colquoit, deeply entrenched in storytelling, and waving his arms.

Lorena paid little attention to him or to Adalwolf at her side. Crossing into the store, she found a seat in the shade and tried to collect her thoughts.

Adalwolf was reading Colquoit's mind, wasn't he? How else would they be here, in this place she'd never seen, in a time they couldn't have known? How was he managing any of it? And what part was she playing for him?

It was all too confusing, and what she really wanted to do was get some sleep, but the irony was that she was *sleeping, and even that afforded no rest anymore.*

And in the back of her mind, a niggling voice tendered the question—why was he digging in the past? She assumed that her exploits of late—peeking into his journal while he slept, arranging lessons with the German lady—would be private. What if he turned his eye to her *past? Would she be able to shield her actions?*

In this anguished state of mind, Lorena rested on the wooden bench across from the patent medicine counter and ignored the prattle of the other patrons.

Some time later, a clatter outside sent everyone running to the shop window. A woman in a voluminous apron shouted toward the back room, "Pa! Come a-runnin'. It's those Reds again!"

Only Lorena was brazen enough to stroll outside into the thick of the action. Confident that she could not be hurt within her own dream, she joined her husband at the edge of the porch.

Every man there stood at arms, some concealing six-shooters behind their backs, others openly sighting their sidearms on the approaching parade. Along the street, every door slammed shut, citizens fleeing the thoroughfare with military precision. Lorena could only see the outlines of these riders on horseback as they galloped into town, but the headwear alone gave them away as savages. She drew in her breath and clung to a post, trying not to faint.

These Indians were nothing like the paintings she had seen in the East. Beyond the shock of seeing them in flesh and blood, she wasn't prepared for the menacing scope of their warrior mentality. Each of the five men had deep battle scars accenting the scowls on their broad, dark faces. Long black hair flowed freely over their shoulders, curling around thick biceps and sometimes entangling in their layers of bead and rope necklaces. Each man wore a black-and-white feather atop his head, making them seem even taller, more erect than was natural on horseback. But what stood out most to Lorena was the passion in their eyes. She spotted no discernable weapons, yet every citizen around her trembled behind a gun. Clearly these men were powerful in a way she did not comprehend.

They drew up even with the sheriff, but he did not step forth, despite some prodding of his companions. At last, another man, a balding merchant-type in faded trousers and rolled-up sleeves, ventured forth, hailing them in their language. The Indians circled their horses around him so they could converse easily without dismounting. Peppered with occasional shouts and rough gestures, the exchange lasted several minutes until, at last, the man was allowed to scurry back to his fellows at the store.

"This ain't good," he said, wiping sweat from his brow. "They want retribution, here and now, or the whole mess of 'em are gonna come sweeping into town in about an hour."

Amid a chorus of "shit!" and similar sentiments, one man articulated the point.

"We can't hold against that many. This whole town'll be buzzard food by morning."

"What'cha gonna do, Jack?" asked the sheriff.

Jack, the man who'd acted as their spokesman thus far, let his mouth drop open. "Me? Bowman, you yellow, back-stabbing snake!"

He hauled back and punched the sheriff square in the jaw. To Lorena it appeared the others hesitated enough to allow him to get a few good blows in before moving to break them up.

"Hold up. Hold up, now!" a grey-bearded man in spectacles called out through the doorway of the General Store as the two men stood panting and glaring at each other. "It don't matter which of ya fixes this, long as you get a wiggle on before they start scalping."

"He's right, Jack," interjected a guy in a faded Stetson. "How do we end this? You ain't yet said what caused all this."

Jack looked over his shoulder at the imposing braves on their stock-still horses. "They say someone ruined two of their Pintos. Some of their braves were bathing along the banks of the Missouri. Left their mounts grazing on the grass. Some kid shot 'em both in the hind legs before the men come up outta the water and chased him off. They want two new horses to replace theirs."

"Well, hey, that's easy," the sheriff answered. "Let's someone give them a coupla horses and we'll get through this."

"And whose property is that coming from, Bowman? Yours?"

The lawman fidgeted. "Hey, now, you know I cain't do that. I've only got the one horse, and what good would I be to the town if I cain't get around?"

"What good are you now?"

He flinched at that but kept shaking his head. "They're just stirrin' up trouble. Don't mean nothin', probably. You boys know that. Bet if we push 'em they'll admit it was Cheyenne or somesuch that messed with their horses and we don't even come into it."

"They saw the boy," Jack said simply. "And strangely enough, he fits the description of that'n."

All eyes followed his pointed finger toward a boy crouched beneath a bench behind them, his mouth and pockets full of candy likely stolen from the store's bins.

Lorena couldn't believe she hadn't thought to look around for Colquoit. Since it was surely his mind, his memory, they were exploring, obviously he would be present. She started to march toward him, to grab him out from beneath the bench, but Adalwolf raised his cane in front of her chest to stop her.

Sheriff Bowman reached him first. He hauled the boy to his feet before everyone and walloped him upside the head. For a moment, it looked like Colquoit was choking on a piece of hard candy, but when that subsided, he went back to his usual scheming smirk.

Lorena wondered how much time had passed since he'd come off the Orphan Train. Young Colquoit looked to be around eleven or twelve with more bone than meat on his form. His brown hair was cut to respectable standards, parted in the middle with a curl at the nape, but that brown buck tooth had already emerged, like a warning fire on the horizon. And Lorena disdainfully noted that he'd never lost his fondness for wallowing in dirt.

The sheriff turned pale under the furious looks of those around him. He thrust the boy in front of himself, trying to redirect their ire, but Jack spoke for them in a clear, arresting voice.

"Was your bad egg what done it, Bowman. So what'cha gonna do?"

Bowman became the picture of pure self-serving panic. "Fetch my horse."

Throwing Colquoit over his shoulder, he marched toward the braves. Jack followed a pace behind.

"Here," the sheriff said. "They can have my horse and they can have the boy. He ought to at least be worth a darn for carrying things."

He stared at the Indian leader. The dark man stared back.

"Tell him!" he spat at Jack.

Slowly, calmly, Jack interpreted the exchange. One of the locals came running with the sheriff's horse, lifting the reins to the hands of the nearest brave. They barely glanced at Colquoit, but apparently accepted the offer. One set of hands grabbed him, flipping him belly-wise over the cloth saddle, then sent the lead horse sprinting out of town in the direction they had come.

35

FRIDAY, MAY 21, 1886

LORENA SAT UP IN BED. The heat of the mid-day sun still burned her arms, but here in this world the day had barely broken. Dawning light congealed in the dense smoke clouds above Adalwolf's rigid form.

"Dear?" she whispered. Was he breathing? Trying to swallow her fright, she felt his chest for a heartbeat.

He knocked her arm aside, muttering in his native tongue.

Undeterred, she felt his forehead. He burned to the touch, wet and clammy.

"You've been up all night, darling. You must rest."

But he was laboring to tamp more tobacco into his smoldering pipe. She watched the workings of his feeble hands and knew he must be as exhausted as she was.

"I need to know the truth," he rasped.

She fell back onto the mattress, hands working at her temples to soothe her own budding headache. "Please. Can't we sleep without dreaming? Just for a short while?"

"Nein. We must seize the time. Colquoit will awaken soon."

Lorena froze, processing this revelation. "He has to be sleeping, too? Are these his dreams, or mine?"

Adalwolf narrowed his eyes, puffed haggardly on his pipe. She could hardly bear to hear the rattle of his lungs as he inhaled.

"Sleep, Mein Treuer," he commanded.

"No." She sat up, surprising herself, and faced him squarely. "Are these his dreams, or mine? Tell me what we're doing."

"Ja, ja, they are his," he snapped. "Now sleep. Quickly."

"But if they are his dreams, what use am I?"

Without warning, he slapped her across the face.

"You will obey me!"

"Yes... just tell me... what do you want? I just want to help you, my love. Please. What use am I?"

Adalwolf's shaking hands dropped the pipe, spilling burning embers onto the bed. He moved to smother them, then wiped his blackened hand on the sheets. As he reclaimed his spot, settling his back against the bed frame, he spoke in conciliatory tones.

"You are Mein Treuer. In this, you are my anchor. You are constant to me. Open to me your mind and from there we travel together. You will ask no more questions. You will obey and remain quiet. Do you understand this?"

"Yes." Feeling a show of submission was called for, she swallowed her pride and added, "Master."

He nodded and closed his eyes. "Sleep, Mein Treuer."

36

FRIDAY, MAY 21, 1886 / SUMMER, 1860

ONCE MORE, she found herself roaming a strange land—among stranger people. Their conversation fresh in her mind, she knew Adalwolf would still be angry with her for failing to fall asleep on cue, so Lorena kept her head down, following dutifully behind her husband.

If she didn't know they were tilling Colquoit's memories, she'd never have believed they were in America. Man-made hills peppered the landscape—squat, ridged, earth-colored buildings that put Lorena in mind of a sand pyramid that had been drenched with water. Between each sod cave hung lines of wash featuring blankets of beautiful geometric color schemes and drying feathers and hides, which seemed to be the staple of their home decoration.

Women of all ages roamed the village in similar buffalo-hide dresses and simple moccasins. Most had babies on their hips or trailing behind them, and all had their arms laden with baskets: clothing, gardening, craftwork—they worked with an intensity that put Lorena's most ambitious tatting to shame.

And around the hills and work areas they chatted incessantly, in high-pitched grapevine shouts or low, rolling laughter.

No men were present save one; an elderly chieftain with a long-plumed headdress draped across his bare chest. He sat in the shade of his sod hut, bent over to rub the calluses on his bare feet. Lorena heard him singing to himself, a queer, loping intonation that the boys in Pennsylvania would have turned into a tavern chantey.

Adalwolf gently lowered himself onto the ground beside him, unnoticed as usual. Lorena wanted to circle the village, even wondered whether she could sample their wares without incident, but opted instead to stand out of the way.

The chieftain kept glancing up at something in the near distance. She assumed it was the lovely young maid strolling through a patch of squash, proffering her curvaceous buttocks each time she bent to add another to her basket. Then a movement in the thicket downstream caught her eye.

She made out the form of a boy, an early adolescent by his size. Shielding her eyes against the sun, she squinted harder and confirmed that it was, indeed, Colquoit. Lying on his back, facing the girl, his right hand thrust down his—

Lorena gasped and turned away.

37

FRIDAY, MAY 21, 1886

A MOMENT LATER, she found herself pressed against Adalwolf's bony back in the stillness of their rented room. He had slumped over onto his side. His ever-present pipe hung from his limp fingers, sprinkling cinders onto the floorboard.

Anxious lest they start a fire, Lorena snatched it and laid it to rest on her side table. She trotted behind the room divider to use her chamber pot, then returned to scrutinize her husband.

He slept, at last.

Every night he stayed up, smoking over her as she slept, running through her dreams. Then in the morning, he stole down to the breakfast table before she began dressing. Sometimes she wondered if he himself slept at all. She guessed the fever must have overcome him at last.

Her stomach growled. She longed to take a sponge bath and go down to breakfast, but how angry would he get if he woke to find her gone?

Indecision immobilized her until she leaned against his dressing crate and chanced to run her hand along his journal. His unguarded journal. And she did have an appointment with Mrs. Tittensor this morning...

Ten minutes later, she snuck out of the room, journal tucked against her breast. A hastily penned note on his bedside explained that she had just dashed out to arrange his morning meal.

38

FRIDAY, MAY 21, 1886

Mrs. Tittensor breathlessly tried to whisk up the chit-chat as she poured tea. Her daughter, still not introduced, flitted in and out of the room in a matching hat and pinafore to serve plates of ladyfingers and cucumber sandwiches. Each time she rounded the corner, the flare of her dress threatened to knock over a set of beaded candlesticks. Those cemented Lorena's suspicion that the family had pulled out every expensive decoration they owned to try to impress her. She was likely the most well-to-do guest this sitting room had ever witnessed.

The ornate effects completely overwhelmed their other guest, Mrs. Schlosser, who had thrice dropped her demitasse spoon onto the rug and not yet managed to sweeten her tea. She muttered apologies as she leaned down to retrieve it again, grey hairs spilling out of her tatted hairnet and clinging to her damp, ruddy cheeks. More murmuring followed as she sat back onto her padded bench, straightening the folds and fluffing the ruffles of her too-tight charcoal leisure dress.

Lorena was quite worried that the older woman would take a fainting spell if she had to bend into her stays again.

"I am so gratified that I was able to arrange this for you, Mrs. Adalwolf," gushed Mrs. Tittensor. Her manner suggested that she was rallying against awkwardness over the older lady's lack of gentility.

"I am indebted to you for it," Lorena returned.

The daughter's mouth formed an *O* as she rushed from the room, and Lorena chastened herself against using vocabulary that might remind them of money.

Meanwhile, Mrs. Schlosser tried again, stretching her short arms toward the sugar bowl, and it was plain she would never reach her target without standing. Lorena clucked her tongue in annoyance and reached for a cake, endeavoring to subtly knock the plate against the crockery, thereby inching it toward Mrs. Schlosser.

The old woman gave a start of surprise and sloshed her drink onto her lap.

Lorena wanted to scream at the way they were squandering her time. As little Miss Tittensor was dispatched for linens and a small washing bowl of water, Lorena kept her eyes on the grandfather clock in the hallway. How long until her husband awoke? How angry would he be with her for sneaking out?

Hoping to expedite their interview, she pulled her notes from her dress pocket and unfolded them onto the table. When perusing Adalwolf's diary, she'd found time only to jot down words and phrases that seemed to come up most often. Some of these she had crossed out on the ride across town. *Tubinger Stift* must have had something to do with the University of Tubingen where his grandfather had taught. *Höhere Kritik* she felt was likely the Higher Criticism line of theology he'd studied. A dozen words remained, including one that had been circled repeatedly in the latest entries, *Todes liebste.*

She was so anxious to get started on the German lesson that she nearly offered to buy the woman a new dress. But the inevitable flusters this would have precipitated stayed her tongue.

"There. There we go," Mrs. Tittensor finally said. She settled into her chair and sipped from her cup, though surely it had gone cold in the interim. "Now, to our lesson, shall we? Mrs. Schlosser, you were quite correct in saying, 'How do you do?' when introduced to Mrs. Adalwolf. Perhaps you could tell us the greeting you would use in your homeland?"

"Actually," Lorena was quick to interrupt. "I had something more specific in mind. Could you translate these lines?"

She attempted to pass the notepaper across the table, but Mrs. Schlosser only looked at her blankly and kept her hands folded on her lap. Thankfully, Mrs. Tittensor accepted it, and glancing over it, nodded perfunctorily. Belatedly, Lorena wondered whether the immigrant woman could read.

"*Buttermesser*," Mrs. Tittensor pronounced with care. "Do you know what this means?"

"Ah, ja!" Mrs. Schlosser smiled with relief. "It is a..."

She pursed her lips, her eyes rolling heavenward. "You push it. In bread. A... a butterknife."

"Oh!" Lorena could not contain her disappointment. Out of hundreds of pages she might have sampled from, to start with such a mundane, useless word!

But Mrs. Tittensor smiled and pronounced it again. "*Buttermesser*. Would you like to say it, Mrs. Adalwolf?"

Lorena shook her head. "No. Go to the next."

"Certainly. Let's see. *Oneiroi*."

Mrs. Schlosser kept a nervous smile painted on her face but did not make a sound.

"*Oneiroi*," Mrs. Tittensor repeated, then tried pronouncing it with a variation. "*One roy*?" When she got no response, she plunged on to the next word. "*Thanatos*?... *Hypnos*?..."

All three women began to look pained. Even young Miss Tittensor had taken to hiding behind the doorway, where only the flare of her skirt could be seen.

"These are English?" Mrs. Schlosser asked. "You wish me to say in German?"

"Of course they aren't English," snapped Mrs. Tittensor, her manners forgotten. "You don't know what they mean?"

"So sorry." The tiny voice that escaped from the large woman underscored her panic at disappointing her betters.

"Keep going," Lorena prompted.

Mrs. Tittensor gave the German lady a stern look before scrutinizing the list again. "*Todes lobster*."

Looking hopeful, Mrs. Schlosser asked, "Lobster? Like *gekochter hummer*? Is fancy dish, maybe?"

"I think you've mispronounced it," Lorena interjected.

"Oh!" Mrs. Tittensor studied her script and tried again. "*Todes liebste*, then."

"No!" Mrs. Schlosser lost her breath and went white-faced. "Is very bad thing!"

"Excuse me?"

"Is bad. Is..." She pointed downward.

"Down?" Mrs. Tittensor guessed. "Ground? Underneath?"

"*Death*," Mrs. Schlosser whispered. "This means... Death's Dearest!"

"Dearest what?" Lorena asked.

"Is bad. Is bad." The older woman looked near tears. Her left hand made a warding sign while the other grabbed her purse. "I cannot help. Please, no."

She jumped to her feet, upsetting the teacup once again, and squeezed past Mrs. Tittensor even as the woman scrambled to clean the mess. Lorena heard her scurry through the house, slamming the back door as she fled.

In the back of her mind, Lorena heard her own laughter. It was getting too bizarre, the ways in which she got thwarted every time she caught the thread of an idea. Meanwhile, the Tittensors were staring at her with those too-round eyes. She pulled out her pocketbook and laid a generous payment on the occasional table.

"For your time. I can see myself to the door."

39
FRIDAY, MAY 21, 1886

LORENA CHIDED herself all the way home for the risk she'd taken. All the explanations she'd had planned for Adalwolf about why she left the boarding house flew out of her mind. He'd never listen, anyway. And if he'd noticed that she'd touched his journal, his wrath would be terrifying.

Outside the door to their bedroom, she smoothed her hair and tried desperately to compose herself. With a shaking hand, she opened the door.

Adalwolf hadn't moved from his spot propped against the headboard.

The pipe smoke still hung in strata so thick her throat constricted. Launching herself through it, she opened the far window. He would be annoyed when he woke—he always worried about chills and drafts—but even leaning against the sill to breathe left her light-headed.

Behind her, he moaned, a feeble rattle adrift of purpose.

Guiltier by the moment for abandoning him in this condition, Lorena ran to his side, perched on the bed, and clutched his hand.

"Dearest, can you speak?"

The folds around his sunken eyes rustled briefly. His lips pursed, then he went still.

She felt his face. Clammy. After drying the sheen of sweat with her handkerchief, she pressed her cheek to his forehead to check his temperature. He seemed every bit as bad as that morning.

Dropping to her knees beside the bed, she folded her hands together to pray. Before the first "Heavenly Father" passed her lips, her husband's eyes popped open and he grabbed for her.

"I awoke," he growled. "You were not here."

"It's well into the afternoon, dear. I left to eat lunch. The landlady offered to send soup and bread upstairs if you're hungry." He was still staring disconcertingly. She fought against spilling her conscience. *Stay calm*, she told herself. "Also, I encouraged Colquoit to take an afternoon nap."

"Ah. Very good." Although his expression did not change, he sounded indeed pleased with her for this last inspiration. "My pipe, Mein Treuer. And sleep."

"Yes, my dear."

40

FRIDAY, MAY 21, 1886 / SPRING, 1863

On the far side of the narrow stream that ran past the Indian village, Colquoit stood, still as a tree. Watching. Waiting.

Lorena scrutinized him. A man now, full-grown as he was ever going to be. Still scrawny. That was apparent even beneath his leather leggings and loose buckskin shirt. But he'd hit his full height and packed a bit of muscle into his arms. His hair, long and shaggy, was held back by a lopsided hemp headband, and he'd tucked a brown feather behind his right ear, exactly the way he would later store his cigarettes. A leather pouch slumped against his hip. It, and his cheek, sported an almost perfect outline of his hand in black mud. Knowing him as she did, she could not guess whether this was intentional decoration or his standard poor hygiene.

Colquoit stared into the heart of the settlement. Lorena craned her neck to see what he was looking at, but nothing appeared to be moving. She guessed the Indians were off eating or sleeping to avoid the mid-day sun.

Whatever he saw made his frown harden. Suddenly,

Colquoit strode forth with purpose. He skipped over the stream without even looking down at the stones he used as a bridge.

"Come," said Adalwolf, setting after the boy as quickly as he could manage. Lorena tried to follow Colquoit's path, but her voluminous skirts made it impossible to see the stones. She slipped and struggled, and in the end, followed Adalwolf's tactic of just sloshing through the stream. It ruined the taffeta, but she was reasonably sure the gown would be spotless when she awoke.

They caught up with him just inside the perimeter of the sod huts, but only because he'd slowed down to a creep, walking erect but noiselessly. Outside the largest home, he glanced around quickly, then darted beneath the blanket that served as a door.

Adalwolf seemed loath to touch the blanket. He prodded it with his cane, holding it agape for his wife before ducking inside himself.

She hadn't thought much about what to expect in an Indian's home, but if she had, she'd still have been shocked at the sparseness of their living quarters. First of all, they had no furniture—unless the furs and cloth bundles spread around the floor represented beds. And instead of using shelving or cupboards, this family appeared to have their every possession hanging from the walls; pelts, pottery, half-finished weavings, clothing, horns, weapons, dried vegetables, strips of meat, bulging leather bags, extremely long pipes, a wooden flute, and a bundle of thin bones hung pell-mell from ropes draped between every pole.

Feeling dizzy, Lorena crouched down to avoid touching anything.

Colquoit crawled over the bedding, searching the crevices

of the wall until he sat back on his haunches with a large bundle in his arms. The Adalwolfs leaned over to watch as he laid it on the ground before him and began working at the copious strings that tied closed the roll of dark leather. His fingers flew, but the last stubborn knot fought him until he got rope burn across his index finger. Lorena wondered why he did not simply cut it with a knife, but he doggedly worked until it fell loose.

Colquoit's breathing came fast and heavy as he unrolled the pack. He scrutinized the contents as though in awe, his hands floating over the objects but never quite touching them. Again, Lorena was at a loss. It looked like assorted junk to her—weeds, rocks, bits of flint, and a few old kernels of corn. But when she turned to her husband, his wide eyes were every bit as entranced.

"You bring only dishonor to yourself when you sneak around like this."

The baritone made all three visitors start and turn guiltily toward the door. The tallest man Lorena had ever seen towered in the doorway—a dark, deeply wrinkled yet virile Indian with kind eyes. He stood erect even though his head touched the roof of the hut. Unlike the other Indians she'd seen, he wore two grey feathers in his hair, each woven downward in the braids framing his face. A large red robe wrapped around his great frame.

"If you wished to see the Sacred Bundle, why did you not ask?"

Colquoit's voice broke in a whine. "I did ask. You said I wasn't ready."

"And you are not. You have no respect for the great ways."

"Do, too."

"Hungry Coyote, look at me!" The old man's voice was firm. Colquoit obeyed, darting his eyes upward for as long as he could bear. "You are not a man. If you hide every time you are asked to take the trials, you can never be a man."

Lorena saw Colquoit's lip quiver, his cheeks burn. She wondered what the trials were that left him so afraid.

The Indian Elder patted him on the head and said kindly, "There are other ways to live. Perhaps it is time for you to embrace the third sex. Live as mixu'ga.*"*

Colquoit shuddered, and Lorena saw the familiar curl of his upper lip over his discolored tooth. "Damn you, Walking Sun. I ain't gonna dress like a woman for your amusement!"

"Listen deep to your instincts, young one. You are not cut out to be a man."

A squawking sound escaped from Colquoit, and Lorena realized he was trying not to cry. "You... all of you..." he muttered as he hastily rewrapped the leather roll. "You all like to think I'm so inferior. But guess what?" He clutched the package to his chest, waving the end at Walking Sun as though it were some manner of musket. "I got the Sacred Bundle! I'm *the holy man now, you old fool!"*

"Stealing a thing is not the same as earning it." The large man stepped forward and in one fluid movement lowered himself to sit cross-legged facing Colquoit. He made no move to take the package—his hands rested palms-up on his lap—but the boy clutched it tighter as though sensing a trick. "You have never learned our ways. We are Chaticks-si-Chaticks. *Men-of-men. We live with pride. You cannot hold your head high if you live in fear. You will always be afraid. Because you lie and loot from those who trust you, you will never be able to trust another."*

The boy who would become Colquoit hung his head. Another prolonged silence crept by. Without wasting words, Walking Sun held out his hands.

"Fuck you, Injun!"

Colquoit leapt up, running past the shocked Elder and throwing wide the blanket as he scrambled through the door.

Adalwolf laughed, clapping with his fingertips. Taking Lorena's arm, he sauntered outside into the bright sunlight. In the distance, they saw the outline of Colquoit on horseback, getting smaller and smaller.

41

FRIDAY, MAY 21, 1886

ADALWOLF WAS STILL LAUGHING when Lorena lifted her head from the bed.

"He told the truth," he said. "For once, he made no lies."

Lorena smiled encouragingly at her husband and wondered whether to approach him with some of her burning questions.

But his next command was, "My journal! Hand it to me, quickly. And leave me alone to work."

❦ 42 ❦
TUESDAY, MAY 25, 1886

"BO, help Colquoit carry my trunk. He's banging it down the stairs again."

Bo hesitated. "Inside the house, Miss Lorena?"

The family they were lodging with, the Gelsons, had laid down the law about Bo so much as stepping onto the front porch. Normally, Lorena acquiesced to demands like this—after all, it was their house—but today, she was too aggravated for such nonsense.

"Yes, and hurry. If they give you any grief, just remind them it will get us out of here faster."

Adalwolf's illness had kept them in Joliet several days longer than they'd intended. Although no one yet had picked up his sickness, the Gelsons were convinced that he'd brought smallpox into their home. Each morning they talked of evicting the Adalwolfs, and Lorena was forced to pay four times the agreed-upon rent to keep the rooms. Now, as they were finally preparing to leave, Mrs. Gelson insisted on stripping, airing out, and scrubbing down their entire room almost before they'd finished their ablutions.

A banging from the house made her hurry into the front sitting room where she found Adalwolf, huddled under blankets in a rickety rocking chair, summoning her by thudding his cane against the wallboard.

"Yes, dear?" she asked, fighting to keep her temper.

"The tickets. You must not forget to purchase them."

"Yes, dear," she repeated. "They're in my pocketbook."

For the first time, it fell to Lorena to arrange their departure. Adalwolf's persistent headaches rendered him incapable of handling the details ... yet, apparently, they did not prevent him from first dictating and then agonizing over every aspect.

"Send your boy to hire a carriage."

Lorena rubbed her temples. "I have, dear. They're loading our luggage now."

He jerked his head up, knocking his pince-nez into his lap. "Don't let them pack my journal! I wish to carry it with me."

"Yes, dear. I've set it aside with my traveling case."

"And tell Colquoit not to pack his medicine case. I will wish for him to use it on the train."

"Yes, dear. I will..." She hesitated, a new idea forming. "I will see to it myself!"

Hiking her skirts, she broke into a trot completely unbecoming of a lady. She had been given carte blanche to handle the mysterious medicine bag!

Mr. Gelson was giving Colquoit's room a much-needed airing-out. When Lorena swept in, he seemed torn between apologizing for the barn-like stench and blaming her for bringing the ill-bred man into his damask-wallpapered home. Breeding won out, and he settled for eyeing her impatiently while she seized the familiar leather bag.

Her hand tingled when she touched it. She turned on her heel, off to find someplace solitary where she could open it. But where? Mrs. Gelson was still turning out her room. Lorena hurried downstairs and took a sharp right into the dining room so she wouldn't meet Colquoit or Bo coming back for another load of luggage.

"Still hungry, missus?" The landlady's sister stopped clearing the table to bob and curtsey, a move that would have been ingratiating if her face hadn't shown such obvious irritation at the interruption.

"Not at all!"

Almost desperate now, Lorena darted back through the hallway, charged into the kitchen—another clear broach of guest etiquette—and ducked into the tiny pantry. No excuses would mollify Mrs. Gelson if she caught her here, so Lorena quickly set to work.

The parcel swung open with a satisfying click, but she found it crammed with disappointment. A tin of drug store tobacco priced at a penny a pinch. A smudged vial of something red and runny. A bag of peppermint leaves she'd seen him buy off a dubious street vendor. And the whole thing was littered with mulch, likely the tallgrass Colquoit was forever pocketing near the railroad tracks.

She pawed through it all half-heartedly until her fingernail caught on a bit of twine, and she realized a smaller bundle was hidden inside.

Freeing it from its cocoon, Lorena dropped to the ground to untie it and spread it out before her. With mounting awe, she stared at the contents, not daring to touch them directly. This was the Sacred Bundle, an exact match right down to the engraved sandalwood pestle. She'd seen Colquoit make off with it in her dream, a few nights ago yet decades ago, and here it sat in her possession.

But why? Why did it matter? She saw nothing great about this rubbish. Colquoit had most of the same ingredients in the outer bag, anyway.

Could that be the point?

A stenciled, wooden bread box laid on the shelf across from her. She lifted the lid and breathed in the familiar, fruity scent of warm sourdough as she puzzled her thoughts together.

When her sister, Anna, got married, Mother Rose instructed her chef to provide a lump of starter dough for Anna's kitchen. Creating bread entirely from scratch took nearly a week and more skill than they credited Anna's new cook of having. But with a foundation of aged yeast, it was easy. Lorena had read it herself in *Ladies Home Journal*. To keep your house supplied in bread, one had to keep tending that starter stock. Each day, you were to add flour and water, knead until your knuckles grew sore, then divide. One half got baked for that day's loaf, while the other half you stored well, to be the base of the next day's dough, and the next. If one tended it carefully and never portioned off too much, then one starter lump became a lifetime of meals.

Was it the same with the Sacred Bundle—these common ingredients, always added in precise amounts, melded again and again with the mysterious starter stock? That would explain why Colquoit always personally filled Adalwolf's tobacco box and why Adalwolf frequently grumbled that he was too miserly in his portions.

At the thought of her husband, Lorena snapped out of her reverie. She wrapped and tied the Sacred Bundle, then thrust it to the bottom of Colquoit's medicine bag. She had to get back upstairs before the Gelsons caught her prowling around—and before Colquoit noticed his bag missing.

No wonder he treated it like a chest of gold, she realized. He truly had stolen the Indians' magic.

She'd never given credence to legends about the natives, but one did hear of their boasts of lucid dreaming and the significance they often attached to the wise men's visions. Surely their dreams weren't equal to Adalwolf's, though. No tales she'd ever heard described seeing into others' minds, viewing events past and present. Or perhaps he was directing this ability in ways they'd never intended?

The only thing she could be certain of was that the answers lay in Adalwolf's private journal, penned in his cribbed hand in his native tongue. If only she could read German! If only she could find a trustworthy translator.

But if she disobeyed him again, would her own sleeping mind confess her crimes?

43

EXCERPT FROM DIEDRICK ADALWOLF'S JOURNAL:

Pawnee Sacred Bundle

To consecrate the bundle:

Eagle feather
Earth
Corn kernels
Tanned yellow hide

For enlightenment, visions:

Tobacco
Hemp weed
Catnip
Mushroom stems—red, from forest
Pigment—red, umber

Add for dream journeys:

Sandalwood
Peppermint leaves
Sweetgrass

For taste:
brandy
clean pestle with salt water

VIII
INTERLUDE

44
LATE SPRING, 1886

"SMITHY!" Sam Beaman waved his bowler hat before hanging it on a peg beside the door of the Riverside Café. "P.H. is looking for you!"

The dogged reporter glanced up briefly at his colleague before hunching over his platter of hot dogs.

Beaman paid this no mind and invited himself to sit at Smithy's table. After calling out his order to the boys in the kitchen, he prodded Smithy again.

"You'd do better to check in sooner than later. Let P.H. chew you out while he's still in a good mood."

Smithy froze despite a mouth full of sauerkraut. "He's in a good mood? P.H.?"

"Shore 'nuff. Sales're way up this week. Everyone I meet's been talking up that story you ran."

"On the crop reports?"

Beaman snorted. "Right. That set the world on its ear. I'm talking about the boardinghouse in Springfield. Whole dang household just up and dropped dead? Where do you get this shit?"

"Eyewitness accounts."

"That a fact? So if everyone in the vicinity died, who's your witnesses?"

Smithy didn't bother answering. Nobody was interested in the bald facts of the obituary. It was the mystery, the shadow of the unknown, the creative additions Smithy peppered in, that kept people talking. P.H. Daniels had made the decision to alter the geography, though, arguing that Springfield had more local impact than some tiny town all the way up near Chicago. And Smithy was more than happy to rewrite it and burn the original. All that mattered to him was that his editor had stopped threatening to ram every wasted inch of copy down his throat.

Knocking back the last drops of his Budweiser, Smithy rose to leave. "If P.H. is in such a stellar mood, maybe he won't start yelling."

Beaman waited for him to turn away before pilfering an untouched pickle from his plate. "Not a chance, kid."

IX

EXCERPT FROM THE GRAND VOLUME OF GREEK GODS AND HEROES

45
TUESDAY, JUNE 15, 1886

George's leg was broken midway between the knee and top of his boot. The men had propped him up as well as they could in the Landau, but every bump in the road sent wild shivers of pain up and down his shin.

Colquoit had been relegated to George's horse, riding between a set of men with his hands bound behind him. But the lady remained in the buggy, sitting across from George. She hadn't spoken since the ride resumed, but her downturned mouth and lowered head were the perfect posture of contrition. He had to remind himself he wasn't that gullible.

As they had no means to properly set the bone until they reached town, the posse made do with what they had on hand: a couple nearly straight branches for splints tied together twice with lengths of cloth. They'd lifted him onto the bench seat and propped the leg up onto a stack of blankets. Each time the landau rocked, the pile threatened to tip over.

Mrs. Adalwolf reached out to hold the mound

steady at one point, and George shied away. It was hell to move his leg even that rough inch, made him suck his breath through his clenched teeth, but it cast the clear message that she was an unwelcome nursemaid.

Withdrawing her hand, Lorena said softly, "I'm not such an awful person, you know."

George grunted and looked away.

Just before setting off, the men had tried to bolster him by teasing him about what a cushy ride he would enjoy while their saddle sores bled worse by the mile. But then the lady settled in across from him, wafting of perfume, and he realized what close quarters they were due to endure.

"If the heat is making you cross," she suggested, "we could ask them to extend the carriage roof."

He shook his head. The humidity could only get worse in an enclosed carriage. Under the baking midday sun, at least they felt a constant breeze.

"Have you asked for liquor? Surely, they could give you something. Even some of that burgundy you keep serving me—"

"I'm fine." He snugged his cap down, covering his eyes with the brim.

"Manners seem to fall out of style here in the West. In the absence of high society, is there no motivation to mend your faults?"

All the world might have seen her at that moment as a refined, sophisticated lady. George squinted, trying to remember just where the blood spatters had hit that morning.

"And your own faults?"

Lorena cocked her head toward him, her long white neck exposed beneath the shadow of her bonnet. "Pardon?"

"You proud of yourself? Mind what they say about your own faults?" When she continued to look blank, he bawled, "the murders!"

"Oh, fiddlesticks." She waved him off in exactly the nonplussed way she would dismiss a servant offering a tray of unwanted canapés.

"Don't mean shit to you, do they?" George sat up straight in his seat, trying to ignore the twinge in his shin. "Just like huntin' deer, I s'pose. One's as good as another. Don't spare any thought towards the families of the men you killed?"

"If you please, Mister..." She sighed. "I have heard the men call you George. In other circumstances, I would not presuppose the familiarity to call you by your Christian name, but you have not yet offered me your proper name. Would I be out of line to expect that small courtesy?"

"George Tremont." His hand twitched to tip his hat, but he played it off by scratching at the back of his neck instead, thinking he'd be damned if he would ever treat this one like a lady.

"Pleased to meet you, Mr. Tremont," she said, her voice smooth as melted chocolate. If her gaze hadn't kept circling between him and the posse surrounding Colquoit, he'd have believed she had no other intention than social chit-chat.

"That name don't mean anything to you? Like the Tremont you killed in Saint Lou?"

The whump-whump of the carriage wheels reverberated as they both held their breath. Crossing the bumpy terrain left them swaying in their seats in almost constant arrhythmic motion. Yet neither moved a muscle. Holding each other's gaze—his intimidating, hers aloof—became the sport of the day.

When she spoke again, her voice held a serrated edge. "Now I understand the disproportionate rancor. You have kin that you think you're going to avenge."

George held his tongue and counted to ten before answering. "Partly true. Philip Tremont was my cousin. But it ain't vengeance I come for. It's justice."

Lorena gave a very unladylike snort. "That man died of his own doing. He was hot-headed, foolish, and underhanded. Justice has already been served on that score."

Breathing in so deeply he got a whiff of fetid horsehair and the triggering of hay fever, George fought down his emotions. Anyone who knew his fool cousin would have conceded this description, but kin was kin. He was not about to be dissuaded.

"Ready for the noose, ma'am?" he taunted, leering at her. "I noticed you been sticking your neck up pretty high in the air. Or are you practicin' that pose so's you can beg for mercy at your trial?"

"There won't be a trial for me. You ought to know that. The moment the newspaper christened me the Hellfire Witch, the jury's minds were made up for them."

He studied her profile, her cool porcelain features unwrinkled, untaxed, as though no emotion had ever ruffled her. He'd have found her beautiful if he wasn't so disgusted.

"You got no soul, do ya? No remorse for nothing you done?"

"Remorse? No." She answered without having to consider the question, her voice a pleasant vibrato. "I'll do what I have to do."

"Was you this cool when you killed your servant boy?"

At last, he'd pierced her armor. A blotchy flush crept from the back of her neck toward her cheeks. She averted her eyes, plucking at the lace of her skirt with both hands as she whispered, "Please don't talk about Bo."

George found himself enjoying her discomfort so much that he bent forward to peer into her face. "I think you like killing, don't ya? I've always heard tell it gets into a man's blood. That true? Does it work that way for women, too?"

She said nothing, but her shallow breathing betrayed her feelings.

"I wonder if it's like dogs," he continued. "They say once they get the taste of blood, they start to fixate on it. Sets them so pretty soon they can't eat nothing else without thinking about it. When do they get their next kill? How long they got to wait? That what it's like for you, ma'am? Couldn't wait to get back to town? Had to get your kill, so you culled the weakest from the herd? Stabbed your little friend in his sleep to get your fix for blood?"

That finally toppled her. She let out a howl and

threw herself toward him. George caught her wrists just before her claws would have ravaged his face. He guessed she hadn't done much fighting, leastways not without a dagger and a clear shot at her victims.

"I didn't want to hurt him! I loved Bo!" As she screamed, she twisted and lurched, unsuccessfully trying to beat her fists against his chest. Again, he held her off, but he twisted to do it, and white-hot pain shot up his leg.

Spurring her on no longer seemed the wise move. As he worked to lower her hands against her own body, George stared into her hysterical eyes. "Then, lady, why'd you do it?"

"It was... the only way..." Her body crumpled to the floor of the shaking carriage, her forehead pressed against his seat. "I have to save my husband."

"Woman, your husband's dead!"

"Maybe," she cried, "but he says he needs my help."

George felt such a rush of electricity churning up his gullet he thought he must've been shot in the back. "What do you mean?"

"He talks to me, in my head. He tells me ways to help him. He makes me do things."

"Like killin' that boy?"

"Yes! Lord help us all. It was the only way..."

46
TUESDAY, JUNE 1, 1886

"GO BACK and talk to him again," Adalwolf told his servant. "I tire of waiting."

Colquoit shrugged. "I offered the man forty dollars, and he said it wasn't possible."

"You were too cheap," Adalwolf snapped. "Offer him eighty. Offer one hundred."

"He said it wasn't possible."

Colquoit pushed Adalwolf's beloved journal aside to make room on the table between them, then lined up three fountain pens end to end.

"This here's the front of the train. And we're here toward the back. The bit that derailed," he nudged the center pen so it rolled askew from the others, "is between us and the engine. So there's no way for them to pull our car on ahead to St. Louis until they get the whole thing realigned."

Lorena sat back on the padded bench, watching the men over the top of her *Harper's Magazine*. She wouldn't be surprised to hear Adalwolf insist that they ride in the engine room if it would get them to the city faster. The train had lurched to a violent stop only twenty minutes ago, yet Adalwolf was as agitated as she'd ever seen him, insisting they needed to be on the move again, no matter the cost or inconvenience.

Since all the man did in his waking hours was read over his notes, she couldn't see the difference between doing it on the train or in his study. But clearly, her opinion was not appreciated.

Nor was Colquoit's. Adalwolf pointed a bony finger at the door. "You will tell them one hundred dollars to take us home now. Tell them I am an invalid and will die if not in my bed tonight."

"You are not dying, my dear." The words fell from Lorena's mouth out of dull habit, the four dozenth time she'd repeated it that week. The fever in Peoria left Adalwolf more curmudgeonly than ever. He was convinced he'd narrowly escaped death, and Lorena, his unwilling nursemaid, had grown sick of hearing it.

However, she couldn't help recalling her father's promise that marrying Adalwolf would soon make her a fabulously wealthy widow. She wondered whether she'd return to Allegheny when that happened or find a new home out West.

As soon as she thought it, she became stricken with guilt over casually wishing death on her husband—both of him. Underneath the crusty old man knelt the heart of her beloved Diedrick. Didn't it?

It would be easier to remember that if the old man wasn't behaving like such a fractious child.

Adalwolf rattled his cane against the table to drown

out Colquoit's explanations. Finally, Colquoit gave in, saying, "I'll tell 'em what you said. But it won't do no good."

He turned on his heel to saunter out just as Bo appeared in the doorway, blocking his path.

"Pardon me, Mr. Adalwolf," Bo said, wringing his cap nervously in his hands. "I heard some men talkin' 'bout findin'—"

"Get outta here, boy," Colquoit barked. "You ain't s'posed to be in this section."

Bo stepped back into the corridor but gave Lorena a significant look before he turned away.

"Just a moment, Bo!" she called. If either man had made any effort to get to know the boy, they'd realize he'd never come into an upper-class berth unless it was important. "Do you need to tell us something?"

"Yes, Miss Lorena." Slipping around Colquoit, Bo stood beside her but made certain to address her husband as he explained, "I heard a man talkin' to the conductor about needin' to see a baseball game today. The way I hear it, the St. Louis Browns are havin' a bang-up season and I guess this feller's one of the muckety-mucks what owns it."

Lorena's smile faltered. "*That's* why you ran in here?"

"Yes'm. You see, them boys on the train got real excited when he said he'd took a notion to watch his boys play today. So they sent runners into town to fetch a stagecoach. And since them coaches seat six people and he's only one man, I thought..."

Adalwolf, who had been studiously cleaning his pince-nez on his handkerchief rather than acknowledging the boy, finally looked up at Colquoit. "Book our passage on the coach."

"You bet," Colquoit said, already on the run.

"I've never been on a stagecoach before!" Lorena squirmed in her seat, then squeezed Bo's arm. "You're our hero."

Bo beamed at her, then looked at her scowling husband and quickly stepped away. With a quick bow to Adalwolf, he exited their car.

In the awkward silence, Lorena dropped her head to her magazine, but her thoughts were miles away.

After weeks of constant travel, she was finally getting a home! True, it was only a rented townhouse in Dutchtown, the manner of unpresuming situation she'd have scorned as recently as six weeks earlier. But she would be the undisputed mistress of the home. No more silly rules about which rooms she could enter at which hour and where she could take her walks. No more cajoling the landladies to get Adalwolf's breakfast served at the hour he expected. And best of all, never again would she find out too late that Bo had spent the night awake on a street corner because Colquoit had "forgotten" to give him money and directions to a flophouse.

"What is the plan?" Adalwolf asked.

"I think a Swedish cook, if possible. And English maids."

Lorena realized belatedly that Colquoit had returned and the question had been directed at him.

"I bought us seats, but we've got to hustle up there to claim 'em."

So off they ventured, Mr. and Mrs. Adalwolf riding in relative comfort with the genial but untalkative stranger while Colquoit sat shotgun above. Bo remained with the luggage, to be delivered home when convenient.

47
TUESDAY, JUNE 1, 1886

LORENA'S first glimpse of the Mississippi River stole her breath.

She immediately clutched Adalwolf's arm and whispered, "See? If we'd come by train, we would have missed this!"

"Stop twitching, "Adalwolf commanded. "You make me ill with the bouncing."

Lorena held her tongue. Her slight movements could not possibly make a difference in the bone-jarringly fast coach. They raced over hills and rounded turns that sent them sliding into each other on the bench seat. Twice she'd fallen forward into the stranger seated opposite her. All in all, it put her in mind of the daredevils who went over Niagara Falls in a barrel.

By the time they drew near the river, loping southbound with the growing city on their right, the day was almost drained. The lowing sun tinted the sky ruby and harvest orange. But it was still bright enough for every crest of the river to glisten with its own private prisms.

Lorena stared, enchanted, lured in by the vivacity of this half-mile-wide swathe of churning current.

The sheer volume of water traffic made her cry out, and it grew denser as they approached the main harbor. Skiffs and sailboats careened between barges and opulent riverboats. As they crossed the famous Eads Bridge, Lorena counted fifteen full-size steamboats anchored bow to stern. All this was but a teaser for the bustle of St. Louis itself. The great river town—the first real city she'd seen since leaving Philadelphia—stretched, sprawled, and staggered in all directions up the hillside. The streetlights were being lit in patches, just enough to draw her eye to the quaint neighborhoods dotted between the industrial centers.

One of them was hers!

She wanted to spring from the stage as soon as they arrived at the stationhouse, to listen to the noises of her new home and watch the street vendors packing away their wares. But of course, her husband insisted that they remain seated until Colquoit ran to the Carriage House to retrieve his private coach.

So, although she was dying to see the city and struggling against the urge to bounce in her seat like a schoolgirl on a hot afternoon, Lorena stayed immobile in the stagecoach for the next twenty-five minutes until, at last, Colquoit reappeared.

Adalwolf climbed into it with his standard grumbling and fussing, but Lorena took her time admiring it under the streetlamps. A landau carriage! Drawn by a pair of chestnut Arabians! And it was new enough that the wheels were yet unscuffed, the brougham folding top still perfectly crisp. She wondered whether Adalwolf would ever allow it to be collapsed into the coupe style it was famous for.

She would at first chance, she decided. This carriage demanded a lady of station to be seen in it.

As she settled into her seat, Adalwolf reminded Colquoit, “Do not dawdle. We have much work to do. I wish you to go to the taverns tonight.”

48

FRIDAY, JUNE 4, 1886

"Mrs. Adalwolf? I shall be sending your boy to the store directly. Do you have a request for dinner?"

Lorena looked up with a satisfied smile. Her housekeeper, Mrs. Berbish, was already adept at managing the household. With only minimal input from Lorena, she kept her brigade functioning in the background, rarely seen or heard throughout the day. And Mother Rose had made it seem so hard!

"Let's do something with roast pork. And a bouillabaisse, not too spicy. Stock up on sweet pickles and find some new flavors of jellies for the fancy cakes. Oh, and that citrus ice was lovely. And perhaps a meringue of some sort for dessert. That's all... Ah, and we enjoyed the pretzels they were selling at the diner yesterday. Could you get your hands on some of those, please? That's all... One more thing, Mrs. Berbish. Tell Bo to bring home another edition of the paper if it has any photos of the president's wedding."

"Very good, Mistress."

Mrs. Berbish withdrew, leaving the lady of the house alone at her writing desk. Savoring the powerful feeling, Lorena stared at the crystal vase of orange and pink dahlias beside the windowsill. She'd always been drawn to the odd starburst-shaped flowers, but little Viola had claimed an allergy to them that prevented the Whittakers from bringing them inside. There was a small part of her that felt a twinge of homesickness whenever she looked at the arrangement, but she quickly smothered it. She had a home of her own to command.

One of the many conveniences she now enjoyed was that while Adalwolf spent his afternoons working in his study, she was free to do the same. No longer did she have to manufacture errands for herself or take walks just to get time alone. No, she could spend an hour at her own research if she pleased, with no one snooping over her shoulder.

It was a painstaking task, but more challenging and entertaining than the mystery stories she'd been passing her time with during the course of their recent travels. During Adalwolf's afternoon naps, Lorena snuck peeks at his journal, copying off as much as she had time for. Then the next morning, she would set about translating it. His poor handwriting was a considerable barrier, and he never seemed to write words like "an" or "the" the same way twice. Worse, the simplistic German-to-English dictionary she'd purchased was almost as bad as relying on Mrs. Schlosser.

Still, bit by bit, a picture had started to form... Although, much like that new Seurat painting the critics kept talking about, it made little sense when viewed up close.

Adalwolf was clearly ravenous for Indian religious works. He'd covered pages with drawings of dream catchers and records of their songs and poetry. Mercifully, these had already been transcribed in English, sparing her from converting them from yet another language. And the Sacred Bundle that Colquoit had stolen and reassembled was detailed time after time.

Apparently, there were any number of similar packs, all descended from a legendary man with a magical eagle's feather. Lorena was skeptical about the magical quotient of a plume, but clearly, her learned husband cared deeply about it.

What did he hope to learn?

She bent over her dictionary, nibbling at her fingernails as she scrutinized the words she'd copied the day before. If she'd misread a single one of his shaky letters, the meaning would be vastly different. Like the word play games in the local newspapers, she had to keep shifting the letters around until they made sense.

One page in particular had caught her eye. It contained a sketch that resembled Colquoit's bag, a stick figure of a slumbering woman, and a word that she had quickly come to recognize: *Schlaf*—Slumber. Beneath that, he had scribbled three words:

Geistfahrer betreten beherrschend

Her initial rendering made no sense: *ghost rider; embarrassed; government*.

She stared at the phrases, clucking her tongue in frustration to ward off her embarrassment at floundering so badly in this language. Not for the first time, she wondered if she could persuade Adalwolf to let her take a language class at the local university. Ah, but she did not have the power to outdebate him like she had her father. And he'd seemed particularly averse to her learning his native tongue.

She was on her own to crack this riddle.

There were multiple ways to decode the latter words, but she browsed the dictionary until another phrase caught her eye. Suddenly she realized that by changing *Geistfahrer* to *Geistfuhrer*, it became *spirit guides; enter; dominate*.

Her throat constricted precisely the way it always did when the first thick gust of Adalwolf's pipe smoke engulfed her each night. That was it! He wasn't just participating in her dreams; he was driving them.

49

SATURDAY, JUNE 5, 1886

"PULL UP, BO," she called. "I see Mr. Christopher."

After a pointed look at his pocket watch, Bo eased the Landau toward the curbside where the handsome young man in a felt Homburg hat and double-breasted Prince Albert frock coat stood waving his salutations.

Another social stop would certainly bring them home late for dinner. Lorena decided not to care. Every evening that week, she'd had to call Adalwolf at least three times and watch her sumptuous dinners grow cold before he arrived at the table. It would do him good to wait for her.

They'd taken a most meandering path home already, going full neighborhoods out of their way just to enjoy the feel of the summer sun and the light breeze flirting between the narrow buildings. Less than a week into their new setting, Bo didn't even trouble to ask before taking down the front half of her coach seat. Mrs. Adalwolf rode in both style and comfort, engaging her new acquaintances in conversation as often as possible. It turned out to be much easier than she'd anticipated to blend into the city's social set. Easy for a woman with both money and breeding, anyhow.

Mr. Christopher bounded toward her buggy, tipping his hat and grinning. He leaned against the frame of the Landau almost before it had come to a rest.

"What a beautiful summer's afternoon! I am so glad to see you out enjoying it, Mrs. Adalwolf. Though I confess, I myself was rushing home to eat and dress. You will be in attendance tonight?"

"Certainly." The young man had tipped her off about the evening's performance, the first of the season for the St. Louis Symphony Orchestra. "If it is anything like you described it, I pity anyone who lets the opportunity pass."

"And will I have the pleasure of meeting your husband?"

"No, no. Master Adalwolf's health does not permit him to venture out in the night air."

"I am sorry to hear that."

Indeed, he did look troubled. Lorena knew that her situation was a matter of mystery to the gossips of town. As no one had yet met the wealthy husband of their newest socialite, it was only natural for them to suspect her as one of the new set of forward single women, those who claimed to be widowed or separated from their husbands as a means of rising above the constraints of single maidenhood. She supposed she would have to produce Adalwolf in some social setting eventually, but part of her enjoyed the hint of scandal.

"I should like to discuss a patronage with your

husband," Mr. Christopher continued. "I am sure he would be most interested in our attempts to promote the cultural arts."

Doubtful, Lorena thought. Adalwolf wouldn't give two second's attention to this clean-cut lad, despite the passionate twinkle in his azure eyes when he spoke about his causes. Mr. Christopher had been introduced to her as the premier connoisseur of visual arts, and he certainly seemed well versed in both the masters and contemporary artists. In only three conversations, he had managed to introduce his plans for an Artists Guild as many as five times now. It required significant conversational skill to continue dodging his requests for a donation.

"I am so delighted to discover that my new home has not only a thirst for the arts but a Mr. Christopher to recommend them. I thank you again for drawing my attention to tonight's concert. I do hope to see you there."

On cue, Bo rustled the reins, shifting the carriage slightly as the horses came to attention. Mr. Christopher was forced to retreat a few paces to avoid getting clipped by the rear wheel.

"And I hope you will consider," he called after her, "attending the unveiling..."

Lorena waved her fingertips at him.

When they had traveled a block beyond his earshot, Bo half turned in his seat to say, "Miss Lorena, I got to ask. Do you really like listenin' to them stuffy orchestras? Or you just tryin' to fit in?"

A pert reply formed on her lips before she remembered this was little Bo she was talking to. With a girlish shrug, she answered, "Both, really. If one wants to be refined and well-received, one must cultivate a liking for such things. And if done well, I do quite enjoy the experience. But I'll admit I hardly expect to find a virtuoso among these rustics. Even if—"

"Pukes," he interjected.

"Excuse me?"

"These Missourians are called Pukes. The state's nickname."

"Oh, heavens! Really?" She burst out laughing and the boy heartily joined in.

As they took a shortcut that ran them along the backside of a brewery, her eyes were drawn to the men taking a break from the heat. All shirtless in their slacks, suspenders dropped along their legs, their pale, sweat-doused skin shone against the filth of the cinders on which they squatted.

"Though I daresay," she added, "it isn't much of a stretch to see where the name comes from."

Bo chuckled about this the rest of the drive home, a deep, pleasant baritone that Lorena found comforting even though it was at odds with her construct of Bo as still a little boy. Similarly, she noted how tall he'd grown over the last year as he handed her out in front of her house.

"You wantin' me to drive you tonight, or Mister Colquoit?"

"Why on earth would I want Colquoit to escort me? No, no! Perish the thought. Please have the carriage ready by seven thirty. Top up for evening. And dress in your Sunday's." She paused, looking at his weather-beaten togs. "We ought to see about updating your wardrobe now that we're getting settled. When you're in town tomorrow, ask around and see where there's a tailor who takes..."

Here she drifted off, unsure how she wanted to finish that sentence.

But Bo gave her his usual broad smile and tossed off a casual, "Sure will!" before he darted off to lead the horses down the road.

Their modest townhouse—a two-room-wide, four-story-tall brick squished between two others of similar shape and size—had not been designed with a carriage house, forcing them to stable their horses a full three blocks away. Indeed, the simple dwelling was no match at all for the airs put on by its current mistress.

As Lorena swished up the lane in her fine bell skirt and matching Eton jacket, she wondered briefly what her new neighbors must think about her. Just as quickly, she dismissed the thought. She did not intend to be on speaking terms with them, even the low percentage who were fluent in English. It would be too awkward. One of her own maids lived just down the street; how could she be expected to converse casually with the girl's mother?

She entered her home and was immediately greeted by an agitated Mrs. Berbish.

"Mrs. Adalwolf," she said simply, then waited as necessary to be invited to speak.

"Yes?"

"Mr. Adalwolf has been calling for you, madam. And dinner is ready to serve."

"And Mr. Adalwolf is...?"

"In his study, madam."

Lorena stared at the ceiling, her mind boring through the wood to spy Adalwolf, unsuccessfully attempting to gauge his mood.

"Do not bring the hot foods out just yet. We'll ring the bell when we are ready."

"As you say, madam."

After the housekeeper rushed off, Lorena turned to the oval wall mirror. She seemed so serene, in control, a woman to be reckoned with. How long would her outward composure last against her angry husband? She took her time removing her hat pin and laying her bonnet on the visitors' rack. She would wear a more impressive style tonight with pretty parakeet feathers to match her evening gown, but she liked the freedom of being able to go as she pleased now and always kept a hat handy by the door. With a few adjustments to secure her stray hairs and a quick pinch of her cheeks for color, she ascended the stairs.

Adalwolf, as expected, was seated in his favorite leather chair, his back to the only window. Hunched over his tome, he looked up sharply when she entered. His hand darted to the unlit pipe waiting on the table as he snapped, "Finally. Lie down. Sleep."

Lorena balked. "What—now? Dinner is ready, my dear. Wouldn't you rather take a break from your work to eat?"

"Nein."

She moved hesitantly toward the divan arranged opposite his desk. She could feel herself giving in, even as her spirit bucked and whinnied. *Don't argue*, she could hear her mother saying, *a woman's place is to follow her husband*. Still, Lorena's jaw clenched as her rear touched the furniture.

"Will this take long?" she asked. "I mean to begin dressing soon for the symphony tonight."

"Nothing of importance is to be learned there. Sit, woman! I have much to see tonight."

Under his scrutiny, she undid the pearl-and-lace collar of her dress, knowing she could not sleep in such a tight outfit.

"Perhaps we could eat quickly—I requested your favorite hot sponge pudding—and then I can dress properly for bed?"

Adalwolf's nostrils flared. He slammed his fist onto the arm of his chair, spilling untamped tobacco leaves over the cuff of his jacket. "You waste my time! Every day I am closer to death and you talk to me of puddings?"

"No, no. I'm sorry. I..." Lorena shook her head, her eyes wide. She hadn't meant to wake the devil inside.

The only option left was to take the plunge and lie down. She squeezed her eyes shut. His breathing filled the room, but at least he'd stopped yelling.

She found the old divan supremely uncomfortable. He kept no throw pillows to cushion the bowed arm, and it was so short she could not lie flat. Her legs were completely unsupported, bent against the hoop of her skirt at an awkward angle. She could not even pretend to sleep like this. It didn't seem physically possible. Her neck got a crick in it before the first waft of smoke sailed over her.

And yet he sat by like a vulture, waiting for her to lose consciousness. *As though it's that simple*, she thought, *to sleep just because someone commands you to!* Of course, she was not tired; she'd taken a long afternoon's nap specifically so she'd be refreshed for the symphony. And now her beautiful new midnight-blue evening gown would go unused so that she could be exploited in her sleep, a dreaming marionette for a shady old man.

She sat up and stared him in the eyes. True, she couldn't fight this. In the end, she'd do his bidding. But perhaps she could do it her own way.

Without a word, she marched toward him, dragged the spare armchair toward his, and turned it to face him. She eased into the plush leather, gathering her skirts between the tall arm rests. Much more comfortable. A slight smile touched her face as she again closed her eyes, sitting in perfect repose.

Their knees were nearly touching. Sitting in her customary upright posture before his hunched form put Lorena directly upwind of his rolling pipe smoke. She felt like it was going to smother her. *Good.* With each breath, she inhaled more deeply.

As she drifted off, she pictured her dream mansion.

50

SATURDAY, JUNE 5, 1886

Her heart erupted at seeing young Diedrick, handsome as ever in his dusk-grey cutaway morning coat, his thick blonde curls tumbling around his jawline. He looked up from the book in his hands and seemed genuinely shocked to find her there.

With a cry of, "Oh, my love!" she leapt into his lap. His work fell unheeded to the floor as he clutched her. "Oh! Darling!" she exclaimed between roving kisses. "Where have you been? You've been gone for so long." She blinked furiously to hold back tears. "And you're the one I love, my darling. I belong to you!"

Diedrick cupped his hands around her neck, kissing her deeply until she melted into him. He tugged at her jacket, helping her shrug it off before working the stiff buttons along the back of her dress; several sprang free and tinkled to the floor, but Lorena didn't spare a second thought for her fashions, not now when they could finally be together. She undid his cravat, her mouth lured to his neck and chest, rediscovering his musky scent, the salty taste of his skin.

As he drew her dress down and pulled her arms loose of the sleeves, she rose before him, then shimmied her hips to help free herself of layers of skirts and hoops. With both hands, she yanked her bun loose, allowing her hair to cascade over her bare breasts.

Diedrick touched her lace-up boots but opted not to waste precious moments removing them. She trembled as his hands caressed the curves of her legs, coming to rest on her lower back. He rose from his chair. In one fluid motion he swept her into his arms.

"Stay with me," she kept whispering as he strode down the hall to their master suite. "I need you."

They clung to one another as he lowered her onto the featherbed...

51

SATURDAY, JUNE 5, 1886

A half hour later, they still could not stop touching each other as they lie, limbs entwined, in the bedraggled sheets. A mist of perspiration not at all ladylike covered her face. Diedrick's long fingers combed the hair off her neck, tickling her skin.

"Oh, my darling," she whispered. His lips brushed her collarbone and her eyes fluttered closed. "My sweet husband."

"Mein Treuer."

That voice—it was different! Her eyes flew open with a horror that left her queasy.

The world had shifted, every detail. She was cold, outside, standing unsteadily—reclothed, thankfully—on the arm of her senescent husband. Those faded blue eyes glared through her skull. Adalwolf wrenched her arm, pulling her along so jerkily that she fell, skinning her knee on the asphalt. Her weight almost toppled him too; he was no longer the man who could ferry her in his arms.

Lorena rested with her palms flat on the street corner, trying to find her bearings. Was anything real, or another dream? How could she tell when the gritty pavement felt so real, a nearby pile of horse droppings so pungent it made her eyes water?

"You waste my time, selfish woman!"

She rose slowly to her feet, still trying to place the avenue or even the office buildings rising in the distance. St. Louis, surely, but which part? Reasoning that she couldn't have gotten this far from home without remembering the journey, she relaxed. A dream, then. Well, that at least was something she could control.

"Keep up!"

She strolled behind him, so tired she could barely keep up with his doddering steps. As they passed a street lantern, she reached a hand out to steady herself.

"I must rest. Please."

"Licentious trollop!" He shook his cane in the air as if to strike her. "Your useless exertions ruin our energy. March! As I tell you! Now!"

Lorena's cheeks flamed red. For a bewildering moment, she felt as though she'd been caught cheating. But the betrayal was on his side—pretending he had felt nothing! And yet... they were *the same man after all, weren't they?*

At the moment, it hardly mattered. Dream world or not, she could still feel pain. His wrath would not expend itself until he got what he wanted. Whatever that was. She mustered her strength and trotted alongside him.

Beneath her obedient veneer, her overtired mind paddled toward one buoyant idea: the mansion, the lovemaking... it had been her idea. She had not only seized control of her own dream, she had shepherded Adalwolf into it.

An hour earlier, she'd have felt a rebellious victory over her feat. But now, still warm from the embrace of her lover, it became a hollow triumph, one that left her penitent. Had she betrayed Diedrick? Even as she was seeking her husband, desperate for a honeymooning moment with the man she loved, had she forestalled his goal? Mislaid his life's work for her own selfish passions?

For, as savage as Master Adalwolf could be when angry, he was still her husband. She could still see his younger self cloaked beneath his wrinkles if she tried. If she concentrated.

"I am sorry, my dear," Lorena said.

He did not acknowledge her.

The intensifying stench of dead fish told her they were nearing the wharf. Fewer gadabouts haunted the doorways this far afield of the Saturday night gambling halls. When Adalwolf stopped to catch his breath, a gent across the street caught Lorena's notice.

Rough and unshaven in his denim bib overalls and broad straw hat, the thick-chested man crouched in the mouth of an alleyway. Every few moments, he would alternately fumble with the money in his pocket and look around to make sure he was not being watched... which he so obviously was, by every skulldugger on the block.

"Gonna get yourself mugged if you ain't careful," muttered a young man passing by.

"Woah!" The man startled, spilling several coins onto the street. In a panic, he dropped to his knees to collect them and managed to spread the mess further. The bystander knelt to help, and when the money was all returned, they shook hands. "Thank you kindly for the help. And for the advice. Can't be too careful on this stretch of road, eh?"

"Nah, it ain't too bad. Long's you don't go flauntin' your money like that. You not from 'round here, then?"

"No, can't say as I am. Just passing through. Or, well, turns out I might be staying after all, now that my luck's turned. Philip Tremont. And you are?"

"Clay. Clay Arthur."

A series of bangs on the next block froze everyone in place for a tense heartbeat. It sounded as though a gunfight had broken out, but from the hoots and hollers that followed, Lorena surmised it was just a run of firecrackers being set off.

Philip motioned Clay into the alleyway to talk privately. Adalwolf pressed his cane to Lorena's back to guide her forward, continuing to eavesdrop.

"Can I ask you something, Clay? A bit of advice? You seem a decent sort."

Lorena agreed with his assessment. No more than eighteen at best, with bright-red hair cropped close to his head, Clay could not have looked more the epitome of wide-eyed innocence if he'd had a Sunday school primer in his hands.

"Shoot."

Philip draped an arm around the boy, drawing him in close enough to drop his voice. "I come into a nice chunk of money since I been in this town. More'n I feel comfortable keepin' under my mattress at night. You understand?"

"Sure. Can't be too careful. There's a bank over at Sixth and—"

"No, no. I'll be needin' my money in the morning. I just need to find a respectable place to spend the night. No, thank you, I'll be keeping my cash close at hand. I've doubled it every day since I arrived."

"Gambling?"

Philip laughed with much more gusto than was warranted. "Gambling, he says! What call would I have to do that when I've got a sure thing? You'll never get ahead in life thinking like that, boy. Now, do you know of any rooms to let near here?"

"Uh, sure." Clay moved to point down the street, but the way Philip had his arm pinned curtailed the gesture. "Mr. Platt nearly always has a room to let. Nice and clean, but he don't serve meals."

"Mighty fine. Mighty fine. I am obliged to you." With a hearty pat on the back, Philip released him and began sauntering down the street, whistling a peppy tune.

Clay watched him with a faltering grin, then bounded forth to block his path. "Mister, you say you got a sure thing?"

Blinking as though he'd forgotten their long-ago conversation, Philip managed, "Did I? Well, I am on the win these days. Investing, that's my line. I found me a -" He stopped himself short, drew the boy backward toward the alley, and continued in hushed tones. "I wouldn't like to bandy this about, lad. Can I trust you with a whapping secret?"

"Absolutely!"

Philip nodded. "Good. I won't be able to keep this to myself much longer, anyway. People bound to start hearin' about it." From his left pants pocket he drew a brown flask with the label torn off. "You ever hear of Dr. Allright's Astounding Elixir?"

"Oh heavens," Lorena whispered to her husband, "he's a snake oil salesman!"

Even the boy looked wary. "No, thank ya. I ain't dropping my wages on nobody's quack medicine again."

"Now just hold your horses, young man! Have I asked you for one plugged nickel?"

"Naw, but—"

"And I don't mean to, neither! Didn't I just tell you I got more money than I can tote around? I ain't selling nothing. I got a partner for that." He chuckled. "And he's pretty damn slick! Let me tell you, he could sell dirty pictures to a blind man."

Clay shuffled his feet, unsure whether to stay in the conversation. "But the stuff's fake, right?"

"Oh, heck, who knows? Who cares? I've heard him say it cures everything from syphilis to bad backs to liver spots. It don't do me no never mind to see how well it works. It sells, boy! It sells like hotcakes! And here's the secret ..." He tipped the bottle up toward the sky, squinting in at the last drop as though he'd found a secret code etched into the bottom. "It's the best drunk you're ever gonna find."

"I don't follow."

"Liquor, boy. That's the main ingredient. Mighty fine whiskey, but it tastes like tea and don't hurt your head in the morning nor make your insides work again' ya. And that's why people can't get enough of it. Keep coming back, handing over buckets of money. And me, all I've got to do is invest. I give him enough money each morning to make a fresh batch and when he's done selling, I get my share of the profits. I tell you, by the end of the month I'll be rich as Midas!"

Clay let out a long whistle. "Sounds like you're set for life."

Almost absently, Philip fell back to counting the money in his pockets. Clay hemmed and hawed until he'd finished.

"I thank you again, friend, for your kind advice. Good day to you." With a tip of his hat, Philip moved to walk away.

It was too much for Clay to bear. "I want in!"

"What'd you say?"

"I want to invest. I got money. I..."

Philip looked him up and down, considering. "How much money we talkin'?"

"I disremember exactly."

With a great sigh, Philip brought his free hand to the boy's neck, pulling his face in close. "Look here, boy. I'm giving you one chance. You run home, gather up all your savings, and meet me back here. We'll triple it for you by sundown tomorrow."

Clay took off like a shot. Keen eyes watching his prey, Philip found a vacant doorway to sit a spell while he waited.

"That is enough," Adalwolf whispered to his wife. "We go now."

He turned on his heel and strolled up the street ahead of her.

Lorena watched him go but could not coax her exhausted body to follow. Her eyelids closed of their own accord. She slumped to the ground.

52

SUNDAY, JUNE 6, 1886

THE GRANDFATHER CLOCK CHIMED THREE. Lorena awoke in the dark to a stiff neck and aching back from sleeping upright in the leather chair all evening. The bones of her corset cut into her torso where she'd slumped into it. Although her collar hung loose, the stiff lace itched her neck unbearably.

Adalwolf had fallen asleep himself, pipe in hand. He slouched in his armchair, mouth agape, looking dead but for the incrementally slow rise and fall of his chest.

Lorena wasted no time stealing out of the room. In her heart, she felt that a better wife would have roused her husband and coaxed him into escorting her to bed. But, though it would be a relief to strip off her constricting clothing, she hated spending her nights one layer of fabric shy of naked next to the man who both was and was not her lover. If only she could feel warmth inside those gnarled fingers, see again the passion within those calculating eyes...

Two oil lamps sat waiting on the hall table, dimmed

to their lowest settings, signaling that the servants had retired for the evening. Claiming one as she passed, Lorena navigated her way downstairs with as little bumping and thumping as she could manage. The lovely meal Mrs. Berbish had prepared was long gone, surely, but with luck, she could salvage something to tide her over until breakfast.

How the servants must be gossiping! She knew full well how her husband's odd, foreign manners and hermit-like ways both amused and repelled them. Now their failure to appear for dinner coupled with her unannounced change of mind about the symphony was enough to set their tongues wagging for a week.

Damn. She'd never see her way into proper society this way. Now she would be honor-bound to join Mr. Christopher's excursion to the art gallery. Most likely, she'd have to pony up a decent donation into the bargain.

She scurried around the corner, mentally rearranging her social calendar for the week, and ran smack-dab into a stranger in her foyer.

She opened her mouth to scream, but a small "Oh!" was all she could muster.

The man, who had been groping his way through the darkness, whirled to face her, holding his heart like she'd just given him the fright of his life.

Lorena cranked the lamp wick to its fullest height so she could scrutinize him.

Her intruder turned out to be a pleasant-looking man, scarcely older than her, with wavy blond hair and a dapper moustache. He wore a loose-fitting grey suit with mud-covered boots and smelled strongly of horsehair and sweat. One hand clutched a leather valise while the other doffed his cap.

"Please, miss," he said, panting, "tell me straight off —is old Adalwolf dead yet?"

Lorena goggled at him. "My *husband*, Master Adalwolf, is very much alive, sir. You broke into my house in the dead of night to inquire about his health?"

"Nobody answered my knock, so I jiggled the lock open. I daren't wait 'til morning, see."

By way of explanation, he drew a telegram from his vest pocket and handed it to her.

2 JUNE 1886
CAHOKIA, IL
ST. LOUIS UNIVERSITY —
EASTERN EXPEDITION

AUGUST BECKER COME IMMEDIATELY.
FINAL PAYMENT.
DYING.
ADALWOLF

LORENA READ IT SEVERAL TIMES, NOT comprehending.

"I got that this afternoon," Becker said, "and rode all night, praying I'd make it to his deathbed before he...

Well, I'm sure it's an emotional time for you, ma'am, but I need to speak to him right now."

"No." Lorena did not waste a moment considering his request. Every moment Adalwolf slept was blissful freedom for her; she had no intention of cutting that short, at least until she'd eaten. "I'm sorry to disappoint you, but he's not dying. Not imminently, at least. He contracted influenza while we were staying in Peoria, which left him feverish and weak. He is convinced that he narrowly escaped death, but trust me when I say he is very likely to outlive *me* at this rate."

Becker perked up. "Really? My gran was that way. Every Sunday for three years she called for the priest to give her Last Rites. Got to be so regular we set a place for him at Sunday dinners. I'd not have rode my poor horse into such a lather if I'd realized that, but, all the same, I ought to speak to him directly."

Lorena considered her predicament. Waking Adalwolf would reduce her to the slavery of forced dreaming. Yet she could not turn Becker away after Adalwolf had gone to the expense of cabling him. Additionally, she had to be mindful of the servants, who could rise at any time. How would it look for her, a young married woman, to be holding a candlelight tête-à-tête with an attractive young man while her husband slept unaware? The fact that she was fully dressed would only fuel rumors that they were absconding together.

And on top of it all, she was weary, cranky, and famished!

"I will not permit you to wake him," Lorena

decided. "But if you'd like to stay and wait, you can help me scrounge up the remnants of our supper."

TO HER DELIGHT, THEY FOUND THE TABLE STILL SET and several platters remaining on the sideboard: cold pheasant, pickle slices, rolls with apricot jam, and what appeared to be beets swimming in vinegar. After Becker nipped into the pantry for a jug of apple cider and Lorena lit enough candles to illuminate the room, they settled into a scavenger's feast.

"I thank you, again," Becker said as he tucked his napkin across his dusty lap, "for the hospitality. And, incidentally, for sparing us both a heap of embarrassment. Nobody told me the old man'd run off to get married. I wouldn't have been so keen to bust in on his bedroom if I'd known I might find... Oh, blast! Excuse me, ma'am. I didn't mean to be indelicate there."

Lorena tactfully let that pass. "How long have you been in my husband's employ, Mr. Becker?"

"What? No, you mustn't phrase it that way, or I could lose my station. The University was quite clear that we are to think of him as a patron only, and not an investor."

Lorena sighed. "Mr. Becker, what is it that you *do*? Besides barging into houses and talking in circles?"

"I'm a professor of archaeology, ma'am."

"Indeed? You don't speak like a professor. And I've never met one with such calloused hands and deep sunburn."

Becker dropped his hands to his lap and went silent. She realized belatedly that she'd shamed him with her careless observations.

"Oh, I'm a ninny! You've been on an excavation, haven't you? Do tell me about it. How exciting it must be to interact with true history."

He smiled. "There is a romance to hunting antiquities. I've been leading a small expedition these past few months."

"Yet you were only a day's ride from St. Louis?"

Becker's eyes tracked to the valise at his feet before he responded. "It's meant to be kept secret, but I suppose, seeing as you are married to The Old Patron—no offense meant. We refer to him as The Old Patron because he didn't want his name bandied about. Since you are somewhat financially involved, I suppose I can share a bit of—"

"This is going to involve Indian rituals, isn't it?" With sudden foreboding, Lorena wished she'd ejected him from her home. "And more Sacred Bundles and special pipes and things that prevent me from getting a decent night's sleep!"

"Well, uh," he stammered, taken aback. "Yes, to the former, but I can't speak as to the latter. I've been studying burial mounds just east of the Mississip'."

Lorena speared another slice of meat. "I know little about such things, Mr. Becker, but it seems as though a few burial mounds shouldn't consume your entire spring."

"It's more intricate than that, ma'am." Becker leaned

forward, eyes shining. "We've unearthed an ancient city."

"Whatever can you mean by that? Indians didn't build cities."

"These did. From what we've found, it was once bigger than London. And it spanned centuries. Might even be as old as the Parthenon."

"But that's absurd. You mean they had buildings? Highways? Civilization?"

"Don't let your imagination carry you a'running, ma'am. They had simple tools and likely lived in huts, maybe earth mounds. But they farmed and traded and prospered. The Mississippi's always been a hub for trade, apparently. We're finding carvings and weapons and pottery that must have originated in tribes all over America.'

"And they buried all this in graves?"

Becker refilled their glasses with cider while he explained, "It's more akin to Egyptian tombs, I'd say. Or, you know how St. Peter's tomb is beneath the Basilica? Think along those lines. These types of burial mounds were also places of worship. And they didn't skimp on construction, mind you. We've found vast underground chasms, chock full of carvings."

"What sort of—"

She was interrupted by a door slamming overhead, followed by plodding footsteps. Adalwolf. Lorena listened intently, calculating his direction. Most likely, he'd search the top floor first, expecting to find her in bed. She had several minutes before he shuffled his way down to the dining room.

"That must be our butler," she lied, dropping her voice. "Quickly, before we are overheard—how does my husband factor into your research?"

Becker had been staring at the ceiling, too. To oblige her, he carefully scooted his chair nearer to hers so they could speak *sotto voce*.

"The Old—that is, Mr. Adalwolf, has financed this whole endeavor. The University wouldn't allot the funds, so I turned to him."

"But how did you meet? He knows almost no one in town."

"It was before he moved here. Perhaps you've heard of my father, Dr. Gerhard Becker? A famous theologian, he was. Many years ago, old Adalwolf read one of his papers and wrote to him for clarification. They exchanged many letters over the years. I read my father's correspondence after he died. Your husband has some fascinating theories on the similarities of Creation Tales—"

"Yes, yes, I'm sure he does. But the telegram. Why did he summon you?"

Becker leaned closer. "*He was right.* He'd theorized about an ancient city in America, long before any of us knew the breadth of this find. When I wrote to him describing the statuettes the old French explorers found there, he not only agreed to fund my research, he packed up and moved to America. He was planning to supervise us. Of course, I didn't know how decrepit he was—no offense—until we met this winter. I couldn't take him along, so he changed his offer. He's paying me monthly, but I have to bring all my best artifacts here so he can view them first."

"And he takes first pick for his private collection?"

Becker's face turned to stone. "The University would never condone that, ma'am. He is our patron, not an investor."

"Save your breath, Mr. Becker. He's promised the final payment tonight. You must have something amazing in that bag."

Becker's fingers twitched to the handle of his valise, now tucked beneath his chair like an affectionate pet. "No, ma'am."

Lorena held his gaze until she heard the old man puttering down the stairs.

"Is that you, dear?" she called. "We're in the dining room. You have an unexpected guest."

Becker bounced to his feet with the valise cradled in his left arm, ready to greet Adalwolf as soon as he reached the landing. Lorena listened to him toadying in fluent German as they sequestered themselves in the parlor.

"*Guten Abend, Mein Herr! Ich habe ein Artefakt...*"

Lorena remained unheeded at the table, languidly swirling her last bite of pheasant through trails of jelly on her plate. The last phrase Becker uttered before closing the parlor's pocket doors was one she'd learned to translate.

Todes liebste. Death's Dearest.

53

MONDAY, JUNE 7, 1886

"While our Mr. Deeghan is still formulating the building blocks of his style," Mr. Christopher said, his hands drifting in the air before the canvas as though being pulled by changing currents, "his budding talents are displayed in the way he contrasts his detailed work with the broad strokes of his shadows. Feel the way your eye is drawn not to the floral arrangements and ornamentation inside this house, but instead to the girl beyond. Why is she pressing her face to the window-pane? What does she want? Why is she wistful?"

"Why isn't she cold?" added Mrs. Henderson.

The other women in the party tittered and wandered off behind Mrs. Henderson and her sister, Mrs. Nelson, who joined in deriding the scandalously bare arms of the featured maiden. Lorena knew the sisters had thirteen children between them; how prudish could they be in their hearts?

For her part, Lorena enjoyed the outing far more than anticipated. It had the appeal of being fresh and unexpected, as Adalwolf's lack of interest in such matters kept her from having to prelive it in a dream. And Mr. Christopher seemed so delightfully earnest, both in describing each featured piece and in his crestfallen looks every time the party failed to appreciate them.

It was certainly worth her price of admission.

Mr. Christopher's goal was to build the foundation of an Artists Guild to foster the local talent. Lorena had surprised him with a very generous donation that morning simply to save her face in society and offset the impending rumors about the Adalwolfs' eccentricities. But watching him struggling to court the interest of this financial base—the overly well-to-do set with nothing better to do on a spring afternoon than join him in a relaxed tour of the art museum—she found herself rooting for him to succeed.

The exhibit was certainly incongruous. Local offerings hung interspersed between well-known pieces imported for the summer, letting styles and mediums intermingle almost at random. Likewise, the gaggle of gossiping wives only occasionally aligned with the small cluster of muttering husbands plodding through the rooms.

Mr. Christopher tried to steer them from the oil painting toward an inked portrait, but Mr. Henderson sidetracked them yet again by sidling toward a marble statue to declaim, "More injuns, huh?"

Mr. Christopher closed his eyes, taking a cool, deep breath, before bounding up with a gregarious smile. "Well spotted. This is indeed a depiction of an incident in the French Indian War in which several American youths were kidnapped. However, while negotiating the peace treaty in which they were to be returned, some of the women chose to stay with the Indian tribe. Thus, the title 'The Willing Captive'."

His audience gasped, pressing closer. While Mr. Christopher described the detailed work of the anguished mother's face, pleading with her daughter to return, Mrs. Nelson wandered ever closer to the Indian brave standing boldly in the center of the work. His body was covered only by a loose cloth at the waist. Lorena had the distinct impression that Mrs. Nelson was looking for the proper angle to ascertain why the wife had chosen to stay with the native.

Good, thought Lorena. *The priggery is only skin-deep*.

Mr. Henderson, meanwhile, continued to derail the examination of the artist's techniques and message by demanding to know who had commissioned it and for how much. He seemed to think the size of the price tag was all an educated man needed to concern himself with.

Lorena drifted up the hallway until a plaque beneath one featured painting drew her eye: *Hypnos and Thanatos*. It seemed distantly familiar, and she tossed the words around her mind for a moment before realizing with a rush where she'd heard them. Adalwolf's journal. *Thanatos* was one of the words Mrs. Schlosser had been unable to translate.

"Mr. Christopher!" she called, waving her handkerchief so enthusiastically that he came running to her side. "Please, can you tell me what this means?"

"Ah, yes. John William Waterhouse. I am intrigued by the symbolism myself. It is based on Greek mythology, as many of his works are. Here you have Hypnos, or Sleep, clutching a handful of poppies," he pointed to the young boy's hands, "as he slumbers in the arms of his brother, Death."

"Thanatos is the name for Death?"

"Yes, that's right. Note the antique lyre resting by his hand. I believe that represents—"

"Great Scott! More injuns!"

Mr. Christopher might have been too much of a gentleman to cuss in front of a lady, but Lorena saw the profanities dancing in his eyes as he excused himself to defend yet another historical artwork from Mr. Henderson.

Lorena stood staring at the painting for several minutes, horrible theories and exciting answers chasing in circles until she felt dizzy. Without a second thought, she aborted her outing, hurrying out the side door without a word to anyone.

TWENTY MINUTES LATER, SHE ENTERED THE ST. LOUIS Public Library, only to be greeted by a persnickety librarian.

"We are closing in minutes, ma'am. You'll have to come back tomorrow."

"I'll be swift," she answered, sweeping him aside with her arm. The years she'd spent roaming libraries in Allegheny made finding the Greek Mythology section the work of mere moments. While the librarian tapped his foot at her, she scrutinized the shelves and seized the most likely tome: *The Grand Volume of Greek Gods and Heroes*.

"Just a moment, if you please," she said in her most commanding voice. Unsurprisingly, he chose that moment to go shoo the other patrons.

Setting the book on the table beside her, she scanned the index and flipped to the only page featuring Thanatos. The Creation Tale. No time to read it thoroughly, let alone copy it off for her records. She ripped the page out, folded it, and stuffed it into the ruffles of her sleeve.

A driving rain met her as she descended the steps outside. Having abandoned her party meant no carriage awaited to escort her home. But even as she confronted the jam she'd gotten herself into, one tantalizing, torturing notion mesmerized her: was Adalwolf's study of dreams merely a gateway to something far darker?

54

TUESDAY, JUNE 15, 1886

LORENA TRIED NOT to meet George's eyes. When she lost control of her emotions, they consumed her completely. She'd surrendered to a good ten minutes of wailing sobs that racked her body, clutching the shoulder of a man who quite obviously did not care about her suffering. Now that she was inching back toward self-possession, her pride felt as thin and faded as an old gingham apron.

All she could muster for an apology was, "I'm sorry to burden you."

"Prisoners generally are a burden," was George's sarcastic response. He labored to keep a gap between them, a losing battle on their toss-and-tumble ride. "But I reckon women are prone to outbursts like that."

"I am not!" she protested, sniffling as she dabbed a handkerchief to her eyes.

"Just get some sleep, maybe. You're stressed out and overtired. A good cry and a good sleep'll do ya right."

"Please stop suggesting that. I'm not about to

sleep." She sighed. Her temples throbbed, and the glaring sun made her want to lay her head down, but to that she could not succumb.

Sleep equaled a world beyond nightmares. *He* was there, lurking, waiting to drag her in. Her only hope was to stay awake until her plan had a chance to bear fruit.

Lorena looked at her companion, the man most likely to drag her to the gallows, and found she couldn't hate him. He was only trying to do what he thought was right. If she'd sat in judgment of herself from afar without being privy to all that she'd seen in the last months, she'd probably be on the posse's side.

"Are you fond of the theatre?"

George's head whirled around as though she'd pulled a sidearm on him. "Am I *what*?"

"The theatre. I'd wondered if you'd seen any good performances lately."

"No, I ain't." Looking increasingly wary, he snugged his hat lower on his head.

Lorena cast about for a better conversation starter. Literature? Fashion? She eyed his battered duds. *Not likely*. Politics? Recent events? *Even worse*—she was the biggest headline news in the state.

In Pennsylvania, Lorena was celebrated as a versatile conversationalist. Here on the trail, her mind became as barren as the grassland they were passing through. What topics had interested her before her life revolved around Adalwolf?

"It seems there are more clouds on the horizon. Do you think the weather will turn before we hit the city?"

Her companion bugged his eyes at her. "I didn't

happen to bring my almanac."

"You wish I'd just shut my mouth, don't you?"

"It crossed my mind!"

Lorena turned away, as much as was possible on the narrow seat, and methodically reanchored all of her hair pins. It was ridiculous, being treated like a common criminal. And the way these crude men eyed her as they jockeyed past her carriage—as if they were afraid of her! Lorena Whittaker Adalwolf! In any other situation they'd have been bowing and scraping at her feet.

Only Colquoit met her eye steadily. And the way he'd risen above his station in the past week churned her stomach.

For the hundredth time that day she grieved for the loss of Bo.

What she wouldn't give for one kind face right now! One person she could trust with the logjam of demons in her head.

"You can talk if you want," George grumbled, not looking at her.

"I wouldn't wish to impose."

He muttered something under his breath that sounded like, "Women!"

She glared at him and saw him twitch and shudder as the vehicle bounded over a large bump. With her own troubles looming in her thoughts, she kept forgetting his broken leg.

"Are you in much pain?"

"Constant and terrible," he answered through gritted teeth. "But if you can refrain from climbing all over me again, I think I'll muddle through."

To his surprise as well as hers, she laughed. How terrible she'd been! How completely out of her mind with rage! Utterly unladylike! Mother Rose would have gone crimson with shame, though she suspected Grandmother Eleanor might have applauded.

"Please forgive me, sir. Though, I must say, you do have an infuriating way of getting my goat. But I will allow that I share the blame. I am quick to temper recently." She fanned herself with her kerchief. "Perhaps it's this relentless heat. I am quite overwrought with emotion."

George grunted. "Oftentimes, cold-blooded murder will have that effect."

"Will you please stop referring to it as murder? I'm sure he'll be just fine." Lorena's eyes drifted over the endless plains, fixing on nothing. "He simply has to be."

A silent prayer tugged at her heart, but in a wink, obsession overtook her—the one thing she'd inherited from her husband. She felt within herself his eagerness for knowledge, the comfort of revisiting his studies.

She dug through the valise wedged into the front quarter of the landau and retrieved Adalwolf's journal. Eagerly, she flipped to the very back, to where she'd added loose pages from her own notes, including the page pilfered from the St. Louis library. *Ah, yes.*

"May I read you a story?" she asked suddenly.

George said nothing but raised his eyebrows. She took that as an invitation.

In the smooth, rounded tones she'd acquired from her literature circles, she began to read, "In the beginning, there was only Chaos..."

55

EXCERPT FROM ADALWOLF'S JOURNAL:

MUST LEARN MORE about these Indians of the Great Plains. Eerie similarities to ancient texts. The Osage speak of wandering in dreams. The Mesquakie seem to worship dreams. The legend told by Colquoit's tribe nearly matches the Ancient Greek Creation Tale. Is this the True Divine Link? I feel, finally, that I am nearing the end of my quest.

56

5EXCERPT FROM THE GRAND VOLUME OF GREEK GODS AND HEROES

IN THE BEGINNING, there was only Chaos.

AND CHAOS YIELDED THE FIVE ELEMENTS OF LIFE:

Earth (Gaia)
Night (Nyx)
Underworld (Tartarus)
Evil (Erebus)
Love (Eros)

AND NIGHT AND UNDERWORLD BORE THESE children:

Death (Thanatos)
Sleep (Hypnos)
And Vengeance (Nemesis)

. . .

YET LOVE AND EVIL PRODUCED
Dreams (Oneiroi)
And in her, Chaos was reborn.

57

TUESDAY, JUNE 15, 1886

GEORGE DIDN'T REALIZE the story was over until Lorena set it down and looked expectantly at him. He hardly knew what to say. She'd read it prettily enough, but it sure was short. And not much of a plot.

"Is that one o' them nursery tales, then?"

"Hardly! It was the Greek Creation Myth. Well, I say myth, but... are you a religious man, Mr. Tremont?"

Again, she'd near enough stumped him. Sure, he dragged himself to church on occasion. Then again, he made his living as a hired gun, a mercenary. So how much of God and religion could he rightly claim to have?

"What do you know about Creation?" she cross-examined. "From the Bible, that is."

His eyebrows shot up under his hat. "Don't you beat all? I never had a murderer quizzin' me on the Good Book before."

He could tell he'd soured her by the way she puckered her puss and went back to holding her book like a schoolmarm. Half amused and the rest sheer curious, he recited as much as he could remember.

"In the beginning... let's see... the earth was still and empty and void. And God said, 'Let there be light.' And so there was. And..."

"Yes, Mr. Tremont. And do you notice anything about that?" She waited half a beat, not long enough to have expected him to answer, before continuing, "Earth. Night. Underworld." She pointed to the names on her sheet. "Evil. Love. It's the same story, just told a different way. Do you see?"

He scratched his head, feeling particularly obtuse and hating it. "Can't see as I do."

She sighed, and that was maddening enough, then gave him a little pat on the hand as though he was a child.

"Most people can't. I couldn't myself. I've had a great deal of education, as I'm sure you can ascertain. Years of studying the classics and I'll confess to you, I never saw any of this as any more than harmless diversions. Silly stories told by the ignorant in times past. But my husband realized..."

Here she drifted off, gazing into the distance. He ought to have let her fall silent for a change, but couldn't seem to stop himself from asking, "Realized what, then?"

"He told me once that he studied the ancient truths. I couldn't understand why he looked for answers within mythology and the legends of the savages. I finally saw that he was looking for connections. And he was intelligent enough to embrace the truths that anyone else would have rejected."

Just as George was resigning himself to one of those long scholarly talks that meanders around a point without ever saying anything of interest, Lorena suddenly nudged his arm conspiratorially.

"Do you want to see something amazing?"

He nodded, mostly for lack of any witty response.

She opened the book again, resting it on her lap, and flipped to a page that had been bookmarked with a length of ribbon. As soon as he caught sight of the intricate drawing, he was hooked. It was a simple dagger, but obviously much more than that, too.

The blade was simple, straight and clean. Plenty good for killing a man, but none of that business with serrated edges that made things so messy.

The hilt, though! It took his breath clean out of his mouth.

To begin with, it was twice the size of the blade, which had to throw the balance out of whack. And it was shaped like a bone—a tibia, in fact, the exact broken bone that George was suffering from. Then there was the scrollwork, and how any feller had gotten that kind of detail—including something that looked disturbingly like a beautiful woman's eye—etched into such a small cylindrical area, he couldn't figure, particularly if the material was indeed a bone.

Then he shook his head clear. It was just a sketch. Of course it couldn't be real!

"What's that, then?" he asked.

And, typical of a woman, she'd engendered his interest only to return an answer that was less than no help at all.

"*Todes liebste.* Death's Dearest."

X
DEATH'S DEAREST

58
TUESDAY, JUNE 8, 1886

"Repeat that back to me," Colquoit said.

Frowning as though worried it was a trick question, Clay Arthur recited, "I demand the vengeance of... Nemesis, upon my murderer."

"Balancer of Life. You cain't leave that bit out. Do it again."

Clay ran his sweaty hands through his red hair again, glancing awkwardly at his reflection in the mirror behind the bar. "This is gonna get me even with Tremont?"

"Didn't I already tell you that? Yes! Do this right, and he'll never cross nobody again."

"And all I gotta do is say this line?"

"Yep."

Waving his arm at the barkeep, Colquoit ordered them each another shot of whiskey. The boy paled, looking queasy, but downed it dutifully. As he tipped his head back, his buttocks slipped from the stool. Colquoit caught him before he fell and planted him back into his seat.

"That's it. Just one line," Colquoit said soothingly. "'Course you'll also have to let him kill you first."

FROM TWO TABLES AWAY, LORENA AND ADALWOLF looked on. Whereas he sat in quiet repose, following the conversation with the begrudging approval of an opera critic, Lorena fussed and fidgeted. She'd chosen a chair so rickety that it creaked and wobbled each time she exhaled, but it was located in the only section of the floor not covered in used chaw. She was almost parched enough to consider a drink of the rusty water placed before her, but a congealed brown puddle glued her glass to the table.

Most discomforting of all, Colquoit kept catching her eye and grinning. How could he even see them?

It took continual effort to remind herself that she was dreaming. At times like this, when everything she witnessed seemed more alive, more vibrant, than her waking day, she felt she was losing her mind.

Batting away a fly that kept settling on her forehead, Lorena stood and scrutinized herself in the mirror. In her bright-red traveling coat and heliotrope dress, she was the only spot of color in the room. But her peacock-feather plumed hat had grown heavy on her neck. She pictured the light straw bonnet she'd debated wearing. Concentrating, willing her image to change, feeling the triggering of asphyxiation that accompanied the laden pipe smoke... She blinked to find an adorable knitted cap perched atop her head instead.

"Attend!" Adalwolf barked, thumping the table.

Clay had mustered his courage and, with some help from

Colquoit in finding his land legs, set himself on a serpentining trail toward Philip Tremont. "You! You stole my life's savings, you son... son... son of a bitch!"

Onlookers cheered and stamped their feet, sensing impending entertainment. Tremont raised his head slowly from the bosoms of the giggling strumpet on his lap. When he saw Clay shaking with impotent rage, he grinned like the cock of the walk.

"Well, lookee here at this young buck what I never saw before in my life!"

"That's a lie!" Clay sought support from the men Tremont was drinking with. "He's lying! He cheated me outta all my money!"

Pushing the whore to her feet, Tremont stood slowly but aggressively. "That's one heck of an accusation, little dude. You sure you want to keep making it?"

His hand patted the six-shooter strapped to his hip.

"Now!" hissed Colquoit.

Shaking so hard he looked about to pitch over sideways, Clay pulled a shiny derringer from his pocket and aimed it point-blank at Tremont's head.

"That's—" Lorena began, then stopped herself. Obviously, Adalwolf knew the distinctive scrollwork on the copper-colored weapon as well as she. It was Colquoit's gun, though to what purpose he'd given it to the boy, she could not be sure.

Tremont's grin had hardened but not entirely given way to the situation. "Now, there. You're as nervous as a long-tailed cat in a room full o' rocking chairs, ain't ya? Siddown, son. Let's talk this out."

Crack!

Clay had gone trigger-happy, loosing his single shot into the rafters. Before he even registered his fatal mistake, Tremont drew his own revolver.

"I can't begin to say how much I hate being shot at."

Young Clay took a bullet to the heart. Adalwolf clapped delightedly.

Lorena woke up screaming.

59

WEDNESDAY, JUNE 9, 1886

LORENA HUNCHED over her papers in unconscious imitation of Adalwolf, working so quickly she slopped ink onto her beautiful writing desk.

"Drat." She dabbed at it with her blotter, hoping a servant could fix the mess later. She couldn't possibly call to them now or Adalwolf would realize she wasn't resting and would demand to know what she was doing.

He'd forgotten about her so far this morning, enraptured with the new artifact he'd obtained from August Becker—some sort of knife made out of bone. And she'd heard him tell Colquoit he intended to test it out that evening.

A chill blew through her every time she pictured the men using the knife. She couldn't say why, for an object couldn't have intent, no matter how long it had lain hidden below the earth, but it felt... evil.

She pictured Mrs. Schlosser curling her fingers in front of herself after whispering the words "Death's Dearest." Lorena wasn't superstitious enough to try warding off wicked thoughts with hand signs, but she was mightily unsettled.

Under the pretense of lying down with a headache, she stole upstairs to Adalwolf's room and copied another passage out of his journal, one full of names she'd come to recognize—Thanatos, Hypnos, and Nyx.

All afternoon she toiled, translating one word or phrase at a time, until the lamp beside her flickered at the end of its oil and the eyestrain had *truly* given her a headache.

When it was done, she hid the German dictionary in her sewing basket and carried the new English text to the window to read it afresh.

60

EXCERPT FROM ADALWOLF'S JOURNAL:

The twin brothers Hypnos and Thanatos, Gods of Sleep and Death, enjoyed working together often. But their little sister, Nemesis, was spoiled and rarely did any work. She preferred instead to sit at the feet of their cousin, Oneroi, Goddess of Dreams, and listen to her intricate stories.

As she grew older, Nemesis took an interest in humans. She studied them and memorized their stories to share with Oneroi. Both girls loved stories with satisfying conclusions, so Nemesis went to her mother, Nyx, Goddess of the Night, to ask her to change the endings for her.

Nyx said, "I will not intervene, for you are spoiled and must learn to work for yourself." So she granted Nemesis the power to exact retribution for her favorite humans.

Nemesis loved her role, balancing their lives in ways that pleased her. But still she was not happy, for often her brother, Thanatos, took the men before their stories were complete. Nemesis demanded that he return a soul he had taken, but Thanatos refused, saying his task was to escort all men to the Underworld, regardless of the state of their accounts.

Nemesis ran in tears to her cousin Oneroi and together they devised a plan. While Hypnos slept, Oneroi stole a bone from his leg and enchanted it. She told the brothers that to get it back they must let Nemesis play a game. Whenever a life story that Nemesis enjoyed was interrupted by Thanatos, she could call upon the power in the leg bone to demand that he return the soul to the living world.

When his dear brother begged for his help, Thanatos consented, yet he insisted that the soul of another would always be sent to the Underworld in exchange for the soul being returned.

They agreed to allow Nemesis to play her game one hundred times, after which she must return the bone to Hypnos.

Nemesis loved her prize and the power it gave her over her older brothers. She engraved it and created a dagger so lovely even stoic Thanatos grew jealous. He tried to steal it whenever she played her game, so Nemesis decided to hide it. In a city far beyond the seas, where few gods traveled, she buried it with the bodies of those he had already taken to the Underworld, knowing that Thanatos never looked at the same person twice.

Nemesis was proud of herself for being so clever, but indeed she was also a careless and forgetful girl. When next she went to retrieve the dagger, she could not find it. Soon, she grew bored of looking and left it behind, never to play her game again.

But Thanatos did not forget, for she had left it in the domain of men, and he knew they would not resist its call.

61

WEDNESDAY, JUNE 9, 1886

Supper still warmed their bellies—succulent roast duck, seasoned to perfection and served in a cranberry-butter sauce, followed by an apricot compote dusted with cinnamon—but the effect was spoiled as soon as the wind shifted. The stench of their neighbors' stewed cabbage assaulted them and sent Lorena fussing for her perfumed fan.

"Close the windows, Bo, quickly. All of them."

He wasted no time and even bolted them for good measure.

Rather less at ease than before, they resumed their positions. Bo sat on the floor polishing silver while Lorena reclined in her settee, reading aloud from the evening paper.

"The Clevelands are back from their honeymoon today. Imagine becoming mistress of the White House at twenty-one years. They say she has violet eyes. I wonder if that's so—"

Her words were cut off with a great banging of the

front door. Colquoit arrived, whistling shrilly, and Adalwolf scrambled downstairs to meet him, answering the summons as though *he* were the servant!

"You dawdle! I wait all afternoon—"

"I found him." Colquoit was smug, more noxious than she'd ever witnessed. He flopped into an armchair and hiked his muddy boots onto her sateen footstool.

Adalwolf inhaled sharply. "We must start at once." His tongue darted out too late to catch the saliva dribbling over his lip. "You shall go now and escort him to the Copper Whistle, ja?"

"I sure will."

"You will not look at me or talk to me."

"O'course."

"And you will teach him to say *what*?"

"The thing about the nemesis."

Finally, his aloof manner crossed the borderline. Adalwolf shook his cane in his fist as though he were strangulating it. "Say it precisely!"

Colquoit ceased grinning and pursed his lips in thought before reciting emotionlessly, "I demand the vengeance of Nemesis, Balancer of Life, upon my murderer."

"Ja." Adalwolf looked him over, every unkempt hair on his balding head, and apparently decided he was up to the task before them. "Get on, then."

Hitching up his pants, Colquoit chased his shadow out the door.

"Boy!" Adalwolf yelled, meaning Bo. "Bring my carriage at once."

Nearly scattering the silverware in his haste, Bo

scurried out and had the horse and landau at the ready by the time the old man's shaky fingers had fastened the clasp on his traveling cloak.

Lorena stood in the corridor, twisting her hands. She knew. And wished she didn't.

Just before he reached for the door, she blurted out, "Will that young boy be killed tonight?"

Adalwolf regarded her as though she were a pauper pestering for alms, then softened enough to say, "It is inconsequential." And with that, he doddered down the walk.

Lorena paced the sitting room, alone and beside herself. Her dream was going to come true. Did it serve a purpose? Some deep meaning? And—*inconsequential*, did he say? To everyone but the lad, perhaps!

And yet she could do nothing. She couldn't disobey him. Except... he didn't actually order her to stay home, did he? It was just assumed.

That loophole was all the impetus she needed to change into her walking boots and slip a cable car map into her coin purse.

62

WEDNESDAY, JUNE 9, 1886

SHE CAUGHT the last cable car of the evening and prayed she'd be able to locate her husband and ride back with him. Here in the seedier sector of town, her limited knowledge of the streets ran out. The Copper Whistle was still vivid in her mind, but only from the inside. It didn't have so much as a wooden plaque hanging over the door. She'd have walked right past it if not for Bo parked catty-corner to the entrance.

His dark eyes widened when he spotted her. She did her best to wave him off as she tugged on the rusty door.

The reek of still-warm tobacco blanketing the floor in disregard of the scattered spittoons almost kept her at bay, but she hiked up her dress and plunged in toward the bar. One of the locals leered at her and motioned to the empty stool at his side. A quick survey of the narrow room told her this was no place for an unaccompanied woman with any sense of dignity. Nothing could be done, then, but to join

Adalwolf. He was bound to discover her soon, anyway.

She crossed the room to take her seat at his table. The same seat as before. Beside the same brown gunk stuck to the table.

Adalwolf whirled on her, eyes bulging. She cringed, expecting him to strike.

Instead he hissed, "I will deal with you later. Do not distract me."

Together they watched Colquoit and his prey. Unlike her dream, it was impossible to eavesdrop even at this proximity. She couldn't filter out the raucous crowd or the nearby street traffic, let alone the relentless pianist in the corner, banging out random snippets of songs beneath an empty tip jar.

And suddenly it was in play—Clay Arthur reeling toward Philip Tremont, and Lorena powerless to intervene. Somehow, she'd thought her presence might change things, might make the men behave themselves. But here the boy stood, waggling his derringer in the gunslinger's face, about to meet his doom.

Lorena knocked her chair over in her haste to move between them, but Colquoit moved faster. He grabbed her around the waist, hugging her to his sweaty body as she struggled. All eyes on the shaking gun, nobody noticed her, even when she screamed, "Don't do it!"

And, just as before, Clay fired into the rafters, sealing his doom.

Tremont looked him in the eyes and put a bullet in his heart.

Colquoit squeezed Lorena's waist one last time

before unhanding her. He and Adalwolf scurried toward the body before the final breath escaped it.

"Where is the knife?" Adalwolf shouted.

Lorena remained rooted to the spot as all hell broke loose in the bar around her.

Every man in Tremont's group started shouting the hasty play-by-play of fellows who knew they'd better get their collective story straight and fast. The barkeep jumped over the bar and ran to the door, shouting for help. Meanwhile, the tart who'd been perched on Tremont's lap lost her mind screaming and climbing across tables to find the exit. She failed to notice when her bodice caught on a nail and so exited the saloon with her right boob flopping free, much to the delight of the pianist.

Running seemed like the best idea to Lorena. This was no place for a lady.

She turned to leave just as Tremont skidded against her, shouting, "You ain't seen where I'm going, men. Just gimme a head start, that's all!"

Then Tremont took one last look over his shoulder and began gibbering like a mad man. His eyes grew round as silver dollars while his skin turned chalk white.

"What's chewin' on him?" asked a man nearby.

"He sees something," Adalwolf said.

But only Lorena held the proper vantage to see the horror bearing down on Tremont. And what she saw was... impossible.

The world ripped at the seams, revealing a jagged wedge of reality that could not exist. Her mind tried valiantly to convince her that a torn mural had fallen from the ceiling, almost smacking her in the face with its red clouds and deep-purple shadows. But the shadows moved, producing the smell of cinder and a heat that blew against her face.

In the midst of this rift stood Clay Arthur, full of life, full of rage. His eyes locked on Tremont. Lorena watched as he raised one arm overhead, holding a knife —*the* knife—the one Adalwolf had been cradling all week. Clay slashed, moving with the same deadly precision Tremont had so recently used against him.

Lorena screamed, turning away, and faced Tremont just as he fell to the ground. No marks on his body. No life in his soul.

Amidst the renewed pandemonium around them, Clay jumped through the opening. Alive again. Blood-stained chest and all.

His shoes barely hit the ground before the portal behind him dissolved in a puff of smoke. Clay stared for one brief moment at Tremont's corpse, then dropped the knife and ran like hell for the door.

"What happened?" shouted a man near the bar. "Where'd the body go?"

"Forget that—look at Tremont! He done dropped dead."

"She give him the Evil Eye!" shouted the barkeep, and he deserted his post, running scared into the night.

Petrified, bewildered, and acting only on impulse, Lorena charged out of the saloon herself. At the door, when she dared to glance over her shoulder, the horrible vision had erased itself. Adalwolf stood precisely where Clay's body had been, marveling at the empty floor.

Colquoit bounded a fallen chair to snatch up the knife. The few straggling hairs falling over his eyes did nothing to obscure the ferocity of his grin. Fresh horror gripped Lorena. She took to her heels, running down the street.

"Miss Lorena!"

It sounded like Bo, but she didn't stop to make sure. She stumbled over the curb but kept moving until Bo caught up with her and grabbed her arm.

"Miss Lorena! Land Sakes, how'd you get yourself all the way down here?"

Dear Bo! He looked at her with such concern, standing between her and madness. Always her savior! She swooned and he caught her against his chest.

"Help me, Bo. Take me home."

"I will, Miss Lorena. But do you have the strength to stand?" His voice grew tense. "There's men watchin' us liable to get the wrong notion if they see me carryin' you down the street. I will if you need me to, but my lifespan gonna stretch a lot longer if you start walkin' *now*."

Her eyes popped open. He was right, of course. All the commotion centered around the saloon, but a handful of stragglers were now watching her and Bo with keen interest. Steadying herself on the heels of her kid boots, she allowed Bo to lead her to the carriage and hand her in.

A minute later, she felt the slight forward roll of the carriage as Bo untied the horses from the hitching post, followed by a gentle lurch as he hoisted himself into the driver's seat. Then they sat, waiting, tense amid the rowdy noises of the night. Much as she longed to give the order to go home, she knew they couldn't leave until Master Adalwolf conducted his business. Whatever business that was. What kind of studies delighted in the death of a foolish, young boy?

For Clay had been dead, she was certain. Whatever happened next, the impossible-but-true events she'd witnessed did not allay her conscience. She felt complicit in every inch of the thing. She'd seen the knife. She'd read the story. She'd even dreamt his death. But she hadn't learned enough to prevent it.

Now Clay lived again while the swindler Tremont took his stead.

Lorena chewed her lip, trying not to cry. Even with her eyes squeezed shut, her retinas burned with the afterglow of the wondrous, terrible image of Clay wielding the knife. Demanding his vengeance.

63
ELSEWHEN

Bo's voice boomed through the darkness. He'd been through every spiritual his pa had ever taught him, and still he sang, taking comfort in the familiar words even as they continued to convey new meanings, concepts he'd never dared to dream.

He clung to his teachings, the un-shufflable truths. God. Light. And the promised peace.

Concentrating on the path beneath his feet, he traded one barren landscape for another. Sometimes he heard cries for help that seemed to come from no direction at all. Just when he was convinced that he was alone again, he'd run parallel to a plantation alive with miserable, chalky-faced laborers toiling over withered crops. Beyond that, the grounds grew wild with thundering beasts he dared not look at.

Once, his road dipped underground into labyrinthine mine shafts where he couldn't see beyond the light of the sporadic lanterns placed far, too far, apart. Bo kept placing one foot evenly in front of the other until he emerged into the lesser darkness of the moonless night sky.

Now a palace loomed in front of him, the twisty sort from his childhood books that just went up and up. A crowd milled at its gates. Bo hesitated, but his road ran directly to the front door, and if he migrated from the path, he'd have no direction, no compass. That would drive him to madness.

Keeping his head down, he continued in as unwavering a route as possible through the joggling bodies.

"You, there!"

Suddenly, all eyes turned to him. Bo kept his eyes on his own feet as he continued toward the door.

The man who'd called out to him stepped forth to block his path. "You. Boy. Why are you here?"

Bo stood his ground, looking up to face the man. He soon wished he hadn't.

At a towering six foot seven with pale, bloodless skin and glowing green eyes, he absorbed the darkness, condensing and concentrating it into a tangible menace. The sleeves of his grubby shirt had been torn off to accommodate his broad shoulders, leaving his thick muscles uncaged. As he leered at Bo, his fingers caressed the blood stains on the coil of whip draped over his arm.

"You got business here?" the man repeated. "Or do I need to put you to work?"

Bo could not remember how to form words. He gaped like a fish, producing only wheezes. This was his end, his failure, his surrender.

His hand touched on the dagger thrust through his

belt, and Miss Lorena's face floated through his mind, whispering a phrase that had seemed so deranged he thought he'd never use it. But, here, now, it resonated through his brain, coming out of his mouth with a timbre he didn't know he possessed.

"I demand the vengeance of Nemesis, Balancer of Life, upon my murderer!"

He sensed a change immediately. The leers and taunting of the crowd faded to a shocked murmur, and people shuffled out of his way. Bo kept his eyes locked on the foreman's, refusing to waver until the other man issued a verdict.

With a queer kind of respect, the giant man nodded and stepped aside.

"Let him pass!" he shouted.

The gate swung open with a force that knocked over several of the loiterers. Two guards inside the palace grounds craned their necks to look at Bo.

The foreman put a hand on Bo's back, guiding him forward. "Go straight through the gates. When you reach the mansion, let yourself in. Don't look around. Don't talk to anyone. Keep your hand on that knife. You'll find him in his garden."

Bo moved to tip his hat, then realized he wasn't wearing one. His feet began to move before anyone took a notion to change their mind. Two steps inside the gate, he mustered another song to buoy him through.

I bless the Lord I's goin' to die

Keep me from sinkin' down

I's going to Judgment by and by
Keep me from sinkin' down

XI

INTERLUDE

64
JUNE 1886

"SMITHY!" Sam Beaman yelled, escorting two yahoos into the newspaper office. "These guys want to talk to you about that bar shooting last night."

At his desk, Smithy sighed and took a swig from his flask before turning around. He'd already written a dazzling account without mucking about with eyewitnesses. But P.H.'s code was to always talk to the locals when they turned up. If they thought their names might see print, those were more papers sold the next day.

He kept his seat, leaning back while they were forced to stand in the cramped aisle.

"And you are?"

The scrawnier man stepped slightly forward, scrunching his cap between his hands. "Cletus Selb. I tend bar at the Copper Whistle. This here's Hall Ross, the piano man."

"Musical entertainer extraordinaire," he interjected, twanging the garter holding his sleeves. "I'm available for private parties, if you could mention that some'ere."

Beaman grinned at Smithy as he flopped into his own desk chair.

"And you saw what, exactly?" prompted Smithy.

"The shooting—"

"The lady—"

They stopped, cutting each other off, then Selb dove ahead. "This Tremont, see, he was a regular. Last few weeks, anyhow."

"Not a man you'd want to get on the wrong side of, see."

"Right," Selb nodded. "Bad seed."

"Didn't tip worth dung."

Selb shot his partner a look, seeing they were losing their audience, and hurried on with, "We think he'd snookered this kid out of a pile of money."

"But we ain't figured where the lady come in."

"No. Right. She didn't seem to belong to the kid nohow."

Smithy held up his hands and made a show of reaching for a pencil. "Can you describe this woman?"

"You bet!" Ross rubbed his hands together as he thought. "She was... real plain."

"But fancy," Selb added.

"Right. Kinda snooty, I thought."

"Kinda the type you'd expect to drink Dandelion Wine."

"Right." Smithy tapped his index finger impatiently on the notepad. "Notice anything else? Hair? Age? Eyes? Did anybody say her name?"

"Don't recall as they did," Selb began.

"I'll tell you about her eyes!" For the first time, Ross looked spooked. "They were blazing. Just before she done it. I looked straight at her. Saw the fires of hell in her eyes."

"Is that so?" Smithy asked levelly.

"Well, I mean, I ain't trying to be poetic or nothing. But she was..." he drifted off, shuffling his feet.

"No, no, he's right," said Selb. "All the fellows said she was like demented. All sudden like. Got right in the thick of things, then went creepy silent—"

"And started screaming—"

"And all bug-eyed—"

"And then she turned to Tremont—"

"Gave him the Evil Eye—"

"And he fell over." Ross slapped his hands flat to illustrate the body hitting the floor. "Dead as a pancake. Or whatever."

"Then she tore outta there."

"I see," Smithy said. "That it?"

"You could put in your story," Ross muttered, eyes dropped to his shoes, "that I chased her for five blocks. Gonna bring her to justice. But she just disappeared into thin air right in front of me."

"I thought you—"

Ross elbowed the barkeep in the ribs then tendered a glance at the reporter.

"Of course," was all Smithy said. "Thank you, gentlemen."

Grinning now and proud of themselves, the two allowed themselves to be shuffled out of the building. When Smithy returned to the main room of the office, he beelined to the typesetter's desk, shuffling through the day's approved stories.

Beaman turned to watch. "You're not really gonna rewrite it, are you?"

"I have to. P.H. is gonna love this." He flourished his earlier copy with pride. "I'm thinking of naming her the Hellfire Witch. What do you think?"

Beaman was visibly impressed, but damned if he would admit it. It galled all of Smithy's coworkers to watch him winning the publisher's favor. Worse still was that he seemed to have a gift for sensationalism. And the only way to wash down a pill that bitter was to concentrate on how well the papers were selling this summer.

"No more foreign dudes, then?" Beaman teased. "I thought that was your forte."

Smithy shrugged. "I never could find a catchy name for that one."

He settled himself into his newly padded chair and flattened the old article beside his typewriter as he formulated a revised headline. This development of people claiming to be witnesses was a mite dissettling, but he flattered himself that it showed the power of the press to have them come to believe such fancies. Here lately, he'd been growing concerned that he was overdoing the queer death angle, but it worked out so well for him he was reluctant to abandon it. Everyone in the city knew his name now. And P.H. hadn't threatened to bludgeon him in almost a month.

He didn't even have to cajole P.H. into running the stories now that circulation was up. Everyone was buying into it so well that P.H. himself thought of changing that last story from Peoria to Springfield on the theory that a larger town would hold more of their readers' relatives, necessitating the purchase of extra copies to send home.

The last thing Smithy had intended to do was set any of his death series in St. Louis, though, where it could so easily be challenged.

Aloud, he speculated, "I can't imagine anyone contradicting such a well-traveled rumor as this, though. I heard everyone in the streets talking about it this morning and I ain't even written it up yet."

Beaman shrugged. "Just got to stick to the truth, right?"

A chuckle made them both start; they hadn't noticed P.H. standing in his doorway. He spat a dollop of chaw in Beaman's vicinity and snorted. "Rookie."

XII

IN THE SLEEP OF DEATH

65

WEDNESDAY, JUNE 15, 1886

George let out a groan as the carriage banged over a rock. He felt like his leg was breaking over and over with every jolt. Still, he told himself, the rattle-trap ride had gotten easier. The powerful afternoon heat had tired out the horses, so the posse was forced to proceed at a lazy trot, still miles from town. Compared to the way they'd careened down hillsides earlier, this jaunt could almost be called pleasant.

"Do you see what I'm saying?" Mrs. Adalwolf asked.

"Uh-huh," he managed, gritting his teeth as he resettled himself on the padded bench. The lady had talked for so long she'd left his head spinning. Nearly everything she said was pure nonsense, but she believed it with such passion. He couldn't help but listen. "Go on, then."

"Why else would every culture have a name for Death? Or stories about Vengeance? How else could the Greek's concept of the Underworld be exactly like the

Indians'? Across the globe like that and to have identical concepts?"

While Lorena talked, she waved her hands animatedly and touched his arm every time she leaned in to confide some new morsel. If he was being honest, he didn't mind the contact. For the first time, she seemed like a real woman, the kind he could sit on a porch with or bring chocolates to.

Yes, this storytelling side was attractive, but bewildering.

"Personification, see?" She continued, "That's the heart of all mythology. Taking some concept and creating a god or demon to embody it. Everything I ever read on classical literature..."

She ran out of either breath or thoughts here, and George thought he'd take a swing at talking.

"You took a lot of education back East, then? That's unusual for a woman, but I don't dislike it."

"They're *real*."

Her answer seemed discombobulated, and he swiveled his neck to spy on her again. Her eyes had a far-off look, as though she was privy to something both spectacular and indescribable. *Uh-oh.*

"That's the part nobody wants to accept anymore," she continued. "The ancients knew it, but we've forgotten. They exist. Even *him*." She dropped into a superstitious whisper. "I've looked Death in the eyes and lived to talk about it."

She's crazy as a loon, George thought, and it took all his gentlemanly bearing to keep from saying it aloud. Any fool could see she was hitched to a crazy stick, but he was beginning to feel sorry for the girl. It seemed almost like she was a good heart burdened with a nutty head.

"That's how your cousin died, you see," Lorena said. "They used Death's Dearest on him. It only worked because your Philip deserved it, of course..."

George felt shivers like centipedes walking along his spine. He withdrew the arm that had been casually draped beside hers. Somehow it seemed blood-soaked just from being in contact with the woman.

He was being a damn fool. As head of this posse, he knew there was only one thing to be done. Justice. He had to bring her in and no going softhearted on the way.

"I don't want to talk about how my cousin died. And I seen how you butchered that boy. What you ain't yet told me is what happened to your late husband."

He caught the liar's flicker in her eyes as she prepared her answer. Guilty men tended to look off to the side like that before trying to sculpt a manure pile of truth into something that wouldn't make him gag.

"Death took Master Adalwolf in his sleep," she said slowly. "That's the best I can describe it."

"Is that right? And you ain't leaving nothing out to save your pretty hide? Like why everybody says you done him in? Something about that just don't sit right with you telling me he died all peaceful in his sleep."

A rumble caught him off guard, made him turn in his seat to look over the driver's shoulder. Thick clouds brewed on the horizon, directly in their path. A summer storm a'coming.

"I never said that he died, Mr. Tremont." Lorena's

words were cool, but when George returned his attention to the lady, the tempest in her eyes wielded its own lightning. “Death took my husband. But I intend to get him back.”

66

WEDNESDAY, JUNE 9, 1886

LORENA DRIFTED AWAKE, blinking at the fall of moonlight on her bedroom wallpaper. Well-rested for the first time in ages, she realized she had slept without dreaming. *When was the last time that happened?*

The events of the evening flooded into her mind, from the horror at the saloon to Adalwolf's unbridled glee on their ride home. He had stroked the dagger like a pet as he and Colquoit compared notes on what they'd seen. It apparently never occurred to him that Lorena held information, so she kept her silence and was able to slip away unnoticed when they returned to the townhouse. While Adalwolf worked in his study, she hastened to fall asleep without being watched, a luxury she'd taken for granted most of her life.

Though she wanted to bury herself beneath the covers and sleep until sunrise, she gave in to her bladder and rose to use the chamber pot.

The shadows shifted, and there stood Colquoit, leering through the thin layer of her chemise.

Lorena grabbed at her blanket, wrapping it clumsily around her chest. "Out! Out, you vermin! You swine!"

"What is this?"

Adalwolf shuffled in, exposing them both with his lamp. Colquoit immediately retreated to the foot of the bed, gesturing to a small table.

"I brung a fresh cut of tobacco, like you asked."

Adalwolf looked him over carefully. "I see. That will be all for the night."

Colquoit nodded and left without another word, but as he crossed behind the old man, he looked back at Lorena, his eyes boring into her body. *Revolting.*

Adalwolf eased into his armchair and began tamping his pipe. As soon as Colquoit's footsteps faded down the hall, Lorena crawled across the bed to clutch at her husband's hand.

"My dear, you must turn him out of our house immediately. He came into my room alone while I was sleeping."

Adalwolf looked genuinely shocked at the idea. "Dismiss him? Of course not. He is far too valuable to me. He knows too much to allow him to work for someone else."

Her cheeks grew hot. "But I'm your wife! You are supposed to protect my honor."

"*Tch*! He will not harm you."

Brushing her hands away, Adalwolf continued sprinkling the dirty leaves into the bowl of his pipe. Lorena watched the feeble movements of this withered husk of a man, thinking how easily Colquoit might overpower him. Was he afraid to risk a confrontation? Even so, shouldn't he try for her sake?

"My dearest," she whispered, "do you still care for me at all?"

Adalwolf glanced up in surprise. For a moment, he seemed thoughtful, perhaps even sad.

But rather than offer her comfort, he turned back to his task. He lit a match and breathed his fire to life, smothering her in the familiar scents of catnip and peppermint.

Lorena turned away so he would not see the tears stinging her eyes.

67
THURSDAY, JUNE 10, 1886

ALL NIGHT, she wandered darkened woods, never sure of her bearing or destination. Leaves rustled with snide laughter while underbrush jeered and poked her. She turned a full circle, slowly, scrutinizing the terrain. Rows of identical trunks stretched in every direction until the isolation grew suffocating. When the wind moaned, she considered ducking beneath some sturdy boughs and waiting for morning, but a dull panic in her chest compelled her ever forward.

Something new haunted her, just on the outskirts of her perception. A presence.

The prickling of her neck told her someone was watching.

Not Adalwolf, surely. He'd have been easy to spot, even in the mists. She'd have heard his boots tromping over the fallen branches.

No, this voyeur moved like the air, never visible, but near enough she felt his boding breath on the back of her head. She was sure she could almost touch him, if she dared.

Where is Adalwolf? Why isn't he with me, watching, as always? Did he intentionally leave me out here alone?

Feeling like bait, she huddled beneath a traveling cloak and chose a new direction, then another. Several times, she thought she'd outstripped him, but when she inevitably stopped to catch her breath, he was there, always just behind.

The worst part was how leisurely he pursued her... as though he knew she could never escape.

68

THURSDAY, JUNE 10, 1886

DRY TOAST FELL from her hand into the runny yolk on her plate. It threatened to drip onto her frilled sheets, but Lorena couldn't find the strength to lift the tray. She'd never been so tired, so weak. And yet she was afraid to sleep, lest Adalwolf set her running again.

"Mrs. Berbish," she called weakly. She couldn't remember her other servants' names, but surely if they could hear her, they'd send for the housekeeper.

Lorena lay immobile for several minutes, waiting for help. Finally, she pushed her breakfast tray down to her feet and struggled to sit up. Adalwolf had left his journal beside the armchair at her bedside, and she longed to wade through it again.

Muscles she'd never noticed before complained as she twisted to reach for it. Groaning, she nabbed it with her fingertips, misjudged the weight, and nearly dropped it to the floor.

At last, she cradled it in her lap, propped herself against the headboard, and settled in. Opening it to the middle, she flipped page by page for only a few minutes before finding the drawing that had caught her imagination the first time she'd encountered it.

"*Todes liebste*," he'd printed below the sketch.

"Death's Dearest," Lorena translated aloud.

That dagger—the curious bone-shaped hilt with the distinctive flourishes that seemed almost to dance in place—was the weapon that had killed Tremont.

With a sudden jolt of electricity, she slammed the tome shut and replaced it on the side table. She told herself she was being heedful, not wanting to get caught should Adalwolf return. What kind of silly woman would be scared of a drawing?

A voice came back to her from across the years... Bo's mama, sitting with Lorena and her younger sisters one stormy night while their parents were attending a formal dinner. "Little girls got no call ta be scared. Not while's you got a man like your pa. He gonna see you's always taken care of. Tha's right."

Somehow that thought had always been enough. Her father had been gruff and conniving with little patience for his daughters, but as long as she lived under his roof, he shouldered all their concerns. Now, however...

There was her husband. She always felt safe when she was near young Diedrick. But as Master Adalwolf... It was still hard for her to differentiate between them, but the man she lived with did not adore her. He hadn't even spared a glance for her in the bar as she ran to safety.

Bo could always be counted on to help her, of

course, but he was only a boy who would always be dominated by those of higher stations. He might bring her occasional comfort, but no more.

Who did she have left to protect her?

The smell of her morning coffee made her queasy. She pushed the serving tray farther down the bed with her foot. Too far. It toppled to the floor with a crash, the china shattering on impact.

Hopefully one of the servants would have heard the noise and sent Mrs. Berbish to check on her. If they did, Lorena intended to have her fetch the notes from her desk. She was far too weak to dress herself today, let alone roam the house. But she thought she might stay awake long enough to study. There was suddenly so much she needed to know.

Still, no one appeared.

While she waited, recumbent in a pool of sweat, she closed her eyes and conjured images of the pages she wanted. She'd invested so much time translating them word by word that it became easy to recall the finished phrases now, just days later.

"Escape renewed from death's domain."

That phrase had come together so easily for her that she'd worried she'd mistranslated it. And yet... yes, it fit perfectly with Adalwolf's fixation with old age, disease, and dying. The entirety of his journal centered on death. Or Death.

"One death can claim another."

This one had puzzled her for days. She'd turned it inside out and still it made no sense. Now she believed she understood. A murdered man had one final chance... provided he knew the ancient lore.

"Nemesis's crafted tool."

That was the inscription below the sketch. Each time Adalwolf wrote of Nemesis, he'd left the word in English, capitalized. She'd thought this was an eccentricity, but now it fit as well. He wasn't using the term for an enemy; he was referring to Nemesis, the Greek god of vengeance. The balancer of life.

That tool... Death's Dearest...

She'd been approaching this all as a sort of parlor game or interesting pastime, like those jigsaw puzzles Mother Rose enjoyed on long winter nights. With precision and patience, she'd assembled the border, patching together abstract concepts gleaned from her husband's research. But suddenly, the gaping middle taunted her.

She had to know everything.

The rattle of the doorknob caught her ear. Adalwolf shuffled in, nearly tripping on the mess at the foot of the bed.

"Colquoit!" he called down the hall. "Clean this."

Lorena pulled the blankets tighter around her neck as the apprentice entered. He dropped to his knees to collect the bits of broken platter and sop up the mess as best he could. Strange, but the more effort he put into cleaning, the more she felt her sleeping quarters were being defiled.

Oblivious to the tensions ricocheting between them, Adalwolf settled into his favorite spot and readied his pipe. Lorena knew she was about to be sent back to the darkness.

69

THURSDAY, JUNE 10, 1886

Her dreams seemed to be going grey.

Lorena lolled unheeded on a circular sofa in some stranger's parlor, encroaching on one of the most personal moments this family might ever share. Directly across from her, an old man orated from his death bed, testifying to the merits of this son, that daughter, extracting promises from the teary attendants.

In another era of her life, this might have moved Lorena. In her current stupor, she could only stare at the ceiling and wait for the dream to end.

A maid swept through, quiet as a ghost, to set out a plate of canapés topped with cream cheese and carrot shavings. Lorena considered sampling a few just to counteract the lingering bitterness of the gruel she'd been served for breakfast.

Apparently, she'd slept through an entire day and the following night. She'd woken in the early hours, famished, and been given a brief interval to do a hasty sponge bath, change that soaked nightshirt, and glom down a serving of cornmeal porridge. Then Adalwolf dispatched her here... to this colorless jumble of pasty faces and pre-mourning clothing.

Someone new shuffled into the room, unacknowledged by the attendants. He carried a bulky camera mounted on a tripod, which he propped carefully in the corner before taking a seat near Lorena. Like her, he seemed unmoved by the scene, although his fee for the post-mortem photo would probably be influenced by the bedside manner with which he treated the grieving family.

Lorena's temples pounded. Lack of rest, she supposed. No...

Her eyes widened. The shadows grew deeper. She felt it.

"He's fading!" cried the eldest daughter.

A quick reshuffling sent everyone near the bedside trying at once to hold the old man's hands. He tried still to speak between increasingly laborious gulps of air.

Lorena sat transfixed, feeling the pulse of darkness as the shadows swept in to absorb the man. When they receded, nothing was left but the empty cadaver.

70

FRIDAY, JUNE 11, 1886

In her two months of married life, Lorena had learned to embrace the ineffable. They'd crisscrossed the northern half of the country, bumping shoulders with all walks of life. But nothing prepared her for this...

This patchwork of fancy dress and dirt they called a Barn Dance.

In spite of her haggard spirits and fatigue, she found herself laughing hysterically at everything she saw. Women in their finest Sunday clothes sat on hay blocks waiting for gents in overalls to ask them to dance. The lucky ones participating in the Virginia Reel spun their boots over knotty hardwood and dodged the posts that sprouted through the center of the room. In place of a proper full-sized band, they had four men playing up a storm on fiddles and one old cowpoke at their side playing the spoons. Wherever nails sprouted from of the walls, they'd hung sprigs of dried flowers bound with twine. She half expected to find livestock in the stalls.

It was exactly like the balls back home—if someone had

stripped out the elegance and beauty and peppered everything with sawdust.

The swirling colors and vibration of the floor as everyone —boy to man along the sidelines—stomped in time left Lorena too unsteady to stand unsupported. She leaned onto the punch table, walking hand over hand toward an empty rocking chair in the far corner. The molded wood fit her body like a swaddling cloth. She leaned back in comfort and resolved to spend the rest of her dream here, despite the poor view it gave her of the goings-on.

She had little interest, at any rate, of a soiree where she didn't know a soul. Boredom alone made her listen to the running commentary of a trio of schoolgirls just behind her. They gossiped about everybody who came near but gave special interest to a recently engaged couple who seemed to be at the heart of the affair.

Lorena had little trouble spotting the girl they meant. Pink-cheeked with a coquettish glint in her deep-brown eyes, she reminded Lorena of her little sister Viola, particularly in the way she swished the train of her dress behind her as she talked. Her fiancé was clean-cut, but Lorena found him tragically gangly. His ears poked out east-west while his cowlick pointed north. Each time they squared off to begin a dance, his beloved ran a hand over his hair to tame it, but this was destined to be the first battle she'd lose in her marriage.

With that thought, Lorena looked around for Adalwolf. He stood out, of course, in his somber clothes and full sneer, leaning heavily upon his walking stick. Lorena waved to him out of habit but did not go to his side.

Dancers stampeded between them while unattached gals paraded their ginghams along the perimeter. One young woman chose to block Lorena's view by standing just in front of her. At an affair that mattered, Lorena would have taken umbrage; here, it was another amusing example of gauche behavior.

Lorena pitied the girl somewhat, for she was a cute young thing with her blonde hair done up in cascades of curls and a becoming glow to her porcelain features, but no men took notice of her. When she moseyed farther down the hall, Lorena noticed she had a slight limp, as though her right leg did not bend properly. Perhaps that was why she jutted her nose up so high, as though daring anyone to laugh.

Lorena watched her pace until a commotion at the door caused the fiddlers to stop mid-song.

"Easy now!" yelled a bald man as he barreled across the room. "Put them guns down!"

Even Lorena jumped to her feet to watch as two men faced off with pistols, not twenty paces apart. To one side stood a newcomer to the party, still in his hat and duster. On the other, the newly engaged couple cowered together behind a middle-aged gunman.

The boy peeked his cowlick over his defender's shoulder long enough to shout, "She ain't your girl no more, Rufus!"

"You spineless little weasel!" Rufus advanced several steps. "Look me in the eye and say that!"

More friends and relatives reached for their holsters. Soon, there was more iron waving in the air between the walls of the barn than there was supporting it. Bystanders ducked for cover.

"Stop! Don't kill him!" The girl who had reminded Lorena of her sister abandoned her cover to run to Rufus, protecting him from her family militia. "Rufus, please, stop waving your gun around. I done chose Johnny."

Rufus grimaced, the edges of his mouth twitching as though he was trying not to cry. He opened his gun hand enough to allow the pistol to fall slack, then bent down to kiss her on the forehead.

The crowd didn't relax until someone stripped him of his gun and made him take off his longcoat to prove he was no longer armed. After that, the band kicked back to life, and the warring parties retreated to separate corners. Rufus ended up in the unfashionable end of the room, beside Lorena, kicking half-heartedly at a post and muttering to himself.

The young lady with the limp drifted by and stopped just behind Rufus.

"He don't deserve her," the lady whispered. "The way he cowered when you came in. Gutless."

Rufus didn't acknowledge her but talked to himself in the same tones. "Gutless. Yellow. And look at him gloating now, as if he'd done anything more remarkable than not piss himself when he seen my gun."

"Daisy must still care about you," the lady said, "to run to your side the way she did."

"Daisy," he repeated. His gaze focused on the young bride-to-be half a room away.

Then, to Lorena's astonishment, the young lady hiked up her dress right there beside the dance floor, exposing herself ankle to crotch... and no one noticed! Two schoolboys walked past and neither spared her a glance.

Two incredible things became apparent to Lorena. First, that she was the only person who could see the lady. Second, that the woman's limp had been caused by the rifle strapped to her leg.

The lady untied the Browning and propped it against a hay bale, all the while saying in her soothing manner, "She'd fall in love with you again if he was gone. Maybe someone left a gun lying around somewhere."

Rufus looked down, puzzled, and noticed the rifle at his feet. In seconds, he'd made his decision, dropping behind the bale like a sniper. He fired once, then dropped the rifle and ran into the night.

Lorena saw the lady squeal with delight before she heard the distant screams.

An even denser crowd formed this time, in pandemonium around the fallen man.

Lorena saw Adalwolf elbow his way in, yelling, "I am doctor! I will save him!"

"No, you wo-o-on't," sang the lady to herself.

Lorena clutched a post to keep from fainting. A shadow dipped into the room, and she knew it was extracting Johnny from his body. The air rustled around her, exactly as it had through the long night in the woods. Then the sensation snuffed itself to nothingness.

"Stop pouting, Thanatos," The lady said to the retreating shadows. While partygoers around her shouted and cried, she perched on the hay bale and retrieved her Browning. Lorena watched as she pulled a knife from her boot and began carving another notch into the stock of her rifle.

"You're Nemesis!" Lorena cried. "You must be!"

The woman's head whipped up in shock—

And Lorena woke abruptly in her own bed.

71

FRIDAY, JUNE 11, 1886

SHE LAY in thick black mud along the banks of a river. Alone.

Glad for the respite, she washed her hands as well as possible and raised a cupped handful of water to her mouth. It tasted of tin and soot. She spat it out, then dredged up saliva to spit again, desperate to rid her mouth of that tang.

She took stock of her ruined dress with a sigh, then climbed the steep bank. From a short distance, the befouled water was beautiful, lined with ancient willows and tiny bushes with clusters of pink flowers that smelled of cherry. It was as peaceful a scene as she'd beheld in weeks.

Humming to herself, she roamed the small trail until she tripped over the body of a small Chinese woman. Mostly naked, her torn and bloodied robes scattered on the ground beneath her, the bludgeoned lady had been left for dead. Though Lorena could see the slightest movement of her lips as breath passed through them, she knew it would not continue much longer.

Death would come mercifully soon. Lorena stayed by her side until the shadows took away her pain.

THE MAN'S SCREAMS SUBSIDED FOR ONLY A MOMENT, then escalated to a higher pitch. He fought so hard on his gurney that the doctor could barely get a hand on his stomach.

"Appendix," the doctor surmised. "I'll bet anything. Let's get to work."

He wheeled the man into surgery while a squadron of nurses hurried to don their bonnets and aprons.

Lorena wanted to tell them not to bother—if he was going to live through this, she wouldn't be here. But intervention was moot. No one seemed to even notice her cowering in the corner, covering her ears with her hands.

His agony lasted until the ether knocked him out. Lorena sat on an empty bed while the doctor applied the scalpel, generating more gore than hope.

A quarter hour later, Adalwolf strolled in, twitting, "This wastes my time."

"I didn't choose this dream," Lorena reminded him.

"I need more deaths. Faster," Adalwolf said to himself. "Perhaps Mars-La-Tour."

"PARTIR!"

The line of cannons fired deafening blows that seemed to shake the hillside. Lorena ducked behind the commander in golden epaulets shouting orders, thankful they were at a far enough distance not to render her deaf.

Adalwolf stood near her, whistling softly as they watched the gunners reload.

The commander continued yelling in French until movement downfield caught his attention.

Through the hanging smoke of their gunfire, the enemy had crept up and now emerged in full charge. Hundreds of dragoons thundered forth, scattering the now-defenseless artillery men.

In the panic that followed, Lorena was forced to watch bodies run through with curved sabers, flattened beneath line after line of charging steeds, pulverized until nothing remained but broken carcasses and a smear of entrails.

72

SATURDAY, JUNE 12, 1886

Lorena's entire body jerked with the heart-pounding sensation of being snatched out of a deep slumber. But she had apparently only traded one dream for another, landing her quite comfortably on an elegant veranda.

"...was no place for a lady of culture. I hope you do not mind," a woman nearby was saying.

Enchanted by her surroundings, Lorena craned her neck to take in the beauty. Someone had cultivated the vast patio into hanging gardens with exotic vines creeping down every post, sprouting flower buds that perfumed the air. Gazing globes on brass stands cunningly refracted the grandeur. Lorena took a seat at a marble-top table to admire the silver tea service laid out upon it.

"A lump of sugar?" asked the woman.

Lorena watched a dragonfly flitting over a cast iron birdbath.

"It is rude to ignore your hostess!"

Lorena jumped as the lady turned to face her. "You—you can see me?"

"Of course. Fortunately, you are not one of those perverted wretches who dream of roaming around invisibly. I would not have invited you here if you were."

The lady smiled, flashing a dimple, and the splendor of the garden dimmed in comparison. Long red hair flowed loosely over her porcelain skin. The simple cotton dressing gown was perfectly tailored to hug her curves. Deep-blue eyes bore down, unblinking.

Lorena could only stare back, thunderstruck.

After a moment, the soft pink lips stopped smiling.

"I had hoped for more stimulating conversation, my pet. You may remain in my home as long as you wish... providing you do not bore me."

Even with the lovely lilt in her voice, Lorena recognized the threat and realized she had better start participating. This dream was not writing itself.

"Please excuse my manners. Were you offering me tea? Yes, please."

Mollified, the lady passed her a delicate china cup.

"Close your eyes as you sip. Try to pick out each sensation as a separate experience. The leaves are from the Pindhos Mountains, mixed with mint and citrus leaves. After it steeps, I add exactly three drops of Attiki honey so it melts against the tongue, warm and inviting as a lover's kiss." She sighed deeply. "I could spend half a century savoring a finely brewed Shepherd's Tea."

Lorena followed instructions, knowing she was expected to comment on the tasting experience, but she was too distracted by the lady's odd phrasing. What woman so young thought in terms of fifty-year increments?

"Perhaps we should start with introductions," Lorena ventured.

"Do you find them necessary? What a mortal notion. You are Lorena Adalwolf née Whitaker, of the new Americas. And I..." Here the lady outstretched both arms, palms up. "I am called Oneroi, Goddess of Dreams, Finesser of Impulses, Knower of the True Self."

Lorena gasped. One of them!

Oneroi stood gracefully and led Lorena across the long balcony until they stood at the railing, overlooking the impossible. A bounding ocean flanked by mountain ranges peaked with quiet valleys. Bustling cities enshrouded in dense forests. It was as though someone had cheated with a jigsaw puzzle, then brought the misplaced pieces to life.

Oneroi stroked Lorena's hair affectionately. "You, my pet, are among the elite who have traveled fully into my realm. The choice to stay is now yours."

Lorena backed away from the dizzying view, trying to make sense of everything she was seeing and hearing. "I can live in a dream? Is this because I've been sleeping so much the past few days?"

"Not merely sleeping. Dreaming! My cousin, Hypnos, guides those boring minds who surrender their consciousness only to sleep. I *touch their lives briefly, giving what they crave, then he guides them back to their droll waking lives." Her lips turned up in a sneer for just a moment, then returned to a radiant smile as she took Lorena's hands in hers. "You have been dreaming for days, the rarest of feats! Only one human in a myriad will achieve that. You are now mine."*

Lorena recoiled. "Your slave?"

"No, dearest. My disciple. And you will discover I am a

most generous benefactor to my favorites. Tell me, what does your heart desire?"

Feeling faint, Lorena asked, "May I sit down?"

Oneroi laughed. "You will disappoint me if all your wishes are as pedantic as that."

"No, I only meant..."

But Oneroi was already leading her through the gardens, toward a pair of burgundy, crushed velvet fainting couches. Oneroi lounged on hers, the folds of her dress cascading over the edge while Lorena sat primly opposite.

Silence stretched taut between them. Lorena felt small under the goddess's penetrating stare but had no idea what she was expected to say.

Finally, Oneroi tutted. "Patience is a virtue for mortals, a hindrance to gods. Now tell me your deepest wish."

Lorena shrugged helplessly.

"Do not ponder too long, child. The answer is always just behind your lips. What is the one thing you want most?"

"My husband, Diedrick." Lorena answered without thinking, then realized how deeply she meant it.

Oneroi looked delighted, her lips forming a perfect O. She shot to her feet and retrieved something from a small curio shelf Lorena hadn't noticed before, then squeezed onto the seat with Lorena, giggling like a schoolgirl.

"My, my, yes. That man was *exciting. I am fond of all my disciples, but he was a particular favorite. How long has it been since he lived with me? Decades, surely."*

"Diedrick came here? Do you mean during his long coma?"

"Why, of course, dear. What did you think a coma is? Here."

She thrust the curio into Lorena's hands, revealing it to be a framed portrait of young Diedrick. Lorena's heart leapt at the rendering of his carefree grin.

"No wonder you crave him," Oneroi said. "He was delectable. Handsome. Robust. Bursting with energy. Always riding his horses and making love."

Lorena nearly dropped the portrait. Forgetting both her manners and the fact she was speaking to a deity, she shouted, "You had relations with my *husband?"*

"No, not me, you silly girl. Look at you, shaking with impotent rage. How adorable you are. No, I was speaking of that foreign bride of his. Oh!" She clapped a hand to her mouth, laughing through her fingers. "That was you, *wasn't it? I had quite forgotten that I bent time for the lad. And it still works? Your hearts are still linked?"*

Lorena nodded, unable to speak.

"And you began dreaming of him without my intervention? How wondrous."

Lorena studied her lover's picture again. "So, my dreams now are his dreams from back then?"

"Yes. I have linked hearts many times but never over such a span of time and distance. Tell me, my dear," she said with a saucy wink, "how vivid have the dreams been for you? I want every *detail."*

Lorena blushed, dropping her head, then realized she must have misunderstood. No woman would want to hear what happened inside the bedroom, surely.

"I met Diedrick months ago, in dreams," Lorena said. "Then this spring he came to me in real life. His older self, that is. Master Adalwolf, I call him now."

"He found you? He remembered you?" Oneroi rose, pacing.

"How unusual. So few humans preserve my gifts. I choose to be flattered."

"I cannot tell how much he remembers," Lorena admitted. "He will not speak of it. But surely, he retains something of our time together. He found me almost as soon as he began using the Sacred Bundle."

"He tries to control me?" Oneroi shrieked. Emotion inverted her beauty, creating a monstrous visage, terrible to behold.

"No, no, of course not," Lorena lied, choosing her words carefully. "He uses it to... honor you."

The goddess appeared pacified. Her features soothed into a becoming pout. "I am bored with this garden and all the stilted formality of modern life. Come, let us bathe together while you narrate your tale of love."

Tugging Lorena behind, Oneroi flounced up the lane to the palatial homestead. Through open French doors, Lorena saw a room-sized pool on the inside of the house.

When they reached the water's edge, Oneroi unknotted the sash at her waist, loosened her dressing gown, and stepped right out of it. She shucked off her shoes and turned to Lorena, utterly, brazenly naked. Mortified, Lorena tried not to stare at the curves of alabaster skin or the jewel piercing her tiny navel. But as the woman leapt with abandon into the water, Greek art suddenly came alive for Lorena. She easily pictured a classical sculptor hauling a 300-pound slab of marble up to his workshop, just for the pleasure of chiseling Oneroi's form into it.

The goddess submerged for a moment, then reappeared several yards out, beckoning. "Join me, Lorena. Now!"

Lorena knew it was a command but felt certain she'd die in her sleep of embarrassment if she had to skewer her modesty like that! Oneroi watched her intently, forcing her to act. Stripped of any better options, Lorena flung herself into the pool fully clothed.

At first, the water was warm and inviting, crystal clear with a sweet hint of grapes—which Lorena discovered because she'd forgotten to close her mouth. It was far deeper than she'd anticipated, too, landing her far over her head. When she realized how heavy her layers of clothes had become, panic set in. Could she swim in a dream when she didn't know how to in real life?

She flailed about, needing desperately to breath, while Oneroi frolicked in the opposite direction. Why did she insist on this? I'd much rather be lying in bed.

Instantly, she found herself buoyed to the surface atop a rosewood Louis XV bed that somehow floated in the center of the pool.

Oneroi splashed her as she swam past. "Brava, my pet! Very inventive!"

Lorena could not help feeling proud of her cunning, however unintentional. She began musing at the power of dreams.

"This spa is exhilarating!" Oneroi gushed. She dove under the bed, then climbed up the other side and curled against the pillows, soaking the quilted comforter. "Regale me now with more tales of your passionate young love."

Lorena made a show of squeezing the water from her hair and clothes so she would not have to face the naked goddess.

"May I ask you about Diedrick's time here?"

"Certainly. You may ask, though perhaps I shan't answer."

"When you asked him his heart's desire... what did he request?"

Lorena stopped breathing as she awaited the answer. Adalwolf had once told her that his vendetta against death began when he woke from his coma, believing the illness had nearly killed him. That obsession consumed his life. But was it already young Diedrick's deepest wish to conquer death?

"Such a troubled young man, our dear Diedrick. He came to me in the throes of a tortuous life. Everyone he loved had been swept away. He lived in isolation. Imagine such a vivacious lad living as a hermit! The poor dear. Naturally, his only wish was for you."

"Me?" Lorena spun toward Oneroi so vigorously she nearly pitched herself into the water again. "But how could he ask for me? We hadn't met yet."

Oneroi's soft laugh tinkled like bubbles in a champagne flute. She clasped her hands between her perfect breasts. "He said he need a beautiful young woman with whom to share his life. Well-educated but not argumentative. Skinny but with an ample bottom. Fair-skinned but raven-haired. Spirited but subservient. Devoted to him beyond reason. And, ah, yes, a most proper lady but ravenous *in bed."*

Lorena blushed at this but could not suppress a smile.

"Indeed?" Oneroi teased her with waggling eyebrows before explaining, "Many young men concoct fantasies like this. They have such little experience with women that they rely on stories, illusions, and their own vain whims to sketch a vision of the ideal girl. Rarely do they realize when they have strung together so many conflicting requirements that it is impossible for one person to be all things. So a god may grant his wish, only to watch it fall apart in doses of reality. However, in this

instance, I decided it would be more fun to honestly fulfill his wish. I had to engage Chronos's help. He searched decades to find the woman who could be Diedrick's soulmate."

Lorena's heart fluttered. She was ready to worship Oneroi, to erect monuments to her benevolence and foresight. Oneroi had given her to Diedrick as his one true love. She'd united their hearts, bound them as man and wife. They could never have found each other without her intervention.

"Why are you crying, my pet?"

Lorena didn't bother wiping away the tears. "He loves me. My Diedrick truly loves me. Oh, thank you!"

Impishly, Oneroi slipped back into the water and swam, pushing the bed like a beaver toward the shore. Lorena climbed onto the tile floor, only too happy to leave the pool, and more than moderately relieved when Oneroi opted for clothes. She donned a black silk robe adorned with golden dragons, which stunningly contrasted with her dark red hair.

Oneroi opened a set of pocket doors and led them into a familiar parlor. Lorena recognized the blue upholstery and hurried to stand on the throw rug so she wouldn't drip water on Mother Rose's hardwood floors.

"Do you know where we are?"

"Yes, of course. That urn beside the furnace is the one I knocked over the first time I wore a hoop skirt."

Oneroi scrutinized her. "No stirrings of homesickness, then? No scenes from your childhood you long to relive? Ah, well. No matter. Nostalgia is a passive trait. We shall forge ahead."

The next door opened to an ornate opera house, empty and silent but lit to the last candle. Lorena sighed, hoping they would not be forced to sit through an entire show as the only audience members.

"I thought this would please you." Oneroi sounded testy now. "Do you prefer the outdoors? Do you long to fly toward the sunset? Name your adventure."

Lorena did not hesitate. "Diedrick's mansion, please."

Oneroi wrinkled her nose. "No. That does not interest me. I have already created that web of dreams. We shall rob a train and live as outlaws."

They crossed another doorway to a dusty barn where two stallions waited for them, already saddled.

Oneroi tossed her a knapsack filled with clothes. "You need to change into britches. We won't get far if you ride sidesaddle on the getaway."

Caught once more under the burden of her goddess's ludicrous demands, Lorena slowly unpacked the outfit, complete with kerchief and holster. "You said before that it is my choice how long I will remain here?"

"Of course, my pet. You may remain with me as long as you like." Oneroi slapped a cowboy hat over Lorena's wet bun. "We shall feast on excitement!"

"Or... I may choose to wake up?"

Oneroi's smile froze, her eyes dangerously dark. "Why would you leave? I can offer you everything. Unlimited possibilities. Bliss."

Lorena wished she had translated more about the goddess of Dreams from Adalwolf's journal. She only remembered seeing the name a few times. What had she read about Oneroi's love of storytelling? Something about wanting the stories to be satisfying?

"It's not over," Lorena blurted. "My love story. There's so much yet to explore with Diedrick. A lifetime together. I know you would find it interesting."

Oneroi kissed Lorena on the forehead.

"I would grant your every wish, child, but Chronos rules time and he is less relenting than I. Diedrick lived with me only 192 hours. I do not know how much of that time you have already spent with him, but the time you have left is finite. You may be destined to be with him again, but such a shame it would be to squander your remaining time by taking it all in one great gulp now. Then all you would have left is that cold, conniving old man."

Devastated, Lorena backed away, hands on her stomach as she nearly doubled over. She had never considered that their time must end. Diedrick's mansion was her haven. Finding him again was her only goal, the notion that made all this madness worth enduring. What if she was already nearing the end of their time?

"I'll be all alone!" she wailed.

Oneroi embraced her, those slender arms displaying surprising strength as she held her close. "Hush, my pet. We are all solitary, each of us. Even though I weave through the minds of everyone in the world, still I am alone." She pulled Lorena tighter for one suffocating moment, then let her go with a gentle pat on the head. "Yet we endure."

Lorena pulled away enough to look the goddess in the eye. "But he is my entire world. Without him, there is nothing to live for. Nothing left to dream of."

"Nothing to dream*?" Oneroi looked as though she had been slapped. "No one has ever threatened me like that." No hostility remained in Oneroi's frown, only a wistfulness that hinted at her stunning age. "And if you leave now, will you betray me? Shall you join Adalwolf's quest to thwart the gods?"*

"No, my lady."

She could tell from Oneroi's narrowed eyes that the goddess did not believe her. In truth, she did not believe herself. Once back in her own world, she would do whatever her husband commanded of her. She always had.

On the other hand, it was Oneroi who had the power to reunite her with Diedrick. And shouldn't she feel indebted to the goddess for pairing them in the first place?

If nothing else, a show of fealty was preferable to leaving an irate Greek god at her back.

"I'll pledge to you! Like they did in Ancient Greece. I mean... I wouldn't be able to build a temple. Plus, I find animal sacrifice barbaric and unpleasant and most of the rest of it seemed to be about drinking too much wine... but setting all that aside, I swear an oath of loyalty to you, my goddess."

Oneroi's radiant smile seemed to infuse the room with sunshine. "My devoted pet, you are a constant source of unexpected pleasure. Come. I shall prepare your departure."

Oneroi grasped the latch of a new door but did not open it. With her free hand, she caressed Lorena's temple, studying it.

"You have been diving from dream to dream recently, watching scenes of death. Tell me why. Do you fear dying?"

"No. My husband is using my dreams to search for Thanatos."

"What a ridiculous notion! Humans remember less about Death than they do Dreams. If you are visiting ordinary people's memories, you will catch only a fleeting glimpse, a shadow, perhaps. You must find someone who has witnessed Death multiple times, on this very night."

Oneroi squeezed her eyes shut, lips pursed. Her hand flew to her own temple, rubbing small circles.

"Ah-ha!" she shouted, eyes popping open. "I have located

someone. You may feel shaky. I am about to merge you with the mind of a man who witnessed horrors this very night, before he fell into a deep slumber."

Oneroi squeezed the latch, and the door jerked from her hand, slammed open by a wind so powerful Lorena fought against being sucked outside. Then the gust reversed, bearing down on them with intense heat and the smell of burning flesh. A tower of flame shot up before them, flaying the night. The protective darkness stripped away just enough to reveal phantom silhouettes.

Over the far-off screams, Lorena cried, "Is that hell?"

"No, my dear, it is only the folly of mortals. Do not be afraid. I shall watch over your endeavors with great interest. Fare thee well, my faithful one. Mein Treuer."

Her graceful arm prodded Lorena in the back, sweeping her forward into the abyss.

73
SATURDAY, JUNE 12, 1886

SHE LANDED ON HER FEET, unscathed. Adalwolf materialized, leaning on his cane beside her, a bored spectator to a fire that appeared to be engulfing an entire city. Block after block of stores, homes, even ancient trees blazed, all competing for the attention of the scrambling townsfolk in the streets.

"Not Chicago again?" Lorena asked her husband.

Adalwolf shook his head. "Canada, I believe. Vancouver."

Someone shouted above the din, "Send the Mounties down Hastings! The sawmill's going next!"

The man's instructions took no immediate hold on anyone. Those who weren't fighting the flames already were running toward a narrow bridge several blocks away.

Adalwolf shuffled nearer, peering into her face. "You did not respond to me. We could not wake you. I was... concerned."

She wanted to believe his disquiet amounted to affection, rather than the loss of his favorite laboratory experiment. But Oneroi's words still rang in her ears: "You'll be stuck with that cold, cunning old man."

"I was comatose," she replied tartly, then tried to evaluate

his reaction. Did he remember his time with the Goddess of Dreams? Would he realize that she had visited that realm as well?

He gave no indication of deeper thoughts but patted her shoulder and decided, "After this, you will rise and eat a hearty meal."

Lorena nodded, but already she could tell his thoughts had moved on. He prodded her—more gently than usual—in the back with his cane.

"Move closer to the fire. Death must be everywhere tonight, yet we are missing it!"

"Missing Death's shadow, you mean?"

As always when she revealed herself as more acute than he had anticipated, Adalwolf responded first with an accusatory narrowing of his eyes. Then he relented to a begrudging, "Ja. You have seen it, as well?"

"I have." She took a deep breath and turned to face him square-on. "And I think you are approaching this the wrong way. You need to stop chasing the deaths themselves. Look instead for someone who has witnessed it."

"I can witness it myself! Be silent, woman."

The fire caught the sawmill. It burned as brightly as a sunrise, pulling everyone's horrified eyes toward the row of men clinging to the scaffolding along the top deck. It appeared to Lorena that they'd scrambled up it to escape the flames, only to find themselves trapped three stories above the road.

Someone on the street shouted up, "Climb onto the roof! You maybe can make the jump to the waterfalls!"

Taking his advice, they hoisted one man onto the roof and started to help another when the scaffold buckled under their weight. One side broke loose, plummeting them straight into the raging fire.

In that instant, a dozen men were lost. The loner on the roof let out a wail, his open arms flailing toward the pit. The shrieks from inside the building were unbearable.

Lorena turned away, covering her ears, wishing none of it was real. But it had to be. Sure, this was a dream, but Oneroi had said she was sending her to the mind of someone who had freshly witnessed the horrors. Did she mean the man on the roof?

Fighting her instincts, she peeked back. He hadn't moved, hadn't yet fled, only clung to the corner of the roof, talking to himself. No... not himself. He was talking quietly to someone below, someone in the midst of the chaos, who could not possibly hear him. And yet...

Lorena knew the moment she spotted him that he could not possibly belong to this city. While every willing hand toiled against the fire in rolled-up shirt sleeves, one man strolled among them all without a care, resplendent in his evening tail-coat and top hat. With a dismissive wave to the man on the mill, he turned on his heel and wandered elsewhere.

With every step, Lorena saw him differently, not as he'd appeared to the worker, but as he truly was. His beard faded away. His hat disappeared, revealing plaited silver hair. The austere profile looked nothing like the painting she'd visited, for that artist had taken liberties to make the god beautiful, but she recognized him anyway.

"Thanatos," she said.

The god startled, turning toward her, and Lorena found herself staring Death in the eye. He blinked first, looking puzzled and perhaps intrigued.

Before he could advance toward her, Adalwolf wrapped his arms around his wife, pulling her to his chest like he had when he was young. Warm and safe in that moment, Lorena relaxed into him and felt him pull her out of the dream.

"Look away," Adalwolf whispered. "I have him."

74

SATURDAY, JUNE 12, 1886

LORENA AND ADALWOLF faced off at the dinner table, warring manners over a feast of roast goose in sage dressing that smelled so good her empty stomach clenched. The only problem was that Lorena did not remember dressing for dinner.

"This feels wrong," she said.

Adalwolf meticulously sliced his breast meat into strips as he replied, "Eat, Mein Treuer. You cannot continue if you deplete your energy fully."

She nodded, seeing the sense of this. And the whipped sweet potatoes dusted with brown sugar were divine. Yet...

"You said you would let me wake to eat. If this is just a dream, eating won't suppress my hunger. It won't help at all."

Her husband said nothing, avoiding her eyes as he slurped his coffee.

She gritted her teeth. Did he not understand how vexing it was not to trust her own mind? Not to delineate reality and these detailed dreamscapes?

Standing, she sought her reflection in the half-curtained window. Her hair was undone, dropping in tangles to her waist, with her ostrich-plumed hat securely affixed to her crown. And while she sported her favorite crushed velvet dropped-waist jacket, the dress beneath it was missing, leaving her corset and shift exposed. It made no sense unless she were dreaming.

Or unless she were going mad...

"This is *a dream, right?" she insisted.*

"Ja!" Adalwolf wiped his mouth and threw his napkin onto the table. Seizing his cane, he rounded the table toward her. "If you have no wish for food, we will go."

She recognized the mania brewing in his eyes. He was nearer his life's objective than ever now. Any promises he might have made about giving her a rest folded under his new zeal.

His shriveled talons gripped her arm, pulling her down the hall and through their front door.

Even in a dream, it mortified Lorena to be wandering her neighborhood half clothed. Everyone along the street turned to stare as her bare feet stumbled against the rough sidewalk. Faces pressed to windows across the way, eager to see this strolling Godiva.

"Wait!" she cried, pulling ineffectually against him. "Let me dress. I'll only take a moment."

But her appeals went unheeded, and they turned the corner toward the older Italianate mansions and cutting-edge Queen Annes of the uptown proper. On these blocks, the well-to-do took their promenades with consequence, never nodding too deeply, always painfully aware which person on the pecking order should initiate a wave, which might dare to shout a hello. A woman running about in her underclothes would never again reach above the bottom rung of the social ladder.

"Be a dream. Please be a dream," she chanted.

Mr. Christopher's carriage overtook them. He had his right arm raised in genial greeting to Adalwolf before he sighted Lorena. His dimpled grin crumpled as though rigor mortis had bested him.

Worse still, the sisters Mrs. Henderson and Mrs. Nelson were heading their way on foot. They didn't appear to have noticed her yet, but their path would bring them directly to her in only moments.

"I want to die!" Lorena wailed.

"Yours is not the death I need," Adalwolf said, chuckling, but at last he released her arm.

Lorena turned back, ready to make a mad dash for home, and found herself face-to-face with her own housekeeper.

"Mrs. Berbish!" she cried.

But before the woman could react, Adalwolf shouted, "Ha!" and pushed Lorena forward with both hands. Lorena stumbled, arms flailing madly, and knocked Mrs. Berbish into the street.

Lorena's forehead slapped the sidewalk just as Mrs. Berbish fell beneath the hooves and wheels of Mr. Christopher's carriage.

75
SUNDAY, JUNE 13, 1886

SUNLIGHT FILTERED into the stuffy room along with the chirping of birds just outside. Lorena took this as a good sign as she lifted her heavy forehead and pried her eyes open. She was lying in her own bed, familiar as ever in her St. Louis home. Good, good. But a strange maid stood in the corner fussing with a set of oil lamps.

"Who are you?" Lorena demanded in a voice so hoarse she didn't recognize it as her own.

The girl yelped and spun around.

"Oh! Missus! I didn't know you was waken up."

"I've never seen you before!"

"I beg your pardon, ma'am," she said with a curtsey, as though this was somehow her fault. "They sent me up to refill your lamps. Should I tell the cook you're ready for your lunch, then?"

Lorena waved off her questions, still trying to get her bearings. This felt real. The nightgown she wore was the same one she remembered putting on after they returned from the saloon. Her bed had formed hard lumps underneath her body but otherwise seemed correct. Sniffing deeply, she caught the stale hint of burnt sweetgrass lingering in the air but nothing fresh from Adalwolf's pipe. He hadn't been around recently.

"What time is it? What day is it?"

"Saturday, ma'am. Teatime. Three thirty, I believe."

"Saturday? It couldn't be!" Lorena tried to remember the events of the past few days, but it was simply a blur since the shooting Wednesday night.

"You've been asleep for days, ma'am," the girl explained. Lorena noticed how she inched backward toward the door with each word. "Taken sick. They haven't sent for the doctor, but your husband's been attending to you each day and night." She attempted an encouraging smile. "Are you feeling a mite better now?"

Lorena hated her for being so annoyingly perky. "Where is Mrs. Berbish?"

"Has nobody told you, ma'am? She's gone, ma'am."

"What do you mean, gone?"

The maid felt the need to curtsey again before replying, "Dead, ma'am."

The room started spinning. Lorena collapsed onto her sheets until the sensation passed.

"I shouldn't have blurted it out like that," the girl said. "I'm sorry, ma'am. I've never been a lady's maid before. Should I go find someone who can talk more proper?"

"No! Tell me what happened to Mrs. Berbish."

"Why, she was run over!" Reluctance to speak to her employer lost out to the girl's desire to tell the story. "By that nice Mr. Christopher. Well, by his carriage. She was walking down the street yesterday, healthy as you please. And next thing you know she falls flat on the ground and gets trampled to death!"

"No!" Lorena ran her hands through her unwashed hair, half expecting to find her hat still tethered there. She was so certain that was a dream! Unable to meet her servant's eyes, she asked, "Have I left the house this week? Have you heard anything... unusual... about me that I should hear?"

"Why, no, ma'am! You've been in bed since Wednesday, like I said. Took sick after your night out with Master Adalwolf."

Holding her breath, Lorena stared at Adalwolf's empty chair. It had been a dream, then. Just another one that came true. But he hadn't been sitting by to witness this death; he'd taken a hand in it somehow. What was he playing at?

"Will there be anything else, ma'am?" the girl prompted after a long silence.

"No. Wait, yes. Tell the cook to send up a meal. Quickly, before my husband returns."

76
SUNDAY, JUNE 13, 1886

LORENA FOUND herself standing in an austere study. A bachelor's home, she guessed, decorated in heavy furniture, yet utilitarian. No wall hangings or doilies, no plants or flowers. And at the long, polished table, only a single chair.

Adalwolf drew open the curtains to let in the hearty afternoon sunshine. She watched him, humming a march and tapping his foot, and marveled at the changes blooming forth in her husband. His stoop seemed less pronounced. His arms weren't shaking, nor was he using his cane for support. When he turned toward her, she even fancied that the wrinkles surrounding his thin lips had faded, leaving room for the corners to turn up in a faint smile.

"Mrs. Berbish died," Lorena said, accusation heavy in her tone.

"Yes!" His voice crackled like a funeral pyre. "It is so easy to me now. Watch this."

He seized a pot of ink from the writing desk and hurled it through the window. Lorena heard screams and raced to his side.

Several stories up, they overlooked a bustling city street. The ink pot had smashed like an anvil into the skull of a passing worker. She could see his faint movements as he lay sprawled on the sidewalk, black ink and blood pooling around him.

Adalwolf cackled and rubbed his yellowed fingertips together. "He will be dead by morning, both here and in our world."

"How can you be happy about that? It's murder."

He paced the room, listening only to himself. "Almost I am there. A flick of my hand and Death does my bidding."

As spacious as the apartment was, Lorena felt more confined by the second. Clinging to the windowsill, she said, "We're in a dream. I can feel it. How can anything here affect reality?"

"Foolish girl!" Stepping so lightly he was almost dancing, Adalwolf circled the table. "You witnessed everything but were too simple to comprehend. This is why I chose your mind rather than a man's. I have entered your mind a hundred times, leaping then to minds of strangers, acquaintances." In a mocking falsetto, he cried, "'It was so real!' Of course it was, woman! We were invading deepest memories. We saw glimpses of the future! But to you it was all pretty hats and dresses."

Lorena stepped into the room, keeping the width of the table between them. "You are going too far! You may have manipulated people that way, but you cannot toy with a god."

"Ach! It is immensely easier! Whose mind do you think we are trespassing right now?"

Lorena turned around slowly, considering the stately room. Immaculate. Expansive. Somber. What felt wrong? Her gaze traced the buffet to the chest to the table, all beautifully matched oak, inlaid with ivory handles and midnight-black scrollwork. Only the desk gave an indication that the room was inhabited, with its tall, tidy stacks of paper. Inching closer, afraid to touch anything, she peered at the sheets and found only row upon row of tally marks.

"This is Death's study," she said, panicking. "We shouldn't be here. It's too dangerous."

"This is his dreaming mind. He cannot harm us. He will never even notice me. That is the beauty. With humans, I plant thoughts and wait, wondering. If I show a man he will win at cards, will that convince his waking mind to gamble it all? Yes, usually, but not always. People have doubts. But a god does not doubt. For thousands of years, he has seen this *is black and* that *is white. Always is order. Never the unexpected. So, when I show him now here is person dead, he does not doubt. He believes the person is to die, so he carries out his task."*

She watched him, power-mad and giddy, nearly crackling with energy. He seemed younger by the second. And for just a moment, the unchecked joy in his voice reminded her of Diedrick. She searched his pale blue eyes, telling herself all would be right if only she could spot that familiar twinkle.

"All I have to do," Adalwolf said, speaking to himself now, "is convince him I cannot die. But how?"

He strode to the framed mirror standing in the corner and scrutinized his reflection.

"Shall I show him I am still a young boy? Can I make myself invisible to him? Convince him I am already dead so he cannot visit me twice? Or simply choose someone else to die in my stead whenever my time is near?"

Lorena shivered, no longer able to cling to the fragile

façade. The last vestiges of her sweet, young husband were trampled underfoot as Adalwolf took the reins of the ultimate mind.

"You don't need me anymore," she said softly. "You have everything you wanted. Please, let me go."

"Do not need you?" He sounded perplexed, as though she'd delivered a riddle. "But of course I do. You are still Mein Treuer. You tether me to my reality. What is the point of living forever if I become anyway a soul without a body?"

She tried to concentrate on his next words—something about a promise to keep her alive with him—but the shadow in the corner seemed to be deepening. The air pressure plummeted, cramping her bowels with a sense of foreboding.

"We need—to leave," she gasped, "before—he knows we're here!"

"He cannot know that." Adalwolf preened once more before the mirror. "No one has ever delved into the mind of a god. I am the first, the only! I am the most powerful being in the world!"

Immobilized by dread, Lorena was unable to tell her husband she was no longer his sole audience. For without footsteps, without a slamming door to announce his arrival, Thanatos manifested between them. He paid Lorena no heed but towered over Adalwolf until the old man whirled around in shock.

The god roared with unadulterated fury. His rage emanated in shockwaves that knocked them both off balance.

With a cunning glint in his eye, Adalwolf grabbed her hand just as Thanatos seized his throat. It seemed to Lorena that everything dissolved into nothingness...

She woke in her own bed, her eyes popping open just in time to see Adalwolf's pipe crash to the floor beside his empty chair.

XIII
FLIGHT

⁂ 77 ⁂
MONDAY, JUNE 14, 1886

SHE LEAPT from her bed and nearly fell against the wall as her legs buckled beneath her. The days of lying in bed had left her body feeble, but her mind raced circles around the room.

Adalwolf was gone.

The pipe was still smoking. She felt the seat of his chair—still warm.

"Oh, my dear," she whispered. And again, when no further thoughts would come, "Oh dear."

A growing commotion in the house below drew her attention—women shouting and running about as though the place were on fire. She pulled on a house robe and threw open her door.

A nearby maid screamed when she spotted Lorena leaning over the stair railing to peek into the front hall. The entire staff milled about with their coats on in front of the open door. More of the young girls followed the lead of the first one, staring up at their mistress, squealing in horror, and fleeing the house.

Only the old cook, Mrs. Olafsson, stood her ground. "Mrs. Adalwolf, I regret to inform you that we are leaving. All of us."

"But why?" Lorena asked, descending the staircase as fast as her feeble legs would allow. "Has something happened?"

Mrs. Olafsson appeared flummoxed. She worked her mouth like a fish for several seconds before stating, "We must tender our resignations. Collectively. Effective immediately."

She pinned her hat onto her head with the bearing of a soldier arming himself before battle and swept through the front door.

The last fleeing maid looked back long enough to utter, "Apologies for your late husband."

"My late...? Excuse me?"

But the entire crew vacated Lorena's life almost as swiftly and bafflingly as Adalwolf. She half swooned, catching herself on the post just before she'd have pitched forth down the stairs. Her stomach growled, leaving her to wonder whether the chef had prepared anything before quitting.

Before she could find out, she needed to get dressed in something more than her unwashed nightgown and robe. She retreated to her bedroom where fresh water waited in the wash basin. She stripped down and sponged herself clean, then rinsed and oiled her hair. Despite her hunger and light-headedness, she felt better than she had in a week. She was in control of her own body, with no one forcing her into nightmares.

With no servants to help lace her stays, she

skipped the corset and opted for a roomier traveling dress over a simple camisole and stockings. She was clumsily adjusting the bustle when Colquoit's snigger made her whirl toward the open doorway.

How long had he stood there, watching?

He ran his tongue slowly over that long brown tooth. Lorena shivered throughout her body.

"Ain't got a friend left, do ya?" he jeered. "Even the lackeys all run out."

"What do you know about it?" she spat back.

He sauntered into the room, and even though she was fully dressed, she ducked behind the dressing screen, peeking out at him over the top.

"I know you got yourself a nickname now. The Hellfire Witch, they call ya."

"You're talking nonsense again, as usual."

Colquoit gazed down at the bed as he moved toward her but settled himself into Adalwolf's chair, crossing his boot lazily over his left knee. "It's all right here in today's paper. Old Mrs. Olafsson was reading it aloud to all of us just a bit ago. They named you for murdering that shyster in the bar the other night." His vile grin widened. "Said you cursed him so's he just dropped down dead."

"Me? But you know I didn't—" She stopped herself short. What Colquoit knew was of no use to anyone. "Let me see that."

She strode forth, holding her hand out for the newspaper. Colquoit held it outstretched, a grown boy playing keep-away.

"Don't mind yourself about the details, girlie. The coppers'll explain it all when they get here."

Lorena sucked in her breath. She rarely trusted a word Colquoit said, but his lies were never this compelling. What else would cause the entire staff to run out the way they did?

Colquoit bent to the floor to retrieve his master's pipe. "Bad time for the old man to disappear on ya, ain't it?"

"How do you—" Again, she stopped herself from falling for his games.

But the apprentice was only too happy to answer anyway. "I was standing right there when he done disappeared. Played too close to the fire, did he?"

She did her best to stare him down, even as he rose and flexed his muscles. With one shove, he sent her backward onto the bed. She rolled over, scrambling to her feet on the opposite side, ready to run down the hall if he made a move toward her again.

But his interest was focused on Adalwolf's journal. He picked it up, weighed it in his hands as though that would determine its worth, and said, "Guess he won't be needing his chicken scratches no more."

A voice in her mind hissed, *Save it!*

"Put that down!" The words came out in a deep, resonating tone she had no idea she possessed. "You don't want to displease Master Adalwolf. Especially now."

Colquoit was still smiling, but the joke didn't reach his eyes. "Don't bullshit me, woman."

"He is at the reins of a greater power than you can

conceive." Lorena pressed on, not caring whether there was a grain of truth in her words so long as they pierced his confidence. "You will listen to me until he returns... or you will not live to share in his glory."

Slowly and with great care, Colquoit replaced the book on the desk. Lorena nearly wilted with relief.

"Bring the carriage around," she ordered. "We'll leave at once. And send Bo up for my belongings. I know *he* hasn't deserted me."

Colquoit said nothing, storming from the room without another glance at his mistress.

As soon as she was alone, Lorena clutched the book to her chest. Wherever Adalwolf was, this journal was the key to his life. She could feel him, both halves of him, the megalomaniacal old man tethered to one end, the loving gallant on the other. And Lorena stood alone at the center, anchoring him to reality armed with only his indecipherable collection of theological theories.

But saving her husband meant saving herself first. Time to run.

78
ELSEWHEN

HIS FIRST INSTINCT was cowardice under the gaze of the god. But as Thanatos flew toward him, ready to strike, Adalwolf dodged.

Another place. Another reality.

He was alone. Somewhere dark yet not forbidding. Pleasantly warm. Cozy.

He scratched his chin, adjusted his pince-nez on instinct, despite the fact that there was nothing to see. Concentrating on Lorena, he pulled at the vision of her dream home, the mansion he'd once built for her in her mind.

Strangely, the setting eluded him. Was she fighting again?

Pursing his lips, he tried to override her will. Perhaps if he allowed himself to fade back in time, become the Diedrick she so loved...

And still nothing moved. This odd space, a doorless, windowless square confine, proved unchangeable. He pressed his hand against the malleable black wall, felt it yield to the pressure of his touch, then snap back. He faced skyward, calling for a light source. Again, he was impotent.

Had he lost his skills suddenly? How could this...

And the truth struck him like a lightning bolt.

"I've done it!" He nearly applauded himself. He had gone where no other mortal had ever dreamt of.

And yet—

"Mein Treuer...?"

Without her, his gateway, he was trapped within Death's mind.

79

MONDAY, JUNE 14, 1886

SHE'D HAD no one to pack her bags and no clear idea what to bring. There was no time to plan where they were bound or how long they'd be gone. She could only give in to the urgent sense of *go, go, go* that left her running to the window every time carriage wheels crunched along the street. The best she'd managed was a trunk jammed full of necessities and a heavy coin purse. The most important package stayed clutched in her arms: Adalwolf's Pullman valise, into which she'd carefully placed his journal, her own notes, his pipe and tobacco pouch, the fateful dagger and—though she couldn't say why, exactly—her Grandmother Eleanor's naughty book.

Finally, Bo appeared with his traveling pack slung over his shoulder, looking like he'd just swallowed a live garter snake.

"Is Master Adalwolf still in here?"

"No, he's..." She searched for an explanation, gave up, and ended with, "elsewhere."

Bo gulped loudly. She couldn't tell whether he was fighting off a crying spell or trying not to puke on her rug. "They wouldn't take a lady like you off to jail! It just cain't be true."

She'd been saying that very thing to comfort herself but knew there was no truth to it. Hearing false hope from the boy made the whole ugly ordeal loom larger.

"Hush, now. Let's get everything downstairs."

Bo charged ahead, taking her luggage to the landing, then doubled back to help her.

"You look all skin and bones. They said you was dyin'."

She waved him off. "I'm fine. Famished, though. Do you suppose there's anything left to eat?"

Together they ventured into the kitchen. She helped herself to a wedge of cake while he located a picnic basket and began emptying the icebox.

"Grab those apples, too," she said over his shoulder. "And the cucumbers. No, leave the meat. It looks old." As she fumbled with the cap on a bottle of milk, she asked, "Bo, why did Mrs. Olafsson speak of my *late* husband?"

His eyes went wide, and she was shocked to hear him cuss softly under his breath.

"It's that Colquoit's fault. He told them all that you..."

She found a tin of peanuts and scarfed a handful before passing it to him. "That I what, Bo?"

He packed the lid on the basket much harder than necessary.

"I don't believe a word of it, Miss Lorena. I tried to tell them all that you couldn't have..."

"Done *what*, Bo?"

"This morning when Mrs. Olafsson finished readin' that awful story about you... Colquoit told them all he'd seen you do it. And that you'd gave the same Evil Eye to Master Adalwolf and made him drop dead, too."

For once, Lorena was too shocked to breathe.

Outside, the bells of their carriage clanged hard enough to draw the attention of the entire street. Colquoit was following her orders but obviously wouldn't mind seeing her caught before he could help her escape.

As Lorena and Bo scurried into the entrance hall, she said, "There is no time to properly explain, but Master Adalwolf is *not* dead. He's... indisposed. And as I cannot rely on him to return in time to exonerate me, we need to flee this city."

Bo held the front door for her but seemed reluctant to let her pass.

"I can drive you, Miss Lorena. Do you trust that Colquoit enough to bring him along?"

"No," she answered immediately. "But I trust him even less at my back."

80
ELSEWHEN

IN EVERY FIELD THEY TOILED, pale hands thundering in the darkness, waiting for a dawn that would never come. A chill in the air whipped at wearied shoulders, but not a soul looked up. The weather in Purgatory never really changed.

Thanatos awoke.

Stretched along a luxurious fainting couch, the immortal was accustomed to unalloyed comfort cradling his existence. Today, however, he had a headache, a nagging throb in his frontal lobe. The god clenched his mighty fists.

The human would fall to him eventually.

But Death was not willing to wait.

81

MONDAY, JUNE 14, 1886

THEY RODE full tilt from the edge of St. Louis to Traveler's Repose, Missouri, where they found a roadside spot that promised, "Ma's best eats, Pa's knee-slappin jokes, and water for your horses."

Ma's Diner served generous portions, but Lorena deciphered the cook's tendency to oversalt the food when she was forced to pay sixty cents for half a dozen bottles of Ginger pop to take on the journey. Still, the bill was worth the price of admission to the outhouse; after four hours winding southwest on apparently random dirt roads, she felt like her bladder was going to explode.

"Whereabouts you folks headed?" asked the hook-nosed old maid making change for their tab. She'd done a commendable job feigning lack of interest in them up to that point, especially considering their odd seating arrangement; Lorena and Colquoit chose stools at opposite ends of the room while Bo ate on the porch, keeping an eye on the horses.

Lorena hesitated too long. It was absurd to claim to be headed west with no specific destination in mind, but she didn't have even a spotty grasp of local geography.

"Omaha," she finally hazarded.

The woman's eyebrows shot up. "In that fancy carriage? Your horses'll give out by Jeff City."

"Oh, well..." Lorena stammered. In truth, she'd been hoping to return to Pennsylvania to the solace of her parents' house, but Colquoit was dead set on taking them West to his old haunts. "They are looking rather peaked. Is there a boarding house in town—"

"We're heading out again now," Colquoit interrupted. He swaggered along the bar in their direction, pausing only to belch and adjust his drawers. "Gotta keep you one step ahead of the law, remember?"

Both women gasped—the waitress at the admission, Lorena at his bald treachery.

"You folks... wanted?" the woman asked.

Colquoit nodded, enjoying himself. "You just finished serving the Hellfire Witch."

Coins clattered on the counter. The lady dropped the handful of money Lorena had just passed her, apparently afraid to touch anything associated with her now.

On her feet, Lorena squared off against her enemy. Her hand rose in the air to slap him, but she stayed it at the last moment.

"Ready the car," she ordered between gritted teeth. Too late, she thought to add, "He's only joshing, of course."

But her pretty smile did nothing to mollify the waitress as they scuttled out to the landau. She whispered the state of affairs to Bo, and he whipped into action, settling her into the back and leaping into the shotgun seat just as Colquoit pulled away from the rest stop.

82

MONDAY, JUNE 14, 1886

ON THEY ROLLED, with no clear notion of where they would wind up for the night or how much more these pampered city horses could take. So many questions assailed her, but the solutions eluded her grasp. Adalwolf's journal lay spread over her lap, but every time she tried to work a translation, her head thudded as dully as the slowing hoofbeats dragging her onward.

Only Adalwolf had the knowledge to lead them, and he was... where, exactly? Not dead, or his body would have been left behind. Not with her, either. That left an alternative that she didn't wish to think about.

They'd been running parallel to a shallow river and now turned to take a covered bridge across it. A minute later, they were surrounded again by greens and browns of endless low rolling hills, ancient trees, and waving grass. Loneliness pierced her spirit.

If Adalwolf didn't return, would she ever be with Diedrick again?

That thought made her cry out. She wished she

could take it back, force it into a locked trunk of her mind.

"Oh, my love!"

When she squeezed her eyes shut, she could feel him with her, taking her onto his lap to comfort her, holding her tight to his chest. Tears streaming down her cheeks, she tilted her head up to receive his kiss.

But there was only air. And when she blinked into the daylight, the memory of his touch dissipated.

She had to get him back.

Stowing the journal once more into the valise, her greedy fingers unwrapped Colquoit's medicine bag. He'd cut a tin of tobacco primed for Adalwolf's use. She grabbed a pinch between her bare fingers and tamped it into the pipe with her thumbnail. Working the pocket lighter took more patience than she had to spare, but eventually the flame lit, and she sat back against the leather seat, inhaling deeply, pulling the fire into the bowl of the pipe.

She hadn't counted on it hitting her lungs so viciously.

For a moment, she could neither breathe nor exhale but spluttered against the burning of her throat. It took several swigs of Ginger pop to convince herself that she hadn't set her insides on fire.

Steadier and more scientifically, she approached it again, thinking perhaps she could get the effect by breathing in only the smoke wafting out of the end, like she had before. But the darned thing didn't want to stay lit without her puffing it.

At last, she discovered the trick of holding the

smoke in her mouth and releasing it in shallow breaths. This worked for all of three puffs before she grew light-headed and nauseous. Even the feeble currents of incense she'd managed to circulate were enough to suffocate her. She leaned her head out the window, gulping for fresh air.

When she was absolutely certain she was destined to remain in control of her bowels, she emptied the pipe's contents onto the road, then dropped it unceremoniously back into the Sacred Bundle.

Her eyelids grew heavy.

83

MONDAY, JUNE 14, 1886

The dining room had been set for two. Intimate candle lighting flirted between crystal goblets over a silver-fringed linen tablecloth.

Lorena could smell the meal being prepared in the next room: a prime rib roast with a horseradish sauce; eggplant perhaps, though the scent was obscured by a strong cheddar; roast chestnuts had found their place in some dish, perhaps a pudding; something chocolaty was involved with the dessert; and a bold coffee finish. Dream or not, her mouth watered in anticipation.

The window view of her flower garden confirmed that this was her dream mansion, though something seemed amiss. She hadn't spent much time in this dining room but felt certain the wall across from her ought to lead to the front hall. Instead, it was an uninterrupted paneling of sheer black that utterly failed to harmonize with the peach-and-pearl wallpaper of the other three walls.

As she stared, a seam split along the center. A pocket door formed and was immediately flung open to reveal Master Adalwolf, wild-eyed and disheveled.

"Mein Treuer!" he rasped, the tinge of delight in his voice so unexpected she would have been sure she was imagining it. But he rushed forth on his tottering old legs to grasp her hand in his, pressing it to his cheek—just like the Diedrick slice of him so often did.

"My dear," Lorena asked, "are you real? How can I tell?"

"Ja. I am here as long as you are."

"But—I'm not really here. You know it's just a dream."

Adalwolf kicked a chair back from the table and sat heavily into it. "You are my anchor. When you are sleeping, I am in control. I have solace in your dreamscape. Without you... Thanatos has locked me in his mind."

"Oh," was all she found to say. Backing away, she graced the chair opposite him.

Idly, she wondered whether any servants would bring food if she summoned them. She had never seen anyone but Diedrick Adalwolf in this mansion.

"I have seen things. Horrible things," Adalwolf said. He drooped baggardly in his chair, clutching the armrest as if it were likely to pitch away from him at any moment. His eyes were tempests, so black it seemed to Lorena the world was in danger of falling into them.

"I've entered his dreams too, you know," she reminded him. "You dragged me along."

"No! His dreams, I believe, are of the deaths that amuse him. They are fast. Simple. But the ones which occupy his waking mind..." He could only shudder to punctuate his thought.

As the room grew colder, they no longer met one another's eyes.

Adalwolf raised an empty water goblet, considered it, then ran his thin tongue along his parched lips before speaking again. "When the god of Death sleeps, I rule over him. Think of it, Mein Treuer. What I have accomplished! No greater glory has man ever sought!"

"And when he wakes?" she interrupted, primarily to trim his megalomania before he started cackling again. He sobered instantly.

"I must hide."

Adalwolf sprang from his seat and crawled inside the china hutch, closing the cupboard doors after him. Her mouth dropped open at this unexpected conduct, but the reason followed quickly on its heels.

Thanatos himself strode into her dining room, and if he was still angry, he hid it well behind a benign smile and a swagger full of sin. She wasn't aware she had outstretched her hand until he took it softly and bowed over it, his radiant eyes never leaving hers. Those perfect peach lips grazed her fingers, giving her a pleasant shiver. When he looked up, he crooked a finger, and she felt him pull a ribbon of words from her mouth.

"My name is Lorena. Born 1860. Middle daughter of Albert and Rose Whittaker of Allegheny, Pennsylvania, America."

Without dropping her gaze, his long fingers twisted at her wedding band. She prattled on again.

"I married in April of this year. Father brought him home. We thought he was just a weird, old immigrant. But I..."

She squeezed her eyes shut, trying to break his spell. The afterimage of Thanatos flickered against her eyelids, his porce-

lain features oozing out of place as his skeleton loomed larger. Suddenly, she was staring at him again, still caught in his web.

"I...I ..."

He nodded, still smiling, cajoling. He wanted the name, the name of his enemy.

How could she refuse?

"He was born in Germany. Württemberg, he said. And he was christened... as... Diedrick..."

"Wake up!" Adalwolf shouted from his hidey-hole, so shrouded that his words barely reached her. "Tell him nothing! Wake yourself!"

Thanatos turned abruptly from her, circling the dining table toward his prey.

Desperate to escape, Lorena slapped herself with violent force.

84
MONDAY, JUNE 14, 1886

SOMEHOW, she saw both the inside of the carriage *and* the mansion for several seconds before succumbing to reality. Just as Thanatos grasped the brass handles of the china hutch to yank open the cupboard door, that world froze and faded to nothingness.

The day was aging fast toward evening with the oppressive heat of the setting sun muffling the tiny carriage. Bo yelled her name, a panicked pitch in his voice she barely recognized.

Lorena leaned out the open window to speak to him, then just as quickly flattened herself against her seat.

They'd been surrounded. Three men on horseback flanked their right side, and she could glimpse at least two more on the left.

"What do they want?" she yelled, almost hoping they were merely highwaymen.

"They told us to pull over, Miss Lorena, so's they can run you in!"

"Shut up, fool!" Colquoit scolded, and for once Lorena agreed with him. Then he tacked on, "You'll never take her alive!"

Bo might have innocently confirmed her identity, but Colquoit had made sure to fill in the blanks for any slow-witted members of the posse.

One of the men shouted for them to stop. Instead, Colquoit spurred his horses to a reckless gait. Perhaps he was trying to kill her Arabians, after all, and leave them stranded in the countryside. It dawned on her that she might be better off taking her chances with the posse.

And the more they careened along the trail, the harder her chest pounded. She had no recourse, nowhere to hide, no options but to plead against fate.

"Diedrick!" she cried, hiding her face behind her fists. And she knew it was silly, calling to a man who may have never existed in this plane, but somehow it helped. Only he could remedy the rest—clear her of his murder, end her dependence on Colquoit. He would take care of her.

Someone fired a rifle, scaring the horses. In a crescendo of shouts and whinnies, they lurched ever faster.

"Mein Treuer," Adalwolf whispered.

She could feel him lurking in her mind, just behind her throbbing temples. Wedged between her mind and Death's, he waited for her to pull him back to reality. *But how?*

With a thump, the carriage pitched onto its side.

Lorena banged her head on the frame as she tumbled from her seat.

Was Death coming for her? She had a vision of herself falling into his realm, the one she would never wake from. He would coerce everything from her—Adalwolf's name and all his secrets. Then what? Punish them both for meddling in his powers?

Nausea surged again as she scrabbled with the door lever. She pried it open, but gravity bested her, snapping it shut like a coffin.

Before she could try again, one of the men opened it for her and peered inside. His weather-beaten face cracked into a wide grin as he shouted, "Alrighty, boys! Looks like we done caught the Hellfire Witch!"

85

EXCERPT FROM ADALWOLF'S JOURNAL:

Behold. I am growing stronger.

As raindrops trickle
Down branches
And join the swift wide river.

See. I am growing stronger.

As the cub born blind
Nursed by its mother
Becomes a great black bear.

Listen. I am growing stronger.

As the summer breeze
Chased by storm clouds
Howls with mighty thunder

Hark. I am growing stronger.

You who would defeat me
When I was weak and at your mercy,
You have power over me no longer.

Run! I am growing stronger.

86

TUESDAY, JUNE 15, 1886

ONWARD THEY PLODDED, the horses slowly succumbing to the torpor of the frying heat beneath riders dripping with sweat. Afternoon humidity weighed upon them, turning Lorena's mind sluggish, laggardly. Even with the top down on the landau, not enough wind mustered up to offset the hot spell, and they were down to their last dregs of water.

She could tell they were nearing St. Louis because she recognized the tiny clumps of storefronts that passed for towns on this side of the city proper. She'd fled through them going the other way less than twenty-four hours earlier.

Colquoit was surely thinking the same thing. She caught him scrutinizing the buildings, craning his neck to see around the man he rode with, which made her wonder whether he would try to escape now that they were near civilization. He wouldn't get far, surely, but it would be an amusing diversion to watch him try.

When the storm finally caught up to them, everyone

in the party turned their faces upward to enjoy the cool water. But the drizzle segued to a harsh onslaught, with winds whipping at them from all directions. They found refuge inside a covered bridge, and the men dismounted to give their horses some respite.

Lorena averted her eyes as they took turns urinating through slats in the bridge. Once they were done comparing distances, they broke into two packs: those too exhausted to ride another mile and those anxious to get home by sundown. George's constant agony left him in no position to settle the dispute that broke out, so after a bit, they worked it out themselves.

Three men mounted up again, saying, "Just sit tight, George. We'll fetch back the sheriff in nothing quick."

Lightning flashed, bringing thunder so loud it made the walls quake. Lorena gave in to her nerves and started gnawing on a thumbnail.

Slouched across from her, a sheen of sweat over his sunken eyes, George managed to overcome his queasiness long enough to say, "Keep your chin up, y'hear?"

"So they can get the noose on more easily?" she retorted.

He shrugged to indicate he was bowing out of the conversation and lolled his head over the armrest once more.

She chastened herself for being so snippy with the man. In spite of his own misery, he'd done his best to be a decent traveling companion. Being able to talk with him had kept her awake. Her body craved sleep, but she didn't dare snatch forty winks, not with Thanatos lurking at the portal to her mind.

Adalwolf had not spoken to her all day—not since they'd killed Bo together. She could not tell whether that meant his hold was weakening or he was too busy playing his cat-and-mouse game with Death.

Her eyelids lolled shut, but she jerked herself awake again. *Hold on a little longer,* she coached herself. *Surely it won't be long now.*

She'd followed Adalwolf's instructions precisely: given Death's Dearest to Bo, explained how to use it down to the specific phrase to utter, then sent him into Death's domain to wield it. Why hadn't he reappeared yet? That boy, Clay, had used it on Phillip Tremont almost instantly.

Picturing the two boys, the difference sprang at her: Clay was furious just before he was killed, hell-bent on revenge. But Bo loved her, had died trying to reason with her. Even after she'd cut his larynx, his lips kept moving until his eyes glossed over beneath a pool of tears.

Would Bo refuse to use the knife against her? She'd spent most of her life looking out for him, and now as adults they'd been taking turns protecting one another. Maybe he wouldn't have the heart to stab her. Maybe she should have used Colquoit after all, but Bo was the trustworthy one. Bo always followed her orders.

But what if he refused? She couldn't reach him anymore to cajole or convince him. Her little Bo had grown up since they came out West, proving himself capable of making his own decisions and sticking to them. If he chose not to use the knife to return to life, then she truly had murdered him.

The notion welled up in her chest. *Don't think of that. Not now.*

But the tears were already flowing. Even squeezing her eyes shut couldn't blot out the image of his broad, smiling face.

It hadn't felt like murder. She knew she was hurting him, even though she did her best to make his death quick. But he was supposed to be returned! She'd promised him this death would not last long.

Oh, Bo, I'm so sorry.

Suddenly, she began bawling uncontrollably.

One fellow, whose hay fever had left him more irritable than the rest, snarled up at her. "You may as well save all that for the judge. You ain't gonna con no one here into lettin' you go just 'cause you can put on a pretty waterworks display."

Lorena tried to protest this accusation, but all that came out was a squeak and a hiccup.

George used his hat to swat away the circling horseflies, then sized her up. "You ain't spoke about that boy all day 'cept when you claimed he was your kin, so I don't believe you're suffering from remorse. This must be fear of what comes next. That usually rears up right at the end like this. I ain't gonna lie to you. What you done will likely land you on the gallows. But you can't say you don't deserve it."

"I didn't kill anybody!" she howled. Since every man present would claim this as an outright lie, having seen her with the knife above Bo's lifeless body, she plunged on, talking faster. "Not my husband, not your cousin, and Bo didn't count! And I was not thinking about my own death. I was trying to..." A slow chill crept through her. "My own death? Oh, Heavens!"

How had she missed that crucial point?

When Adalwolf gave her the instructions, everything flowed so logically she accepted it without question. Give Bo the knife and instructions. Kill him. Send him to find Thanatos. Wait for him to bring himself back to life.

When Bo opened the rift, Adalwolf would be freed as well. Both men would return to her, safe and sound. Unless...

Her own careless words haunted her, niggling at her mind. *My own death*. She knew how Death's Dearest worked: it allowed one soul to trade places with another. Someone had to die. And as Nemesis's tool, the balance of retribution meant vengeance. Lorena had murdered Bo. To come back, he would have to trade places with her.

How had the missed this enormous hole in their plan? Even now, she felt like she was groping through a dense fog, shrouded from the truth.

She reached to adjust her pince-nez, then froze, staring at her own traitorous fingers.

"I do *not* wear spectacles," she said slowly, thinking each word as loudly and deliberately as she could. "You... rotten... scoundrel. You've been *possessing* me? After all I've done for you, you're controlling my mind? So you could *sacrifice* me to make your escape? Adalwolf, you are *not* the man I loved. You have ties on me no more. Out! Out! Out!"

Screaming now, she bounded to her feet in the small

carriage. With both hands clutching her hair, she shook her head violently, hoping to dislodge him.

"Begone, you filthy demon!"

With the flat of her wrist, she pounded her head just behind her temple, again and again. The carriage rocked beneath her. She kept beating until her mind went silent and the fog receded. Whether she'd truly exorcised him or merely left him cowering in a darker apse of her mind, swift repossession of her faculties left Lorena woozy.

She found herself towering over a spooked posse—or what was left of it as more men rode off, promising to fetch the law. The few still hunkered down trained their twitchy trigger fingers on her. Without Adalwolf tamping down her fear, those sidearms seemed like the most menacing beasts in the world.

Shaking, she eased herself onto the leather seat and took great gulps of air.

"I've been studyin' on it, ma'am," George drawled, "and I reckon if you hire yourself one of them fancy Eastern lawyers, you got a decent shot at a plea of 'Guilty but Insane.'"

His words walloped the tension. One by one, the men turned the noses of their rifles into the air, like ladies snubbing her at a social.

Lorena offered a tremulous smile. "Thank you, Mr. Tremont."

For the first time that day, she saw him clearly: suffering through the pain with clenched teeth; sweat adding a patina to his green-tinged skin; the poorly-set bone reeking of blood under a thick grime of trail dust.

At the outset, his men had done their best to prop his leg on a cushion of threadbare blanket, but the bumpy ride left it about to topple off the seat.

"Let me help you," she whispered.

George fidgeted like a nervous bridegroom while she readjusted the padding. Never quite moving nearer or farther from her, he succeeded only in distressing the fracture.

"Leave him be, woman," one of the men growled as he walked past the carriage. "We'll get ya to a proper doctor, George, soon's the rain lets up."

George nodded to the fellow, then sank heavily back into his cushion, his eyes squeezed shut.

Lorena retreated to her own bench, lost in thought, and discovered too late that she had inadvertently tucked the hem of her dress under his pile of blankets. In moving away from him, she launched an avalanche that sent George's poor leg crashing to the floor of the carriage.

George bellowed like a stuck bear. Two men scrambled up between them, fussing over him and trying clumsily to reset the bone. All the while, Lorena ineffectually swore that she would never have hurt him on purpose and begged them to believe her. Soon, George cussed a blue streak that drowned her out.

Amid all this commotion, she did not notice the returning troops until someone jerked her arm, pulling her toward the ground. Everything went topsy-turvy and she flailed to catch her balance, but rough hands latched around her waist and lugged her along the road.

She wrenched herself free for just a moment, but a

second man showed up to catch her. Each grabbing her under the arm, they half-dragged her to the mouth of the bridge, where a makeshift mob teemed toward her. At least a dozen strangers assembled in a semicircle of grim faces. One rough-whiskered lout peered into her face, their noses almost touching.

"This here's the one!" he announced. "I seen her do it."

She gasped, recognizing him and a scattering of other faces from the night Phillip Tremont was killed.

"Kill the witch!" The crowd took up the chant until one of George's men stepped in front of her, palms raised up for silence.

"Wait, wait, wait! You're all wrong," he said. "Unhand her."

Panting and ready to faint, Lorena moved toward him as soon as her captors released her. In one swift move, he spun her around and looped his left arm around her neck, pinning her against his body with his right.

"You can't let a witch look at you," he explained conversationally. "We learned that on the trail. Evil Eye."

From inside the bridge, George's shout carried over the rest. "You sons o' bitches! I didn't go through all this for no pay! We was hired to bring her to the law, not turn her over to a lynch mob!"

87
ELSEWHEN

He heard them whispering as they trailed him through the mansion, but no minion dared venture into "the master's garden," so Bo picked his own way between the creeping brambles and stagnant pools. As promised, under the barren boughs of a copse of dead cherry trees sat a gazebo draped with desiccated grape vines. No wind rustled. Even the sunlight filtered down queerly, as though it had given up trying to add beauty to this landscape.

As soon as he stepped onto the gazebo, two figures he had taken for statues suddenly broke apart. He saw they had been hunkered over a board littered with black and white tiles.

The man nearest him, a silver-haired fellow in a natty suit, slapped his palms on the table and rose, saying, "I detest these time-squandering diversions."

The younger man laughed, a rich booming baritone at odds with his cherubic face and mop of blond curls.

"You always bemoan my games when you start to

lose. Do not fret, Thanatos. I promise to let you win... at the end."

The blond glided across the floor to block Thanatos's exit, and it took Bo a moment to work out that he was in a chair with wheels attached, like palsied men used. Beneath his nightgown, one leg dangled limp.

Thanatos looked up suddenly and roared, "Who dares trespass in my garden?"

Bo jumped at being spotted. As Thanatos bore down on him, he lost his voice entirely. With the knife still clutched in his hand, he raised his arm like a shield.

"My leg!" cried the cripple.

"Another human come to demand favors from me? Run away, fool, before you unbar the gates of my fury."

"But Thanatos!" The other god rolled forward to clutch his arm. "Perhaps we can get it back this time."

"They will never return your tibia, Hypnos. She sent him here to taunt you. And to manipulate me like a puppeteer."

"True on both counts." A pretty young woman appeared behind them, grinning wickedly. She doffed her Gambler's hat at them, releasing spirals of curls over the shoulders of her cotton dress. The Cuban heels of her leather boots clicked on the hardwood as she sauntered toward them. "But this time, as a present, I offer you a taste of your *own* retribution."

Her delicate fingers ensnared Bo's wrist in a steel grip. She turned the blade of his knife upward until both he and Thanatos were reflected in it.

"Behold, your tormentor!"

In a flash, the blade showed the reflection of another world. An angry mob. A struggling woman.

"Miss Lorena!"

"Her?" Thanatos grabbed Bo by the scruff of his neck, pulling him close as they stared at the image together. "Is *this* your murderer?"

88

TUESDAY, JUNE 15, 1886

SHE COULDN'T SEE the man holding her, pinning her arms behind her back while the crowd spat at her. But the man tying the noose remained in direct view, as was the young guy who'd shinnied up the bridge with the other end of the rope.

Lorena perched on the rim of hysteria.

She'd *believed.* Sure, Adalwolf's plan depended on arcane magic, most of which she had culled from amateur translations of *his* translations. But she'd seen Death's Dearest work before. With all her heart, she'd trusted in it.

Adalwolf always said she was his tether toward reality, the only one who could pull him back to their plane. Mein Treuer. His constant. By sending Bo, she would save Adalwolf, who in turn would save her.

They lassoed the noose around her neck and pulled Lorena up, cinching her windpipe. Her legs kicked empty air while her fingers fought against the rope cutting into her skin. Sheer panic took over. She gulped for air, more desperate with each pounding heartbeat, but it was no use. Her world blackened into spasms of helplessness.

If she died now, she'd damned them all.

89
ELSEWHEN

"Name your murderer!" Thanatos demanded.

Though he'd never been one for the jitters, Bo's body shook until he feared he'd faint like a woman. Between Nemesis stretching his arm into the air and Thanatos's vice-like grip on his neck, he was afraid to speak. One false move and he was sure they'd truss him up like a Christmas goose.

"You must make your request," Nemesis hissed. "I cannot help unless you make your wish aloud."

Through the vision in the blade of Death's Dearest, Bo watched Lorena struggle against the ropes. Each movement seemed more labored.

"She's dyin'," Bo cried. "You got to help her."

"No!" Thanatos waved a hand over the blade. "No one dies until I command it. No other god may interfere. I am still the ruler of my realm, whether my sister respects it or not."

Nemesis released Bo's arm, then tilted his face toward hers. He stared into eyes the color of jealousy as she said, “Use my weapon, boy. Punish the one who sent you here. Do you not understand? You will return to life!”

“No,” Bo whispered. “I want to live. But I don’t want *her* to die.”

The gods stared at him, fascinated.

90

TUESDAY, JUNE 15, 1886

DESPITE HER NEED TO fight against the knot, her limbs grew heavier until she hung limp before the crowd, waiting for the end.

They watched her. She blinked back.

It seemed to be taking a long time.

Colquoit muscled through the crowd to peer at her, a mixture of confusion and awe in his scrunched-up face. His hands worked furiously at the knots around his wrists, and he darted back inside the covered bridge, unnoticed.

"Why ain't she dead?" someone cried.

Another man jostled the rope, making sure it was taut.

"You sure you did the knot right, Jarvis?"

"Maybe we need to drop her down and retie it?"

"It's fine, it's fine," insisted another—presumably Jarvis. "Just give it a minute."

But strangely, Lorena no longer believed she was dying. She still could not breathe, and her neck hurt something fierce, but... beyond that, she had nothing new to report.

She felt a bit silly, dangling before them like that.

"We ain't got time for this. Shoot her."

And then the world zippered open.

91
ELSEWHEN

"ENOUGH, Nemesis! Your game binds me not. The woman dies either way."

Thanatos pulled on the sky like he was opening a great velvet curtain, and suddenly, Miss Lorena was right there before them. Not a vision nor an illusion but *her* right there in the flesh, through some sort of jagged window in the air.

Thanatos snapped his fingers, and Lorena's eyes bulged. She twitched again in agony.

"I shall have her in my realm within moments."

It seemed to Bo that everything was speeding like a locomotive, leaving him no time to think.

Nemesis clasped his shoulders and steered him right up to the edge of the portal, screeching, "Do not let my brother win. When she dies, you are trapped here. Say it, fool! Take your revenge!"

Bo raised the knife, his mind spinning like a weathervane in a twister. Lorena's eyes locked on his again, and with blue-tinged lips, she mouthed: *Help me! Kill me*!

The words spilled out of him in one long breath, "I demand the vengeance of Nemesis, Balancer of Life, on my murderer."

He plunged the knife, nicking her somewhere along the midsection.

Thanatos gave him a mighty shove, and Bo tumbled forward, his arms closing on the emptiness where Miss Lorena ceased to be.

As he stumbled to the wet ground, alive and breathing in a world alarmingly full of movement, Bo dared a look behind him. The window to the realm he'd left contracted to nothingness. Just before it disappeared, a withered ghost floated through the aperture. It materialized into Adalwolf, who touched the ground lightly then jackrabbited past Bo onto the bridge.

92

TUESDAY, JUNE 15, 1886

George saw what he saw, even though it was impossible.

Sure, it coulda been his imagination run amok. It coulda been hallucinations brought on by his fever. It coulda. But he saw what he saw, sure as he was breathing.

First, the lady—the Hellfire Witch—got sucked out of the world, leaving an empty noose and a cluster of flummoxed vigilantes.

Second, something pitched to the ground a few yards behind her, inside the mouth of the bridge where only George remained. With all the confusion out yonder, nobody else commented. George wouldn't have paid much mind, neither, if it hadn't charged at him in the form of a haggard old man who took one look at the carriage and started climbing into it, telling George to get out.

Then Colquoit, who even George had forgotten to keep an eye on, charged up on a horse and told the old guy to hop on with him, since they weren't likely going to maneuver the landau through that mob.

As the old guy scrambled from the carriage to the horse, George protested, "That's my best Appaloosa, you damned horse thief!"

"You may keep my carriage and both horses," the old guy said. "You will prosper from this deal, *ja?*"

Colquoit kicked the horse into action, and they hightailed it westward down the trail.

George turned his head to shout for help from whatever remained of his posse, but the next apparition made his mouth run dry. The slaughtered boy—the one he'd helped bury that morning with his own hands—crept along the bridge, sticking to the shadows, still coated in blood from neck to navel.

George got the willies like an epileptic fit.

When the specter drew even with George, he mustered all his gumption and reached out to touch its hair. He'd expected his hand to pass right through it. What he hadn't reckoned on was for the boy to yelp and round on him with his fists raised.

"I ain't got no trouble with you, mister," Bo hissed. "So how 'bout we go separate ways now, no questions asked."

George raised his palms to show he had no intention of attacking. With his leg split open, he would not even be able to defend. And the kid had never been under arrest, anyhow. He had no qualms about letting him go. But the "no questions" bit was too much to ask.

"Ain't you dead?"

"Not currently. But I ain't stickin' around amongst

these worked-up crackers with a spare noose on their hands."

Crouching down again, Bo started running. He darted into the storm and made for a woody patch down the lane. George craned his neck to watch, wanting to see whether the kid cast a shadow, but he stretched too far and pulled his bad leg out of alignment. Gasping pain shot through him, and George fainted dead away.

XIV

INTERLUDE

93
JUNE 1886

"LISTEN UP, boys! I got one to beat all this time!"

There were, in fact, no boys to be found in the *Democrat* office, just old, grey-haired Sam Beaman bent over the bottomless pile of papers on his desk. But Smithy swaggered in, undeterred. He was three sheets to the wind tonight and feeling like a true newspaperman.

He flopped into his chair and kicked his feet up on the desk. Or tried to. Depth perception being a bit dodgy just then, he missed and jarred himself when his shoes slapped the floor.

Grumbling a bit, he adjusted his spectacles and bent over his typewriter. With effort, he managed the T and H, but his finger got pinched in the gap between the E and R keys. Around this point, he realized he'd forgotten to feed paper into the carriage.

"Take dictation, B," he demanded, slapping his old buddy on the shoulder. Sudden inspiration made him blast a shrill, wet whistle and yell, "Hoo there! P.H.! Come on out and hear this. You're gonna love it!"

Beaman's eyes widened. "Shush, you fool!"

But the damage was done. The feared and revered publisher, P.H. Daniels, stomped out of his office, crossed his brawny arms, and leaned against the wall to listen.

"Title it, 'The Undeath of the Hellfire Witch'," Smithy began.

Beaman scrambled to insert a fresh sheet as the younger reporter tipped back his chair and launched into a narration.

"Not since the grand days of Salem has a witch's trial proved so conclusive. Cornered at last after her legendary murder spree, the Hellfire Witch ought to have met her end at the hands of St. Louis's most concerned citizens. But the rope could not hang her, nor could bullets pierce her leathery skin. Before a score of onlookers, she unloosed the gates of hell, stirring up a twister on the outskirts of town to ferry her away on her broomstick—"

"Stop," mumbled P.H.

That syllable was enough for Beaman to cease his typing, but Smithy continued undaunted.

"Whither is she bound, ask those left in the wake of her occultish killings, and when will she strike again—"

"Hush your half-witted ramblings, boy! We aren't printing crap like that."

Smithy's powers of comprehension came several seconds behind the curve. "What are you talking about? This one's a beaut!"

P.H. eloquently spat a mouthful of tobacco onto the paragraph before him. Beaman scrambled to jerk it from his typewriter before the gunk had time to trickle onto the gears.

Turning on his heel, the publisher moved back toward his private room.

"I'll stake my reputation on it," Smithy squealed. In desperation, he ran ahead to block P.H.'s path. "You don't know what you're doing here. You can't kill—"

His backside hit the floor a moment before his head. P.H. had been feeling charitable; he'd pushed him flat-handed and let alcohol and gravity conspire to take him down.

"Listen up and just maybe you might learn something. Some voodoo doctor in Peoria is fine. People eat that bull up. Unexplainable deaths here in town? Well, it was against my better judgment, but it all panned out. And now you want to get every nincompoop with a pitchfork rioting in the streets to your witch story?" P.H. grunted and turned his attention to Beaman. "Get me that piece on the two-headed duck."

XV

DEVOUTLY TO BE WISHED

94
WEDNESDAY, JUNE 15, 1886

LORENA THRASHED ON THE FLOOR, ready to sell her soul for one last, tortured breath... until it finally came to her that she no longer needed to breathe. And her soul was the only possession she had left.

She pushed herself onto her haunches and surveyed the dismal gazebo and its unearthly occupants. The dashing gallantry Thanatos once wooed her with seemed eons away, replaced by fearsome rage. She would have fainted if it was focused on her. Fortunately, he thundered at Nemesis, who merely laughed.

"He is gone! Where is he? Tell me now, Nemesis, *where is he?*"

Nemesis turned away, fussing with her hair.

Hypnos rolled his chair past Lorena to tug on his brother's wildly gesticulating arms.

"Calm yourself, Thanatos. You played her game and the boy returned to life. You know the rules. Why does it vex you so? You will beat him... in the end."

Bo! Lorena shuddered with relief. *He got out.* She'd

fulfilled her promise to him and maybe, just maybe, he would live to forgive her.

He had even managed to save her one last time, she realized—he'd plucked her from the throes of death, staving off the worst of the pain. *Bless you, Bo. Wherever you are.*

"Not the boy!" Thanatos shrieked. "The Necromancer. The one who haunts my dreams. He is gone! Escaped!" He spun Nemesis to face him. "You tricked me!"

Dimples appeared on her rosy cheeks as she answered, "Nonsense, brother. You fooled yourself. I showed your tormentor in the blade. Did you not realize I said that while it still showed your *own* reflection? You had him trapped here… until you opened the portal and released him."

With an inarticulate roar, Thanatos scooped up Nemesis and flung her head-first over the gazebo wall. Without pausing his stride, he seized Lorena by the throat, dragging her like a limp rag doll. She found herself arcing through the air, then slammed onto the stone table, where she flailed like an upended turtle, pinned down by his powerful arm.

"Make her sleep," he commanded.

"What, *here*?" Hypnos squawked. "Why would the dead need sleep?"

"Their minds may still be linked. If she dreams, I may find him."

"I can only make her sleep, not dream. Wait, I will fetch Oneroi."

"No, not her!" Thanatos spun to grab his brother,

but Hypnos faded from being.

As soon as she was released, Lorena propped herself up on her elbows and scooted away, raining black and white playing tiles in all directions.

"Rein in your temper, brother," said Nemesis. She had scaled the wall rather than walk around it. Dead twigs littered her hair, and smudges of dirt hid her perfect dimples, yet she lounged on the rotted boards with a devil-may-care smirk. "If you seek my help, you must ask. Nicely."

For just a moment, Lorena thought Nemesis was addressing her. Then the girl slid from her perch and the two gods began circling each other.

"Where is he? I demand your full answer."

"Now, now. Is that the proper supplication for a goddess?"

"You promised me retribution!"

"I offered you a path which you chose to ignore. Single-minded as always, Death. You limit yourself by your lack of respect."

"Respect?" Thanatos looked genuinely baffled. "For whom?"

"All of us!" Nemesis spread her hands wide toward the heavens. "The myriad of gods you sneer upon—even I, with the same noble lineage. One day you will be the last of us, the destroyer of worlds. That does not make you the most powerful *now*."

"I assure you, it does." Thanatos uttered a shallow ghost of a laugh to punctuate his retort. "Now, if what you require is a display of genuflection..."

He bent his knee with a graceful, sweeping bow and took her hand like a courtier.

"Oh, lovely Nemesis, Purveyor of Whims and Settler of Human Deeds, consider what a boon it will be to use your meager gifts to aid the great Thanatos in exacting his revenge."

Fury boiled in Nemesis's eyes as Thanatos gallantly kissed her hand.

"I will help you."

The goddess had definitely been looking at her that time, Lorena realized, jolting to attention. What was she playing at?

Thanatos dusted himself off, then rose to his full height. "Show me the man in your knife, that I may hunt him down."

"Alas, I cannot." Nemesis waved both empty hands. "I do not have Death's Dearest."

Her gaze flickered to Lorena once more and Lorena gasped. She had it! Sticking through the layers of her skirt and the fatty part of her thigh, the knife remained where Bo had plunged it. Her death and her salvation.

Gripping the bone handle, she extracted it from her flesh, then tucked it beneath the folds of her dress.

A shimmer of lightning bugs heralded Oneroi's arrival. The goddess of Dreams appeared before them in a scandalously gauzy white sarong and dainty beaded slippers.

"My, my. It is not every millennium that I am summoned to Death's door." She looked around, wrinkling her nose. "*Ugh*. How do you endure this feculence? Have all the cleaning wenches ceased dying?"

"Oneroi!" Lorena cheered, warming to her marrow at the sight of one friendly face.

"My pet! You still remember me?" Oneroi lit up, then grew wistful as she realized, "What a shame to find you *here*. Oh, Nemesis, you would have loved this one while she lived. So full of fire! So willfully unpredictable!"

Emboldened, Lorena said, "Perhaps I shall dream again. And perhaps I will yet find revenge."

She raised her arm, brandishing Death's Dearest, and monitored their reactions. Nemesis burst into laughter. Oneroi clapped in delight. And Thanatos leapt straight into the air, looking like a lightning bolt had snuck into his drawers.

"Yes!" he yelled. "Say his name! Help me to summon him!"

"My husband is Master Diedrick Adalwolf of Württemberg. I believe he is currently hiding near St. Louis."

Thanatos immediately went to work, plucking dust motes from the air and scrutinizing them.

Nemesis, however, smiled no longer. Her eyes narrowed to tiny slits as she crossed to Lorena and forced her to lower the knife.

"This is *my* game. There are rules you must follow. You may return to life, but only as an act of revenge on he who has most wronged you. Do you hate your husband?"

"I..."

"Quite the contrary," Oneroi answered for her. "She is devoted to her husband—mind, body, and soul. She would never betray her lover."

Lorena swished that thought around in her mind. Betray her lover? No, that couldn't be right. Adalwolf was never her lover, in any sense of the word. Diedrick had won her heart, and she'd been devoted to him long before her father brought Adalwolf home. But they were not the same man.

How had she ever confused the two? Young Diedrick was caring, passionate, strong, charismatic, and deeply affectionate. Adalwolf... was not.

Everything now seemed so clear, yet distanced, as though she were viewing her life through opera glasses. Marriage had transformed her into something cold, terrible. Enslaved to her husband. Ensorcelled, perhaps. She had even hatcheted sweet little Bo for him!

His filth coated her soul.

"I have unearthed the infidel!" Thanatos shouted. He pulled at a fleck of dust, stretching it the width of his body, then warped it to create an opening between the worlds.

Lorena anticipated the rift he created, but even the goddesses ducked away from the sight of a horse charging directly at them. The steed whinnied and stumbled. When it keeled over on its side, Thanatos had to extend his portal downward to view the two tossed riders rolling in the dirt.

"You! You have found me," Adalwolf said, staring wide-eyed at Thanatos. "I have yet more means of defeating you. I warn you! I have learned all the ancient methods."

"Silence!"

Just as the horse struggled to its feet, Thanatos

clapped his hands, and it dropped dead. Its heavy body flopped over both men, pinning them to the ground. Adalwolf screamed. Colquoit launched a torrent of cussing.

Thanatos bowed to Lorena. "You may play your game, milady."

As Lorena inched forward, Nemesis sidled behind her. The goddess's delicate fingers combed her hair into loose braids, a comforting, sisterly caress.

"Think before you act," she counseled. "You have only one chance at revenge. You must make it count. What did he do to you?"

Bouncing on tippy-toes to see around Thanatos, Oneroi answered, "Why, he stopped loving her. What greater betrayal ever pierced the heart of a young maiden?"

"How did she lose his favor?"

"He grew obsessed with death," Oneroi said. "Small wonder, after enduring that great famine. Locked away from the world, he turned in upon himself and surrendered decades to his single-minded goal of evading Death. My poor pet was foolish enough to marry a memory."

Lorena held her tongue, thinking.

She could still feel the way Diedrick clung to her after they made love, as though she was the only person in the world. Perhaps to him, she was.

If she traded places now with Adalwolf, she would lose her link to Diedrick. Would she be granted another lifetime only to spend it alone, aching for her lover?

"Mein Treuer," the old man called, his rheumy eyes

searching hers as he reached out, supplicating. "You must not do this. Consider—if you return, they will hang you again as a witch. It is better you stay dead. One day, maybe, I will find a way to bring you back."

"She ain't buyin' it," Colquoit said. "Work on one o' them gods instead. Maybe trade away some o' your book-learnin' for a way out o' this."

Lorena tightened her grip on the knife. Colquoit was maybe the craftiest cuss she'd ever met. She longed to get even with him, but the rules of Nemesis's game were finite—one soul could trade places with another. One stab would seal her choice.

"It is time, fair lady," Thanatos said. A hint of impatience crept into his voice despite his brilliant smile.

Still braiding her hair, Nemesis tugged lightly at the sides of Lorena's temples, the way one would rein in a horse. Lorena froze, alert, as Nemesis spoke again in her ear.

"Think. What do you want most?"

"I want my life back."

"Wrong, my pet," said Oneroi. "That is *not* your heart's desire. What is it that you crave *most*?"

Lorena met Oneroi's gaze, and the truth gushed forth. "I want my Diedrick!"

"Good," Nemesis whispered. "And who has stolen that from you?"

Lorena studied the wretch scrabbling in the mud, the aged remnant of her former husband whimpering in terror. More alone now than when he'd lost his family, he'd spent the better part of a century retreating from the comfort of human touch. Death became his enemy then, the general of an invading army mowing down his countrymen, and Adalwolf built a solitary fortress in which to hide.

She pitied him now, this egomaniacal wisp of a man.

"He twisted everything up," Lorena said. "He used me as a pawn, then killed me. ...He'll kill us all."

"She is ready," Nemesis announced. Unknotting her fingers from Lorena's hair, she nudged her forward.

Thanatos draped an arm around Lorena's waist, her escort to the execution. At the brink of worlds, he repositioned the portal, then thrust his arm through it. Grabbing a fistful of thin grey hair, he stretched Adalwolf's head back, exposing his wrinkled neck.

Quaking head to toe, Lorena stammered, "I re-request the justice of Nemesis, B-Balancer of Life, upon the one who torments my soul."

She dared a glance at Nemesis, who gave a tiny nod of encouragement.

As she raised the knife, Lorena closed her eyes and directed one last prayer along the tender thread that tethered their souls. *Stay with me, my love. Always.*

Then, before she could lose her nerve, she turned on her heel and plunged Death's Dearest into the heart of her greatest enemy—Death himself.

95
A DIFFERENT TIME

SITTING stiff-backed in a Baroque wrought iron chair, Lorena waited for the last remaining member of the posse to find her. He picked his way clumsily up the hill, his steps agonizingly slow, with only a curved wooden cane to offset his limp. She saw him turn back several times, scratching at his thick grey hair as he studied the quiet railroad station below. But each time he steeled himself, one hand clutching at the heart that had so recently failed him, and continued the winding path.

From her vantage, cloaked by the vine-covered trellis just beyond the front gate, she could see for miles without being spotted herself. She spent most of her waking hours in this garden, so she'd stocked it with nosegays from her travels, perfectly preserved mementos to make it seem less lonely. Clumps of lilac blooms with sprays of spearmint roosted in a glass vase beside her—the smell of her front porch in Allegheny. Pink magnolias and gardenias from her Carolina childhood lined the arbor.

Perfectly content to lurk in shadows, she waited until her visitor was within spitting distance before rising to greet him.

"God almighty!" he shouted. "It's the Hellfire Witch! I *am* in hell!"

Hands on her hips, she treated him to her best schoolmarm tone. "Let's try this again, George. First, you will greet me with pleasantries. Then I shall invite you to tea. After that, if all goes well, I may explain why you are here."

He backed up a step. Then another. Just when she thought he was going to flee into the night, he doffed a nonexistent cap to her.

"Ma'am. It's... it's right good to see you again."

"Is it? Imagine that. Do sit down, George."

He planted himself in the armchair opposite hers and accepted the bone china cup she offered. It rattled against its saucer as he tried to balance it on his shaking knee.

Lorena studied the deep lines in his face, the paunch of his belly. She'd been anxious to see him again—but not in the hungry way she'd felt for the others. This wasn't about retribution, just a reunion.

"It's been a long time," she said.

"It has."

Lorena laughed. "Still a man of few words, I see."

"Yeah."

George's rough hands fumbled with the tiny teacup. He slurped it down like a shot of whiskey, then grimaced.

"You were the only man on that trail who was nice

to me, Mr. Tremont. I have never forgotten the way you tried to stop them from hanging me."

George looked at his ragged nails, at the waning moon, everywhere but her.

"I spent most of my life wonderin' if it was just the fever that made me see all that."

"You don't really believe that."

"Ma'am, a man can convince himself of anything if he sets his mind on it hard enough. I didn't much want to believe..." He dropped his voice. "That boy you stabbed. I saw him again. Walkin' and talkin'. As solid as you and I. If he was dead, he sure didn't know it... I gotta know, ma'am. Did you really kill him?"

She winced at the one scar that would not heal.

"Oh, I killed him, sure enough. But he managed to bounce back from all that unpleasantness. He lives just a few towns over from you, in fact. One of his daughters-in-law passed the collection plate to you last Sunday while you were bouncing your grandson on your lap to keep him from crying."

George shrank away from her, paler than the marble statues at his shoulder.

"How could you know that?"

"Oh, I pay attention. It's my job now to... see to things. I happened to be in your church just then, so I... took notice."

"Old lady Dilly died that day. Fell asleep during the sermon and for a change she didn't start snoring. That's how we knew she'd passed."

Lorena nodded. George had always been quite

perceptive. She sensed him on the precipice of what she wanted him to know, yet he did not ask.

"Tell me what you remember of the day I was hanged."

"Not much, truth be told. Between the pain of my leg and the fever from the infection, I fell delirious. My buddies forgot they was supposed to fetch a doctor. Left me on that bridge for two days. Everyone says it's a miracle I didn't die."

"You cannot blame them, George. Most of the escaping members of that lynch mob were killed when an errant tornado dropped over them. The rest died of fright. That was my first miracle. You were my second."

The teacup fell from his grip, shattering against the paving stones.

"What *are* you?"

Discarding gentility, the way a snake sheds its skin, Lorena rose before him with outstretched arms. This practiced move caused her woolen shawl to ripple like thick black wings.

"I am the Goddess of Death."

He sprang to his feet, ready to bolt, but she blocked his path.

"If you were paying attention, Mr. Tremont, you would realize that you needn't fear me."

"I'm dead, ain't I? That's why the train I come in on don't have no tracks leading away from it."

"I'd have thought that was obvious."

On instinct, Lorena slipped her arm through his to lead him along a cozy lane. He startled, then found the grace to shuffle in step with her without screaming.

"You were meant to have died that day, George. I gave you a second life, another forty years. I felt I owed you a debt."

"I'd hoped for a few more years," George said, but he grinned before her temper had a chance to flare. "I'd never figured on you as my guardian angel, ma'am... but if that's the case, I reckon I couldn't have asked for none better."

The unexpected quaver of emotion in his voice managed to dab a schoolgirl's blush in the fledgling goddess. Cheeks burning, she feigned sudden interest in a cluster of azaleas.

"If you don't mind my askin'," George said, "if you're the goddess of Death, why were you so scared of bein' hanged?"

"I was human then, George. It was shortly after I died that I took this role. The gods granted me the liberty to trade places with another soul. I chose one of the immortals and wrested this position away from him."

George gave a low whistle. "That right? So you been doin' this the last forty years? How long you figurin' to keep at it?"

Lorena twisted her hands, contemplating his question.

By all accounts—and my, how the gods loved to gossip!—speculation ran wild as to how long she would last.

Chronos, god of Time himself, had manifested at the moment of Thanatos's death. Though Lorena only saw him once, it was said he returned dozens of times to witness her coup d'état, delighting at their reversal. It had long been foretold that Death would come to them all, for even Time must end. Seeing Thanatos die first thrilled him to his core. Like most of the gods, he embraced Lorena as a pet, the quaint little human who spiced up a dull millennium by daring to don the mantle of a god.

She knew, though, that as long as she remained chained to the task of culling all life from the worlds, Thanatos's power steeped within her. His obligations became hers.

So, although Chronos decreed that she was not to be harmed—and though Nemesis vowed never to grant anyone revenge against Lorena, still she remained vigilant, trusting no one.

The moon drooped closer to the horizon by the time she found an adequate answer for George.

"It seems a woman's work is never done."

They strolled on. The land ended abruptly at a twenty-foot-high thicket from which emanated a hideously prolonged wail.

"What the blue blazes was that?" George shouted.

"Surely you remember Colquoit, my husband's assistant?" She leaned closer to whisper conspiratorially, "Purgatory is nothing compared to my hedge maze."

George's mouth dropped open. Lorena snorted in a most unladylike fashion.

"By the way, George," she said brightly, leading him along a side path, "what ever became of my husband's journal? Were you tempted to read it?"

He replied slowly, choosing his words.

"I read the bits in English, ma'am, but there weren't many of them. I never forgot the stories you told me about Chaos and all that lit'rature and the picture of the bone knife you said killed my cousin. To be honest I thought you was crazy as a loon at the time, but after I seen you vanish, I got to wonderin' was it maybe true. I kept your book safe all these years, just in case."

"Good man. And did you leave instructions for it in your will?"

"I was persuaded to loan it to my pastor this Christmas, ma'am. He'd taken a keen interest in the ideas I was spoutin' to him, and he wanted to read them himself. Only..."

He faltered, stealing worried glances back at her maze.

"Tell me, George."

"Only... he went missing a few days after I gave it to him. Left behind everything he owned and... skipped town, they say."

Lorena rounded on him, staring into his soul while the dead man sweated bullets. He wasn't lying. *Damn.* She should have killed him sooner.

"I am truly aggrieved to hear that," she said, fighting to control her temper. Grasping his forearm with both hands, she hustled him to the end of the lane. "Our reunion must end now, Mr. Tremont. Straight down the hill. You know the way."

"You mean... I'm goin' back to the train station?"

"Of course. A stagecoach will meet you there to ferry you the last leg of your journey. It shan't take long." She managed a polite smile. "This land is not meant to be anyone's final destination. I do hope you enjoyed this sojourn as I did, George. Fare thee well."

Thunderstruck, he regarded her with the queerest look she'd seen in many a year, then gave a little shake of his head and broke into the rapturous glow of the newly devout. Bowing and tipping his imaginary hat, he shambled out the gate. She watched until he faded into the gloaming.

One debt repaid. Only one to go...

She'd promised herself once to give Bo the best life she could manage. Perhaps a long life could substitute. Sweet Bo would live to hear his great-great-great-granddaughters singing the gospel songs he loved. If she could summon the power, she'd make him a second Methuselah. But her motives were driven more by cowardice than love. How could she possibly face him again until she knew he'd forgiven her in his heart? And how many centuries would that take?

Alone in the unbroken silence, Lorena sat at her desk in the empty gazebo and attended to her daily reaping. She closed her eyes and marked all the sentient souls due to die that day, then reached for quill and paper to leave instructions for her minions on sorting them. She found this method so much more efficient than Thanatos's means of queuing the troubled souls at his gate, with the added benefit that she never had to look into their doleful faces until she at last had good news to reward them with, as she had with George.

Her task completed, she rolled up the parchment and stuck it in the birdcage just outside her grounds. This was the farthest she ventured out of the garden most days. From the apex of the hill, she surveyed her realm. Day after hour, year after month, the grey flatlands remained unchanged but for the constant flow of souls.

She shut her gate with a decisive clang, locking her worldly problems out for the night, and retreated to her most private quarters. Deep within her courtyard stood a crypt, its double doors exactly her height and width, even allowing for her bustle. The doors had no handles, for they opened only to her touch, and even then, only while she hummed their waltz. "Mephistos Hollenrufe."

Dee-dah-daah, BUM-de-BUM dah-aah...

Darting through the portal, she closed the door behind herself, then stopped, as always, to ensure she hadn't left a crack. A single sliver could be her undoing.

Satisfied at last, she stepped onto the moors and allowed herself to feel human once again, if only briefly. She always entered here, on the moonlit hill where she'd lost her virginity, then jaunted up the wandering lane to their mansion. Tonight, a single lamp flickered in the window of her husband's study.

She'd caged him here, for Adalwolf was far too dangerous to be allowed to return to the world of the living. She'd promised to keep him alive. Indeed, every ordeal she'd been through had been spawned by his fear of death, so it seemed wasteful to discard her oath now. As long as he remained in his trap, she could keep him alive forever.

He got his wish.

Lorena got hers as well, owing to a little help from Oneroi and Chronos. Adalwolf had bucked and wrestled with all his mental might when she sucked him into her mind for safekeeping. But once she molded him into the proper shape and time, he acclimated beautifully.

The scent of cedar logs burning in the fireplace enveloped her as she burst through the entrance of their home. Preening in the antique mirror above the mantle, she pinched her cheeks and began unpinning her hair from its bun.

Before she could finish, Diedrick stole into the room, slipping up from behind to grab her waist. His long blond locks tickled her skin as he nuzzled her neck. When she squirmed, he spun her around, his crystal-blue eyes twinkling.

"*Mein Liebling.*"

They clung to each other, kissing fervently, the buttons of her bodice sacrificed to their passion.

This version of her husband was every bit as single-minded in his pursuits. Fortunately, his current desire was something she was willing to surrender... again and again.

And so, the man who sought to master death pledged his eternity to Mistress Death.

THANK YOU

Thank you for reading *In the Sleep of Death*.

Please consider leaving a review to help more readers find the book.

ACKNOWLEDGMENTS

It's probably bad luck to cross off your entire bucket list in one stroke – especially while taunting the god of Death – but publishing this novel was the entire list for me.

I want to thank everyone at GenZ for their help and encouragement through this process. Their goal is to find and promote fresh young voices. I'm not sure how young mine is, but I'm honored to be part of their selection.

I want to share this moment with my family, the whole, generation-sprawling lot of you. Browns, Van Ginkels, Klauses, Rozinskys, and Brockerts. I love you all!

A huge shout out to the Nebraska Writers Workshop. I wish I could list you all by name, but there are so many people who helped in different ways. Thank you for listening, for your suggestions, and especially for the laughs and encouragement. I've never been part of a group that worked so hard to build each other up, both emotionally and professionally.

Hugs and high-fives to Jeremy, Hans, and my friends back home.

Tom, Katie, and Jacob, thank you for everything. You are my world.

ABOUT THE AUTHOR

Kimberly Van Ginkel is 5th-generation Iowan. Her meandering career path has included TV Programmer, Newspaper Webmaster, and Printing CIO. She divvies up her time between gaming, coding, researching, logic puzzles, genealogy, crocheting, staring into the abyss, baking cookies, and a flagrant lack of exercise. She lives in the Midwest with her husband and two children. She is an internationally published short story author. This is her debut novel.

Learn more: kimberlyvanginkel.com

OTHER GENZ TITLES YOU MAY ENJOY

The Space Between Two Deaths by Jamie Yourdon

The Smoke in His Eyes by Shane Wilson

The Murder of Edward VI by David Snow

ABOUT THE PUBLISHER

GenZ Publishing emphasizes new, merging, young, and underrepresented authors. We're an indie publisher that focuses on mentoring authors through each steps of the publishing process and beyond: editing, writing sequels, cover design, marketing, PR, and even getting agented for future works. We love to see our authors succeed both with the books publish with us and with their other publications. That's why we call it the "GenZ Family."

For more information, visit Genzpublishing.org or contact us at info@genzpublishing.org. Connect with us on Instagram, Facebook, Twitter, and LinkedIn for our latest news and releases.

Made in United States
North Haven, CT
25 March 2024